CW01267223

The Last Man of Thebes

By

Michael Colucci

Chapter 1 - Leksi

A gentle rocking in the darkness. Warm, wet. This might be the womb, if I could remember that far back. He's here with me, thank the gods. My face pressed into his chest. My legs intertwined with his. The harsh odor of stale sweat and the perfume he uses to cover it up. It makes me laugh, the thought of Sigorin wearing perfume. I'm grateful for his smell, stale sweat and perfume. It's how I know him in this darkness.

Not now, not yet. I hear his voice. *Open your eyes, Leksi. Open them.* I do not want to, but I will not deny him, and I fight to open my eyes, to see clearly what this place is. I see stars, at first, but these are not the constellations of my homeland. They mark a different time, tell a different story. These are not my stars. But in the next breath I see that these are not stars at all. Gems? Yes. It is not the sky I see, we are underground. This is a cave. And these are not stars, but crystals, embedded in the rocks above.

And this is not the womb, but a boat.

Confusion washes over me. *Remember. Come back to your own.* I hear Sigorin's voice order me, and I fight for the last memory I know to be true. The pounding of hooves, the sparks that fly when swords and spears crash against shields and armor. War. But I do not know the battle. I do not remember who or what we fought. And as for the why? That could not possibly matter now, if it ever did.

He pulls me into his strong arms. If he is here, then I am right, none of it matters. I relax into his chest. Nothing in all of Earth and Hades feels as good as his chest and his arm firm against my back. My eyes defy his orders and drift closed.

No, open them. You must see. And I obey. I see him this time. His full, brown beard, his powerful jaw, his curly, untamed hair. At the sight of him any desire to make sense of this eternity leaves me completely, and yet my gaze drops down to his neck, his chest, and then all solace is lost.

A gash across his stomach, bloody, ugly and—I've seen enough wounds to know—fatal. Aries drives his spirit through me and like a puppet I am erect. And I see...

The Sacred Band of Thebes, all three hundred of us, fill the boat's massive hull. Each wrapped in the arms of their partner, holding each other in death poses. We die as we lived, together. I throw my gaze to the rear of the boat to find a helmsman, cloaked in all black, steering us to what I know is home. Then I remember, only in pieces, but I remember, curse the gods, I remember. I have a country. Thebes. I have an enemy. Macedonia. I am angry.

Aries, be still, I pray. Let me fall back into the trance that has my brothers. Let me fall back into Sigorin's arms and sleep until the next life, and then I will do your bidding. I will fight by his side for lifetimes, but now let me rest with him. I do not want your fury or your purpose.

I fight the god and rest my head back down on my lover's chest.
No, I am sorry, my love, but this will not be your fate. I lack the strength, I hear Sigorin whisper as he sits up. His massive hands wrap around my arms and lift me to my feet with him. I pray for a kiss, but I've seen this look in his eyes before. That look that is the reason we battle by our lover's side: *You will not fail me. You will not show cowardice. You will not sleep when your duty is to fight.*

And then Sigorin does that thing that only he could do to me, the reason I fear him and love him. He overpowers me. He picks me up as if I were a child, as if this were a hug. I pretend it is as he steps to the side of the boat and releases me overboard into the cold, dark water.

I kick and stroke towards the surface when hands come up from below and grab my ankles—curse those hands—pulling me deeper into the depths. My lungs demand a breath. My mouth opens to let the water consume me, but it doesn't. Instead, mud, blood, and the entrails of men and horses push out of my lungs and onto…dirt? Earth?

And I'm back. I know where I am. My memory is intact. Chaeronea. The bitter sun, blazing in its fury, greets me as those hands pull me by my ankles from the heap of bodies that surrounded me a moment before, my brothers, the Band, my womb. But I reach out for only one of them, Sigorin. His eyes are still open, still watching me. I won't waste time pretending he's not gone. I want to be gone, too. I want death. But dead as Sigorin's eyes are, they still give orders. Violent orders. And at violence, I excel.

As I'm pulled past him, I take Sigorin's sword from his hand. This is the first time I've touched it. It's the one thing he never shared, but now, in death, he insists I take it, and I do not deny him. I swing the steel, and, as if by a will of its own, it removes the hand seizing my ankle from the arm it was previously connected to.

The shriek of pain fills the day. Carrion birds dart into the sky before Sigorin's sword finds the Macedonian's throat, silencing him. I never liked killing. It was never a joy, but a duty. But this death, this killing, this is different. This is revenge.

I relish in the blood raining down on my flesh as the other Macedonian runs, screaming his terror as he goes, "The Band lives! They live!"

Not they. Only me. But all Macedonia knows that as long as the Sacred Band lives, even a single member, so does Thebes, and therefore so does Greece.

But I do not want life, not without Sigorin, not without my brothers. I look up to the blue, still sky. All is well there. The gods above care not about what's below, the smoking hills of Chaeronea, its meadows littered with abandoned banners of fallen city-states, pierced and ravaged by Macedonian spears. Among them, I wait for death to come.

Three more Macedonians arrive, but not their elite. The red of the Macedonian uniform is stained brown by the Greecian earth they upend, but the blood of their victims blends in well enough. They see me and freeze. This is the clean-up crew. An old man, maybe capable in his day, but past his best now and two others, too green to survive me. Their hands shake as they reach for their standard issue blades. I feel the tip of Sigorin's sword rising, deciding its preference.

Three against one, I think, *maybe they'll surprise me. Maybe they'll sort it out.*

"To the death!" I call out. Let there be no question about how I plan to proceed.

"There's no need for that, son, the battle is done," the old one says.

Fool. Clearly the battle is done. We are surrounded by death. Why it swept over us, only the gods know.

A green one draws. The old one calls out, "Hold," but this boy has no training, and he charges forward. May he face Hades with the same courage. May he tell Sigorin of my final deed. Sigorin's blade chooses his throat, a merciful death, fast, painless compared to the lower options. More Macedonian blood spills onto Grecian soil.

The other green one loses his nerve, races off. The old one gets a battle horn to his lips and blows. The crows balk at the sound, but the dead stay dead.

Sigorin's sword calls me forward—*Silence this man*, she demands—but his look stops me. He wants life, this old horn blower. He wants to see this night and the next day. I hold, refusing the sword her bounty. May my brothers forgive me this hesitation. The man runs. He'll tell this tale to his babes, I hope. How he looked the last of the Theban Bandsmen in the eyes and blew his horn, certain it would be the last sound he heard, but lived.

Suddenly there is the smell again, the smell of sweating horses. I remember now.

The battle had been going our way. The Macedonian hoplites were brave and well trained but the Greeks were fighting to defend their homeland against a forign invader and the Sacred Band was their vanguard. We were pushing the Macedonians back to the north, one dead body length at a time. Then their horns blew. We knew what it meant. As we expected, the Macedonains had waited to call in their cavalry until the Sacred Band was already engaged in battle.

The Athenians had said they would face off against the horsemen, led by the King's own son, Alexander. They would fight to the last, they said. Should the Cavalry reach the Band, it would be with but a fraction of their numbers—that was the promise. But the Athenians had lost their nerve, or worse, someone had betrayed Greece. After the sound of the battle horn came the pounding of hooves, filling our ears, and the same smell of sweating horses. Hercules himself could not have withstood the number of Macedonian horses and riders that stormed us, cutting down upon us like giants.

And here is that smell and the pounding of hooves again. Five war horses neigh their greeting, their riders in shining armor. Our battle is not even a half day to history but someone has already polished their armor. I can see myself in its shine. I stand, waiting for them to charge and finish me off, but they rear up and stop.

"To the death!" I plead. They're the only words I know. The Cavalry does not advance.

Sigorin's sword rises up, points its tip at the middle rider, wanting his neck.

"For Thebes! For the Band!" I beg, the usual jargon returning to me, but the horses still do not advance.

The middle rider lifts up his mask, and there he is. Alexander himself. No older than I am—sixteen, seventeen. His eyes shining as brightly as his armor. Those eyes…where I want to see hate and wrath and a need to slaughter, there's wonderment and awe and compassion.

"To the death!" I call out again—*for the love of Zeus, man, are you deaf? If that is compassion in your eyes, then command your steed forward. Send me home.*

But no.

"Take him," the prince says.

And then I see the masses of soldiers behind these horsemen. As if the whole of Macedonia has rallied to the will of this one man. And they do his bidding. A wave of men falls upon me. Sigorin's sword drools at the feast. A stab to the stomach for the first to arrive, a slash to the throat for the second so that it squirts out, so that the others can taste their countryman's blood as they overcome me, pounding and kicking me back into the earth.

Blackness does come, but I know it's not forever. This sleep will not last. Their prince does not will that for me.

I will awaken.

Chapter 2 - Petros

The armorer sure got his snickers in when he was fitting me for this damn helmet.

"Aren't you a tiny little thing! You're swimming in the littlest helmet I got!"

What a wank he was. But now I'm about grateful for this stupid helmet. If I don't stay perfectly still, with my head titled just so, the thing will slide off, and my commander will smack me silly.

This is good, see, because I have something to focus on during his speech.

"This was a member of the Sacred Band of Thebes, one of the most elite warriors..." Blah, blah, blah...

Balance the stupid helmet on my little head.

"Only Alexander and those in his inner committee should have access..."

Yes, got it, understood, thank you, keeping the helmet steady.

"If anything happens to him, your punishment will be death..."

Well, that seems a bit harsh, but this is not a negotiation. Better to focus on balancing the helmet. See what I mean?

"Do you understand why you're being chosen for this assignment, soldier?"

So, I gotta process that one. I was assigned to be a prison guard after being dismissed from my position as a medical officer and because I am too short for the phalanx, not that I wanted to be on the phalanx, gods no. Of the prison guards, I'm the only one who knows how to clean his own arse, let alone watch a prisoner, but I can't quite say that, can I?

"Soldier, you've been asked a question."

"Might it be because I'm of relatively normal intelligence, sir?"

A roll of his eyes. He hates it when I speak. I don't sound like I wrestle oxen for a living, and it makes this one heated. I usually get on better with girls, but good luck finding any of them in a Macedonian Army camp. We are here to take over the world, men's work, women stay at home.

But Captain grumpy has nothing to add, except, "Right, so, be smart. If he escapes, he'll take from you more than your life."

Not sure what that means, but I'm not exactly in a position to ask questions, am I?

"Dismissed."

Thank Athena. I about-face. I'm usually good at the little dance moves they make us do, but my balance fails me, and that blasted helmet slips over my eyes as I walk off. I rear back and manage to keep it on, but…

"Soldier."

I stop, adjust the helmet, turn back to my commander.

“Are you kin?” he asks.

Drat. Just about the cruelest question a man could ask another, at least in Macedonia. Not my first time being asked, either. I’m asked all the time if I'm kin. Or told I'm kin. Or asked why I'm kin. All to my father’s great shame. He hoped the military would straighten the swoosh out of my step. Won’t he be disappointed.

“No, sir.”

“Then walk like a Macedonian. Lest your loyalties be put into question.”

Right. The walk. They always spot your walk. May Zeus curse them all.

Chapter 3: Leksi

Not a whisper, not a scratch from his beard, not even a trace of his scent. Only darkness before I woke up tied to a stick, swaying back and forth like a kid-goat to be roasted. I saw their camp, nothing more than a swarm of pitched hide tents, the odd fire, the quick-propped corrals for the herds. Wagons, too.

Not that I was making a list. I was more concerned with *where* than *what*. East, they were carrying me. Away from my brothers. *When I escape, I will go west, back to them, and face my death there*, I vowed, so that I may find my rest besides them.

This moment of orientation was brief, for soon the bludgeon fell upon me, and the darkness returned.

But this darkness lacks mercy, for it too relents. Even so, I keep my eyes closed, to play at the idea that perhaps I have found my death.

I am warm now; there must be a fire near. There is no breeze so I must be in some lodge, or tent. I am bound, my hands tied behind me with a large pole running between them and my back. The position is meant as torture, but I know how to command my muscles to relax. This is no great bother. At least these binds don't cut into my flesh like the ones before.

And someone wipes my brow with a cool rag, drips water into my parched lips, and hums a soft tune.

False kindness? *That* is torture. I jerk, pulling against the rope, and hear, "None of that, now. No need to fight," from my captor.

My eyes demand an image to put with the voice. They take control, and my eyelids lift, straining to find their focus, but they cannot.

"Hold still now. This might hurt just a bit. I'm sorry," he says.

I'm sorry? No one in my life has ever said they were sorry for causing me pain. He's the first. And still his image is blurred. But then my eyes find their focus: a knifepoint a fist length from my face. I refuse to move from its path. *Do your worst.* It comes for a point right above my eye, a swollen mass, a bruise from the bludgeon. It makes its puncture. Blood trickles from the wound, a cloth wipes the warm fluid from my cheek, and with that I can see clearly again.

And I see him. He's Macedonian, but unlike any man I've seen before. He's small, sure, but it is the kindness in his face that confounds me.

"But now you can see, right? That's something good, aye?" He speaks Greek in that choked dialect of the Macedonians, but there's a rhythm to his words. He's like a drummer, steady and reliable.

I offer him the only kindness I can. "Kill me," I say.

"Aye, go-to, with that," he responds.

"Kill me, or I will break free and do you the service."

But he only wipes my brow once more. Hands bound, I have no choice. I cannot consent to his touch, but I enjoy it nonetheless.

A shuffling outside, and the tent door opens. A captain—I know his rank by the gaudy armor Macedonian officers wear—enters the tent with an ogre of an escort beside him. A freshly stitched wound marks the captain's cheek, but it can only be an improvement on his looks. At least they had the courtesy to send a soldier to do this work—one who has spilled his blood for their cause.

The small guard jumps to attention. He's ignored, of course; the captain isn't here to talk to him.

"Our reports indicate that you are, or were, as they no longer exist, a member of the Theban Sacred Band. Will you confirm or deny?" the captain asks without really asking.

Choke on your cock and die.

"We will mark your silence as a confirmation. As a member of the Sacred Band—"

"My apologies, sir, but I have to ask you to leave," my little captor interrupts.

I do not expect to experience a splinter of pleasure until my death, but the look on this captain's face gives me just that.

"What?" is all he can muster in response.

"I was given clear orders that only Prince Alexander or those of his inner committee are to have access to this prisoner. Sir," my guard says, withholding sir as an afterthought. My heart warms at the subtle slight in that pause.

The captain turns to his ogre and commands, "Deal with him."

How I wish my hands were free so I could fight by this little one's side. The ogre is too much for him. Before my captor can get his dagger out of its sheath, the ogre has him off his feet and on the ground, pressing his massive forearm into the guard's cheek. The guard can't move, can't scream, but his eyes find mine. I don't look away. I stay with him.

"As I was saying, as a member of the Theban Sacred Band, you would have been made aware of contingency plans in the event of a Greek defeat, locations of armories, assigned partisan leaders. That sort of thing."

I do not care what the captain has to say. Nothing could cause me to break eye contact with my little captor, except the Captain's leather-clad hand around my chin, as he forces me to meet his gaze.

"I suppose we'll skip the pleasantries and go straight to the main course." He pulls back and introduces me to the back of his hand. It amazes me that the most masterful horseman or swordsman or military strategist are unable to execute a simple punch. Sigorin hit me harder during foreplay.

Sensing my lack of a reaction, the Captain darkens and pulls a dagger. So this is my end. While I've wished for this moment, I find myself wishing for a moment more. I want to know how my small captor will fare in this mess. And the gods grant my wish.

The ogre hollers in pain, his arm dripping blood as the guard wiggles out from under him.

"Alexander!" the tiny man yells with a titan's voice. "Alexander!"

The ogre grips his own arm over what must be a bite, as my captor draws his blade and dives in front of me.

Oh, the look on the captain's face! This battle is joy.

“Alexander!” my little guard shouts for the third time.

Call your prince, little soldier, and may your own children be of royal blood.

Chapter 4: Hephaestion

His head submerged in sun warmed water is the greatest luxury Hephaestion has known in almost five weeks. Not a proper bath, or an elegantly served meal, or a massage, or a chess match with Alexander, his best friend and prince. No. His head submerged in warm water, washing away the blood of a battle won, a battle done. He holds his breath for as long as he can to extract as much pleasure as possible, until his lungs burn. He withdraws and breathes out the stale air.

His bliss ends immediately when he senses, in that way not even Hephaestion understands, Alexander racing towards peril. Something vibrates inside Hephaestion when his prince charges towards danger and, with water dripping from his ears, he hears what has drawn Alexander out and caused Aries to seize his prince: a booming voice ripe with desperation calling, "Alexander! Alexander! Alexa—". The last shout is cut off and Hephaestion is helpless to do anything but run towards the call.

Hephaestion wipes the water from his eyes and becomes aware that Alexander, or Alex as Hephaestion alone is allowed to call him and even then only in private, is only a few strides ahead of him. To watch Alexander run, one would think he was half lion. He moves with power and grace, with the form and singular focus of an apex predator.

Not a man on the planet could keep up with the prince, except Hephaestion, who has a supernatural speed of his own when he's at Alexander's heels. They race past rows of tents; the huge steaming cauldron, where the army doctor hands out hot rags for men to clean and wrap their wounds; and a pen full of screaming hogs being butchered for the victory supper to come. All the while, Hephaestion, in incremental fractions of the distance, diminishes the gap between them. He is desperate for a touch.

Just before Alexander reaches the tent from which the call of his name presumably came, Hephaestion does make his touch. It's a shove, in fact, because Hephaestion is not a gentle person, and Alexander tumbles into the dirt. Hephaestion's allowed to do this. The two of them agreed long ago that when their play grew rough, they would handle it themselves. And for that, Hephaestion is grateful. He might not be of royal birth, but he's allowed to shove the prince when the prince needs to be shoved.

Hephaestion doesn't wait to see if Alexander is hurt as he's seen him fall worse than that before. Hephaestion charges into the tent. *Perhaps Aries has him, too*, he thinks, but it does not matter, this is what Hephaestion was born to do.

While Hephaestion does not hesitate to enter the tent, his mind does scramble to set aside the thought that this curtain he throws aside is a threshold to more than a tent, for this is the tent where the Band's survivor is held. Alexander is keen to interrogate him on his own, learn any secrets the soldier will part with, and keen to offer him the death that he desires. Alexander respects the Band, at least that's the word Alexander uses. Hephaestion suspects that respect is more accurately a fixation. Alexander is careful how often he calls the Band into conversation, careful only to discuss the Band when they're alone, careful not to seem too interested, too curious. But at each mention, Hephaestion's heart fills with a hope that's mysterious even to himself. By pulling this curtain aside, what of this mystery might be revealed? But this to be considered during a less perilous time. Now, there is work to be done.

Hephaestion enters to find Captain Tam, standing before the bound Bandsman with his blade drawn, threatening to steal him away before Alexander can have words with him. The smallest soldier Hephaestion has ever seen stands fiercely between the captain and the captive. He must be the one who screamed for Alexander, Hephaestion deduces. The guard holds out his blade in a poor mimicry of a serviceable fighting stance. What he lacks in experience, he makes up for in commitment, however, and the man at the other end of the blade, Captain Tam, seems almost grateful for Hephaestion's interruption.

"Your presence is in direct violation of the orders of our prince. Sheathe your dagger, Captain," Hephaestion announces, resisting the impulse to call him a fool.

"Or else what?" Tam laughs.

"Or else I'll rip off your arm and feed it to the hounds," says Hephaestion as he suddenly becomes aware that he's speaking to someone of equal rank. He is in no position to give orders to Captain Tam. What's more, Hephaestion is half naked and unarmed, without a shred of steel on his person. And while he's certain he can manage the feat, albeit with lesser odds, Hephaestion's heart quickens and his muscles tighten, all on their own, preparing to battle.

Captain Tam growls and takes a quick step towards Hephaestion when someone grabs Hephaestion from behind, and violently throws him to the ground.

He looks up to see this new assailant, Alexander, he should have guessed, squaring off against Captain Tam. Confused by this sudden switch, the old captain still holds his dagger up.

"And now you hold your blade to me," Alexander says. He has a talent for making hard men, three times his and Hephaestion's age, shit themselves.

“Prince,” the captain stammers.

“Sheathe your dagger, Captain!” Alexander demands.

And finally, Tam does. Alexander does outrank him after all.

“Atten-tion!” Hephaestion blurst out, and the room’s other two occupants, perhaps the biggest and the smallest men in the Macedonian army, are on their feet, hands at their sides.

The respect Alexander garners isn’t all by birthright or the force of his personality. Yes, he’s impressive. Had he been born a beggar, he would have risen to the wealthy class, but Hephaestion creates the shock and awe by calling the masses to attention. At the sound of Hephaestion's voice, even old Captain Tam stands dutifully stiff and awaits his orders.

“It was made very clear to all that this man was to be interrogated by me and me alone. Explain yourself,” Alexander says, calm. Alexander always appears calm, but barely so, as if at any moment he might unleash Hades on the world.

“I was acting on the orders of my king,” the old captain blurts out.

“And do you know who I am?” Alexander says. Hephaestion loves when Alexander plays this game. Alexander’s pride is not at all tied up in his birthright, it is one of things Hephaestion loves about him, but the prince will use its perception to his favor when it suits him.

“Prince Alexander,” the goat blats.

“The very well-liked king’s son, eldest son, in fact. Who will be king upon the death of his father, do you not agree?” Alexander adds.

“A sad and glorious day it will be," Captain Tam lies. Hephaestion at leasts respects the man's knowledge of the game.

“Perhaps for your sake and the sake of your children and your children’s children you should learn to be more political when faced with conflicting orders. Do you not agree?” Alexander says.

“Sir,” the captain says with a nod of his head.

“Get out. Take your troll with you,” Alexander concludes.

Captain Tam does not speak another word as he leaves the tent, the troll stumbling behind. His next stop will be the king’s barracks, no doubt. This will put Alexander in mortal danger for certain, and perhaps Hephaestion could have stopped this. Perhaps he could have grabbed him and held him down before they arrived at the tent. Except Hephaestion wants to know two things: Exactly how great will Alexander become if no one stops him, if no one forces him to play it safe? And what are the mysteries on this side of the curtain? What does the last remaining member of the Sacred Band of Thebes have to offer them? Alexander’s Father, King Philip, was a captive in Thebes as a young man. He knows all about the Sacred Band of Thebes and their secrets, but he would only speak dismissively of them, referring to them as kinsmen, as if they hadn’t been the most formidable fighting force in all of the known world.

But before Alexander turns to the captive, in an effort to bring these mysteries to light, he turns to the tiny guard and notices the wet patch on his pants and the puddle at his feet.

“Are you not accustomed to conflict?” Alexander asks.

“I’m too short for the phalanx.” That he is able to verbalize a response at all surprises Hephaestion. “He fought bravely, Sir,” Hephaestion says, aware that he only saw the man stand before danger and not confront it, but this was another one of Hephaestion’s duties; to keep Alexander moving forward, to not allow details to slow down his progress.

While Alexander is at least partially aware of this role, he still fires Hephaestion his *how dare you speak* look. Hephaestion fights back a chuckle. This too is part of the illusion that they both participate in wilfully.

Alexander turns back to the little guard and officers a merciful, “Well done, then.” And the man grows taller.

And finally Alexander brings his attention to the man tied to the pole. He is no older than Alexander and Hephaestion, but he is a specimen. Alexander and Hephaestion are fit and strong, stronger than most men, even their elders, they are not accustomed to being in the presence of one who makes them feel physically inferior, but that is how they feel in the presence of the Bandsman, even bound as he is. It isn’t just his size, his muscles, the scars on his body, but the look in his eyes. Even tied up and bruised, that look says, *I would ruin you in a fair fight, my hands unbound, my will unleashed, you would be no match for me.* And Hephaestion wouldn’t be. Even as a child, he never had that thought about another before.

Alexander experiences the same thought. If only for a brief inhale, Hephaestion sees that look usually reserved for Hephaestion after being bested in a wrestling match or a foot race. A look that says, *I surrender. Thank you. In this moment, I can hand over the burden of my greatness.*

But that look has a short life as Alexander collects himself.

"The Band fought bravely. You did not deserve that treatment. My captain will be punished, I assure you. We kept you alive because I have questions and they do not apply to future military campaigns. I know you would not reveal those answers, and we have no real need for them, but we do have questions about the Sacred Band. We, uh..."

Alexander falters, and Hephaestion's heart races.

He continues, "We understand that in Thebes, the partners of the Band live openly as lovers. Is this true?"

The man eyes him, then he turns his gaze to Hephaestion, as if he knows all the secrets of his heart.

"We have kin in Macedonia, of course, but they live in the shadows," Alexander says, coming to Hephaestion's rescue by pulling the Bandsman attention back to him.

"The shadows are no place for men like us."

Like us, the Bandsman said, *like us*. Hephaestion repeats it as a thought, a mantra. *Like Us.* Hephaestion feels as if he's being attacked by a blaze of light, hot, searing, burning off the mask he's worn his entire life. *Like us!* He almost dares to say it aloud as his heart rejoices.

"Like you," Alexander responds, throwing cold water on Hephaestion's flames before they can illuminate their truth. "Like you," Alexander repeats in that calm voice. "But you imply with your answer that it's true?"

"Yes," says the Bandsman. "It is true and no secret."

“And you’re paired with your partner? You take no wives?” Alexander asks.

“It is true,” answers the Bandsman.

“And you have no children of your own?” Alexander asks.

“All children of Thebes are my children,” the Bandsman responds.

“I see. Our historians will note it,” Alexander concludes.

With that, Alexander turns. What he sees inside Hephaestion in this moment, Hephaestion does not know. Does Alexander see his pain? His desire? Does he feel it, too? Hephaestion can usually hear Alexander’s every thought, but the noise of his own heart strikes him deaf now.

Alexander turns back to the Bandsman. “Do you wish it to be by my hand?”

“As good as any other,” the Bandsman responds.

Alexander’s jaw tenses. If there’s an Achilles’s heel on Hephaestion's best friend, it’s the suggestion that he’s ordinary, that he’s as good as any other.

Hephaestion wants to hug the bound man. He feels avenged by him, even if he cannot fully understand why.

Alexander turns to the Bandsman once more. “So it will be done tomorrow. I’ll return you to your brothers.”

Alexander marches out. And Hephaestion follows. He always follows.

Chapter 5: Petros

My knees buckle before the prince and his captain, Hephaestion, take their final step out of the tent. I land in a heap at my charge's feet. Mercifully, my prince doesn't notice or doesn't care to turn back. My breath leaves me, and my lungs collapse, forgetting the simple operation of air in, air out, air in, air out. I hate myself. I'm weak.

I look up to my charge, bruised but unfazed, his eyes as warm as embers. He is everything I'm not, everything I'm supposed to be. And he is kin. And he admits it, freely and openly.

I am his captor. And should I unbind him, I would be dead. This I know.

But his eyes tell a different story. And he says, "Breathe."

Did I hear that right?

"Breathe."

Calm, peaceful. I fight, not wanting him to take over my will, but…

"Breathe."

My lungs do as he commands. A violent inhale as air floods into the vacuum of my insides. I hold on tight, until he commands, "Breathe out, now."

And I do. I shake with sobs and coughs, but he doesn't look away. As shameful as it all is, I don't either. And he holds me with his eyes.

"Battle well fought, soldier. Battle well fought," he says.

Chapter 6: Alexander

Alexander has long believed King Philip to be no more his father than the newt he just saw a soldier roasting up for breakfast. Alexander is quite sure the king suspects as much. He'd be a fool not to. And unfortunately for Alexander, King Philip is not a fool.

Alexander looks nothing like Philip. Alexander's mother, Olympia, agrees with those who point out the lack of resemblance. She spun a tale to explain it. He was conceived by a god, she tells them, and not just any god either, Zeus himself. His mother has a flair for the grandiose. It's her not-so-secret weapon and one that has saved her and Alexander's life. King Philip's marriage to Olympia came at a time when the Greecian states held power over Macedonia. King Philip himself had been a captive in Thebes as a young man and his marriage to the Greecian Princess was a political choice to ease the simmering hostility between the regions. Times always change, however, and over the course of their marriage, the military upper hand shifted to Macedonia. King Philip would take on second and third wives of noble Macedonian blood, even siring a son with the third five years ago. While Alexander is the eldest, there have been calls from the Macedonian elite to do away with the half-breed and his Greecian mother as to keep the royal bloodline pure. The rumors that Alexander may not even be Philip's son, fortified by the lack of a physical resemblance between the two, give the supporters of the movement to oust Alexander from his inheritance even more foder. Enter Olympia's stories of divine conception. So adept is she at spreading rumors of her powers of sorcery and her relationship with the gods, that she has become a folk hero of the plebeians and Alexander is regarded as Hercules himself. Children play with toy dolls sculpted in his image and expectant mothers pray to Olympia for a safe birth. The people want and expect the son of Zeus as their next king, regardless of his relation to their current king. Should Alexander be struck down in a political ploy, riots would ensue. And yet, Alexander and Olympia both know riots are a temporary condition. The threat of riot does not ensure Alexander's path to the crown.

Sometimes Alexandr fancies his mother's story. He likes that people believe Zeus to be his father, and his mother to be a mortal vessel. Growing up, Alexander would venture outside the walls of Pela to visit the plebian villages with his mother. They would bow to him and offer gifts, which he would graciously receive and offer fine gifts in return. He developed an understanding of his people in this way. *If you know to bring a farmer bags of seed and a herdsman a nanny or ewe, but not the other way around,* Alexander learned, *they will feel as if you yourself have heard and answered their prayers.* You will be as a god to them. But Alexander is not one to live in fantasy, himself. He respects the power the story gives him, but, as his tutor Aristotle taught him, he holds tightly to the truth. The most likely truth, in his mind, is that Alexander's father was the strongest, most handsome slave amongst his mother's lot. She paid him a generous stud fee, promised him his freedom, and then had his head chopped off so that he could never tell the tale, and then took back the stud fee.

Alexander busies himself with the possibilities of his parentage as they march, the men of the cavalry rank and file behind him, off their steeds, towards the man Alexander calls father, and the man his men call king. And as Alexander thinks of him, the man in the way.

Upon Alexander's arrival at the large olive wood table, shielded from the sun by a silk canopy, King Philip does not look up from his maps, nor does he regard the cavalry, standing at attention behind the prince.

“Father, I was hoping…” Alexander says, before Philip cuts him off.

“Continue hoping.” Philip's eyes stay locked on that map of Persia. If anything could distract Alexander from his current objective, it is this mission. The gods have seen fit to allow this king the honor of conquering Greece, but Persia belongs to Alexander. He feels it in his heart. That this lesser man would point his arrows towards what Alexander has decided to be his very purpose, makes his heart pound in doubletime. But Alexander calms himself. He remembers the point of today. And so Alexander waits. And his cavalry waits with him.

Finally, “Speak,” Philip says.

“In regards to the surviving member of the Sacred Band—"

“It’s a shame any survived at all, isn’t it? What could they possibly have to offer?” Philip says, cutting Alexander off again. Philip never lets a moment to defame the Band pass by. *As if to do so would put his own swordsmanship into question*, Alexander considers.

Alexander pushes on. “The Cavalry wish it to be their commander’s hand that sends him on his final journey. They fought with tremendous—"

“The Cavalry, hm?” the king says.

“The Cavalry,” Alexander confirms.

“Where’s Hephaestion?” the King asks, as he glances to the vanguard behind Alexander. “Oh, there he is. I see him. So the rumors are true? Where there’s one, there’s the other?”

Alexander understands the implication. It is a subtle schoolyard tease meant to incite his anger, reveal his insecurity to his men. It accomplishes neither. The thing that scares Philip the most about Alexander is not that he’s probably not his son, or that the people love Alexander more than they do himself, it is that Alexander is smarter than Philip. He can not manipulate this prince.

“Where there’s one there’s the other,” Alexander says, and he flicks his head back ever so slightly, prompting his cavalry to snap to their parade rest. They worked this trick out earlier and it serves its point. These are Alexander's men.

Philip's lips tighten as his insult fails to achieve the desired result. He recovers quickly, stands, and calls out, “The commander of the cavalry, heir to the throne, Prince Alexander of Macedonia’s hand shall execute the last survivor of the Theban Sacred Band, if that is the Cavalry’s wish.”

Alexander flicks his head again, sending his men to attention.

“Clever trick,” the king offers privately.

“I thank you, your majesty,” says Alexander. *It is a clever trick,* Alexander thinks, as he decides to push his luck. “One more matter. There was a letter from my mother.”

“The answer is no,” Philip says decisively.

Alexander suspected that would be the answer. In her ongoing mission to weave Alexander’s legend into the mythos of the people, Olympia desires that upon their victory over Greece, Alexander should be brought to Delphi to take a Pythia as a wife. Alexander knows her reasons. The rumors that Zeus was his father, that he is divine, will only be further ingrained in Greecian thinking if Apollo allows him the honor of taking one of his wives as his own. It's too clever of a plan not to be realized.

"We'll find you a suitable bride in Athens or Sparta."

"Of course," Alexander says dismissively, as if he knew the answer all along and agreed with it. In truth, he likes the idea of a Pythia, and he will marry one no matter Philip's wishes.

"You'll stay in Thebes for the next year as the Macedonian convoy to Greece, so a political marriage is favorable to a religious one, of course. Let me tell your mother. I know how much she had her heart set on a Pythia for a daughter," Philip says.

Alexander is suddenly afire with indignance. *What blasphemy is this?* He thinks. *Refuse the marriage, sure, but leave me here, while the glory lies to the east in Persia? No.* If the campaign to Persia could not wait until after King Philip's death, then Alexander would have thought he'd at least be at its helm. *Should I be there surely the King would die en route,* he rationalized to himself. If not by the will of the Gods, then by Alexander's own trickery.

"Father, the Cavalry—"

"Will be fine under Captain Tam's command."

Immediately, Alexander regrets not letting Hephaestion rip off Tam's arms and feed them to the hounds.

“Oh, but you can keep Hephaestion by your side. I’m sure the Thebans will appreciate your closeness,” Philip adds.

It’s a funny enough jab, but Alexander has already decided his plan. No need to win this battle. He will not be governor of Greece. Much too small.

Chapter 7: Leksi

I wake from a dreamless sleep, my limbs frozen in their binds. Even my ability to fend off this pain has its limits, my shoulders cramped and pleading for release. My back contorts, trying to find an escape from this stillness, but my nose detects something.

A bowl of food.

My little captor holds an olivewood spoon filled with gruel to my mouth.

"It's good," he says. "They're bits of goat and olives in it."

He moves the spoon closer still. I turn away.

"Go-to with that. It might be your last meal, might as well enjoy it."

He's right, but, "I've never eaten alone before." I haven't. It doesn't feel right.

I see his eyes questioning, wondering.

"I always eat alone," he says.

"You eat it, then."

"I won't eat what's yours. I did nothing to deserve this," he says, even as his mouth waters.

"You do deserve it. You earned it. You fought bravely." I offer.

"Bravely? I pissed myself," he says. He doesn't know how common that is.

"No matter. There were more of them, and they were bigger. You did the best you could and better than most," I say. It's the truth.

He blushes, smiles, then brightens. "We can share it. If I have some, will you eat?"

I nod my head. I'm not sure why.

He takes a small bite, refills the spoon, and brings it to my lips. I honor my word and open my mouth, allowing him to put the gruel between my lips, and gently, more gently than he needs to, he pulls it clean.

I wait for the food to travel down my throat before I ask, "Are you kin?"

"Go-to with that," he says, my words causing that Macedonian shame to flare up in him. That tension in the jaw, the darting eyes. I've seen it before. Prudes, the whole lot of them. But this one fights it back, returns his gaze to me.

"It's not like how it is in Thebes," he says.

"But I am Theban. And I ask you. Are you kin?"

"Of course, I'm kin," he says. He considers for a moment, as if he is deciding if he enjoys the taste of a wine, before he smiles. He does enjoy this flavor. "I've never said it aloud before."

"What's your name?" I ask.

"I'm not supposed to say."

"Who will I tell? I'm on my way at sunrise, won't have the chance. Would you tell me your name?"

"Petros," His name is Petros.

"Petros," I say. "You are a very capable soldier and you are kin. And that is good."

I see the shame batting down another fire deep inside him. A fire that I lit, I know. Perhaps it wasn't fair of me, considering how our world is changing, but I don't care.

"I wanted to be assigned to the hospital staff." He says, diverting my line of questioning. "I was a doctor's apprentice back home, but the head doctor here did not like me. He said I cared too much. That I spent too much time on small things. I shouldn't be telling you all this." He looks down, bites his lip. He's lonely. He's wanted someone to talk to for a long time.

"I am sure you will make an excellent doctor too." I offer, trying to return his kindness. Kindness is not a skill I've learned, but he brightens at my words.

"If you feed them secrets, little by little, they might let you live. You bide time, you never know what tomorrow holds," he says. He likes me. He wants me to live. The officer who assigned this man to guard prisoners should be executed, I think to myself. He wants to be my friend more than my captor. I consider using this to my advantage, except that, despite myself, I like him, too. He deserves a chance, at what, I don't know. I would like to see him become a doctor, a kin doctor, maybe. I would like to see that very much.

"I want to die. I want to return to my brothers, and my lover," I remember as I say aloud, and this too is true.

"I want to go home," he says.

"Then I wish you safe journey home, Petros."

"You, too…"

"Leksi," I offer.

"You too, Leksi." He says my name.

Chapter 8: Petros

I dream Leksi holds me in his arms so tightly I can't breathe. I'm afraid, wondering why he's unbound, how he broke free, but I'm stiff as a sword, too. Why deny it?

"Petros." He calls my name.

"Petros." A hard whisper, not a dream. I open my eyes.

I see Leksi in the dull flame of the torch, on edge, listening, smelling the air, like a hunting dog held back from a chase.

"Unbind me," he says.

I'm gripped by fear, and I don't know why. My instincts scream to cut this man loose, against all logic. I have good instincts, always have. Self-preservation is something I excel at. But this makes no sense. I have orders. I have a duty as a Macedonian.

"I can't," is all I can get out.

"Then run," he says.

Run? What does he mean? I know what he means, but I'm too busy silencing the voice in my head screaming *Trust this man!* to make sense of what he's actually telling me.

"Run!" he screams this time.

I stand and hurry to the tent door, but I'm pushed back inside. A man, the same ogre as before, is on me. I don't have a chance to inhale, let alone scream out.

Not so with Leksi. “Alexander!” Leksi gets out one mighty howl before Captain Tam, who followed the ogre in, manages to stuff his mouth with a wet rag.

And then I listen and watch, under the weight of the ogre. I listen to Captain Tam explain. “Orders from my king… leave just a fraction of life for my son to extinguish.”

I struggle. I fight back. But I’m too small. The ogre even manages to reach down and strip off my belt, pull aside my tunic. I feel his member, hard against my leg, slip its way upward, but I don't care. I fight for my charge, as useless as it is.

“Which is fine by me. I hate the Band,” says the captain, as he drives the handle of his sword into Leksi’s stomach.

The ogre’s member finds its target, and he thrusts, but not hard enough. I don’t want him inside me, and I couldn’t will myself to open to him even if my life did depend on it.

“I hate all kin,” I hear the captain say to Leksi. And he drives a fist into Leksi’s ribs.

No, I think. *Not like this. Gods hear me, not like this.*

And then my thoughts fade. The ogre's arms around my throat, the lights dim around the outside. All I see now is Leksi, unafraid, angry, furious, as my body relaxes, and the ogre's member finds its way inside. With the last bit of light and consciousness, I stay with Leksi, suddenly more my countryman than any Macedonian has ever been, as Captain Tam's fist finds his face, driving his head back into the post with a hollow thud.

And when Leksi’s eyes close, so do mine. Perhaps I’ll dream of him.

Chapter 9: Leksi

I awake in a rage. I don't want death. I want to kill. Kill.

I drive my feet into the earth as I bite down on the fabric lodged in my mouth, and the post gives. The captain's beating had some worth. My head bouncing against this pole had some value. I loosened it. It's enough. I know what to do.

Petros's knife, lost in his struggle, is a foot's length from his unconscious hand. And I can reach it with my feet if I extend out my leg.

The pain across my back should be unbearable as I spin my leg to face him and the rough wood tears against my flesh, but I no longer feel pain. I extend my leg and pull the knife close with my feet. I spin around again so that my bound hands are near the blade. Though they have no feeling and no eyes to guide them, they manage to reach down and find the handle. Aries is working through them. Aries is my eyes. Aries knows what is to come if I am unbound. Aries saws at the binds with this tiny blade and he smiles.

The knife does its work, little by little, the type of work where you can't see the progress, incremental, strand by strand, until...snap... Aries has his puppet back.

My back collapses, and I fold over. I hold my breath to stop myself from screaming. This mission will be as silent as it is deadly. I roll onto my knees, let my blood flow back into my fingers.

I stand, find my feet. I feel the strength of the fallen rise up into me, and all at once I am strong again.

I stand over Petros. I watch as the small of his back rises and falls. He's breathing. I hold the knife up. I know what Sigorin would do: slit his throat, let him silently choke in a pool of his own blood. One less Macedonian. One less Theban that needs to be revenged.

But I won't kill him. It's not a question. He's kin. He's kind.

I return the borrowed blade to the floor next to his hand and leave the tent.

With only the sandals on my feet and the fabric around my waist, unarmed, I walk out into the Macedonian camp.

Three long rows of simple, cloth tents. Torches illuminate the path, but there are plenty of shadows in which to hide. The Macedonians do love their shadows. And for now, I exist in them.

I'm to walk east, I remember, back towards the battlefield, back towards my fallen brothers, I know that, but my heart will not point out the way. It's not where my present purpose calls. There is work to be done elsewhere. *There is another deed that needs to be revenged before I answer your call, Sigorin,* I think to myself. I know he would approve.

I hear him singing, a low, Macedonian, drunken singing that does not sound unlike his grunting when he took Petros the way that he did. And now I have a destination. It is not east. I go to his fire, isolated, on the outskirts of the camp, in the shadows.

I hear clay dice hit a shield. I look more closely. This kind of killing was not a part of my training. The Band faces our enemies with battle cries in the blazing sun. But I am devoted to this death, even if it means a murder in silent darkness.

It is my shield the dice hit, my shield, emblazoned with the club of Hercules. This man throws dice against the shield of the Band, after performing such an act against my kin. I feel nothing but the pull towards him. I would use my bare hands, but the gods have granted me the means to fulfill my desire. My shield.

The ogre and his unfortunate companion look down as they collect coins from a pile. Their song reaches its climax. It is all the distraction I need as the shield finds my forearm.

My foe looks back as the blade hidden along the bottom of my shield rides across his throat. He makes no sounds as he dies. His comrade does not have a chance to scream as my shield shows him no mercy either.

Hermes comes to escort their souls down below. *Stay close to me, god, there will be plenty more who will require your service.*

Now I feel the tug of my brothers, Sigorin, the Band. *Find them now,* my heart says. I take my shield and the coins. These dead don't deserve them. Let them wander the shores of Styx and beg for their fare. The tug moves my gaze upward. Stars, in the night sky. And these are my constellations. This is my home. They point the way. East.

Chapter 10: Petros

It feels like eons as I wait for the strength to just open my eyes. It's the only movement I can ask of my pathetic, cowardly soul. Just open your eyes.

But I can't. And I wait. I'm an old, damned man now. Finally, when they're ready as if they had a separate will, my eyes open. He's gone, of course. I see the knife, my knife, the knife he used to cut his binds to free himself. The words of my captain—*"Should he escape, you will have no opportunity to explain yourself, your punishment will be death"*—ring inside me.

And my hand, as if it too has a will of its own, reaches for the blade and grabs the handle. So bold, this hand, as if it had a slightest clue how to wield the weapon.

The other hand pushes my torso upright, and I'm on my feet. I reset my clothing. I pretend I am a man. I leave the tent and I enter the night, grateful for the darkness.

If I ring the bell, is my punishment still death? I'm unsure, and rational thought isn't ruling this night, so I do what my heart demands. I walk alone, and I search.

I walk and search until I find the ogre, dead. I find what's left of him and whoever the poor fool was who kept his company smiling from a place on their throats where there should not be a smile. There is more blood than I've ever seen. It's in pools, too much for the earth to absorb. Can I pretend I don't know who avenged me? Is that an option? Sure. Obviously, the ogre and his friend slipped and fell on a sword, slitting their throats. Tragic accident.

I pretend it doesn't feel good. I pretend I'm not glad. I pretend I don't feel more loyalty to Leksi in this moment than I do for my country. I pretend that all those things are untrue because why not just make up my own reality for the rest of this evening. I keep pretending and I walk away, a little taller than before.

There is a camp filled with captains, a king, a prince, too! I walk by them. They sleep well, content, their necks intact. Only two men were slain tonight. I know why but pretend not to. Still, I walk a little taller. I can't help that part.

I know where Leksi's going. I'll find my charge. This is all going to work out just fine. I like this game. I pretend I'll be able to apprehend him and bring him back to the tent all on my own so that Alexander can terminate his life. Why not? That is how I envision the future and so let it be true.

At the edge of camp, I see him in the distance, barely visible in the moonlight but even if that full moon were new, I'd still know he was there, exactly where I knew he'd be, in the heart of the battlefield, where the Macedonian Cavalry rode down and murdered the Sacred Band of Thebes.

I think that I should consider blowing a trumpet or ringing that bell now. But the thought of a musical instrument being turned into an instrument of war bothers me this evening. I'm going to pretend that I've forgotten where they stash the trumpets, and that there's not a bell on the other side of that tent that I've walked by hundreds of times. Alright, perhaps it is there, but I'm quite sure it's broken.

Armed with only my little knife, I head out onto the battlefield of Chaeronea, still musky with the smell of death. I step over the stunted mounds of earth and pretend I cannot hear the forms under the thin layer of dirt calling to me, *breathe easy, Petros, it's not long before you will be one of us.* Fine, I'll confess. My ability to pretend is waning now.

At least I'll die knowing I made my father proud. I've admitted my perversion tonight. I'm kin. I've allowed myself to be entered by another—against my will, sure, but still. I will battle this great warrior of Greece in man to man combat. He will be the death of me, or I will be the death of him. The latter is most unlikely. I think of my father again. Does he think of me? Is this what he wants for me? Marching to my death, a soldier of the North?

Leksi hears me coming, I know he does, but he stays on his knees. I stand behind him now. I can reach down and slit his throat if I were fast about it, but he's earned this moment from me, or at least that's the reason I give myself for not doing it. Instead, I look over him and see what he sees.

The decomposing face of a poor Grecian soldier, his mighty beard still distinguished, even in his death pose, lies unearthed before Leksi. Two coins rest on the corpse's eyes.

What must it feel like to know real love as a kin and then to lose it? I feel sorrow for Leksi. I force myself to think of my duty to my country. I could bury my little blade in Leksi's back or I could slice at his ankles so that he cannot run, but it's all too far from what it is I want to do. I want to kneel beside him. I want to take his hand in mind, to mourn by his side, to comfort him, to tell him how sorry I am for his loss. I fight that back, and manage to get out, "Stand up, prisoner."

He rises to his feet, casually turns, and chuckles to himself, not cruelly. He's crying.

"Walk. We're going back," I demand, or I try to.

"No," he says, sweetly.

"Now," I say, in the voice I was trained to use.

"Do it." I know what he's asking, but I don't respond.

"Please, Petros. Lay me here by his side. There's nothing left for me," he says.

"I can't. I don't know how," I say, noticing the tears streaming down my own cheeks.

"Stab here." He points to his heart and drags down.

I will not stab this man in the heart. I will not.

"Come back to camp. Alexander himself will do the honor," I say, as if he cares about Alexander.

"I don't want him to. You. You're kin. My kin. You, by the gods, please," Leksi says.

"No. I won't. I won't kill you," I say.

"You should never have come to war," he says. There's an apology in his voice, but what is he apologizing to me for?

"No shite!" I offer back. "If you don't come back with me, they'll kill me. You want to die, I only want to make it through the—"

My thought wasn't through. I barely see his arm, only a blur of bended light, flash out, and then darkness, and then cool mud on my chest. And then the inability to move. Everything's different now. Am I dead?

Chapter 11: Hephaestion

Hephaestion awakes to a trumpet tapping out an alarm, a prisoner escape. That's the tune. He knows at once who it is. He is glad.

Alex must have dreamed of the Bandman's escape, Hephaestion thinks, for Alexander is on his feet and dressed by the time Hephaestion shakes off sleep.

But Alexander does not run out the door. He stares at Hephaestion, as he wraps a shawl around his shoulders and slips sandals onto his feet. It is a look that Hephaestion has only caught sight of once before. Just as he does this time, Alexander turns away the moment he realizes Hephaestion's aware of him. Hephaestion wonders how often Alexander looks at him this way and he does not notice. How often does Alexander not get caught with this look of desire? This look that says, *I want more.* Alexander thinks Hephaestion doesn't feel it, too, but he does; and Hephaestion decides that Alexander looks at him like that ten thousand times a day. That's how good it feels to be desired by Alexander. And yet this look is extinguished the moment it is observed, so is it real? Hephaestion is unsure.

And yet the Band lives, Hephaestion considers, *and we are to go to Thebes. I can't be ignored for long.* But Alexander says nothing. And Hephaestion says nothing for now. And they exit into the morning stars.

Chapter 12: Alexander

Alexander has these thoughts from time to time, once a day, he might deduce. The desire to lie by Hephaestion's side, to become one with him, to hand over half of his burdens onto Hephaestion's willing shoulders, *to make my life about Hepha, as he has made his life about me.* He does not approve of these thoughts.

They were born into that paradigm where Alexander does not give to Hephaestion, not gifts, not burdens, nothing. But Hephaestion gives all to Alexander. Neither is to blame. To their credit, they have it made it work as best they can.

As they arrive in silence on the field of combat, where the tracks of the escaped prisoner have led, Alexander utilizes the training of his famed tutor to set these thoughts aside. There's work to be done and these thoughts impede this work. The objective of this mission is to re-capture the bandsman. His freedom represents hope for the Thebans and hope is an enemy to the Macedonian state at this present moment. The bandsman's freedom represents something different for Alexander. It gives him another kind of hope as it pertains to Hephaestion. This confuses the prince. He does not understand himself or the thought, so this thought too is set aside.

Alexander identifies the most prominent threat on the field, per his training, first: his supposed father, and his cohorts around him, observing the operation. King Philip is always the biggest threat. Alexander turns his keen eye now to the hounds, sniffing, seeking out the scent trail. This is indeed a task for dogs, but not these dogs, Alexander considers. These are large hounds that sniff the air, noses up, picking up pieces of the trail here and there. They work alone with a single human handler, one dog, one man. There are small hounds in the kennel, too. They work as a pack, their noses on the trail, following the scent as if it were a path, taking turns clearing their nostrils while the others keep their noses to the ground. When their prey is tracked down and confronted, it is confronted by a pack of dogs and a team of men. The chances of at least one of the larger hounds tracking their quarry is greater, they are working independently versus the pack that works as one; however when the large hound finds their target, they must finish the hunt as one man and one dog. With the bandsman, they will find that, in the end, they are not the hunter. Alexander knows better than to explain this to King Philip and instead considers how this misstep on the part of the King might well work in his favor. Perhaps the value of the Bandsman alive is worth reconsidering with more seriousness. *How else might this man serve me*, Alexander considers.

One savvy bitch sniffs about the grave site of the Band. She lands on point. Her handler, a particularly large man, bends down to pick something up. He looks about to see if he's been seen. He has been but he does not notice Alexander watching him. He gives his hound a stiff nod and she bolts into the trees, her handler hot on her trail; one man, one dog, neither understanding the strength of the quarry they chase.

Alexander deduces that there's been a bounty offered to the tracker who brings in the escaped prisoner and that this man with the savvy bitch wants the reward for himself. Even if his bitch would allow for the company of another dog, her handler would not. *Fool,* Alexander thinks, and then he turns his attention to his father.

King Philip looks up from his maps as Alexander approaches. "Father, he'll serve these men to the crows. Please allow the cavalry the duty of bringing him in." Alexander says. He knows there's no point, but he wants his opposition to the operation noted by those in attendance. They will be taking orders from him one day.

"No, you've done enough." The king answers before he turns to Hephaestion.

"Hephaestion, my son doesn't always take my orders as seriously as he should so I put them on you. See him to Thebes. It's where the two of you belong."

Alexander takes in the responses of his father's men, remembering for future reference who dared to smile and who manages to repress childish giggles.

But then Alexander turns to Hephaestion and his heart hurts for his dear friend. *He should not have to endure my father's teasing*, Alexander considers.

But if Hephaestion feels shame he does not show it. If anything, he seems content with that order. "Sir." He responds to his King. Alexander likes that he did not say *your majesty*. Little jabs have their way.

Chapter 13: Leksi

I never would have thought a man as tiny as Petros would be this heavy. Perhaps it is my injuries, the broken ribs, the wounded arms, the various parts of my flesh that won't stop bleeding. I manage to carry him, still, my shirt slung over his head so he will not know our direction, but there is only one direction to go. I trudge through these woodlands and make it to sunrise before my body screams *enough* and I cannot will it to take another step. I set Petros down beside the river that we follow. It's only a stream in this place, water flowing gently over stones.

For a moment, with my shirt covering his eyes, I look upon Petros kindly before I press the tip of the knife, his knife, into his back. He whimpers. I let the guilt ride through me before I strip off his blinds, still holding the knife between his shoulder blades.

He squints at the morning sun.

"Where are we?" His voice is cracked and dry.

"You walk from here," I say.

"Where are we going?" he replies.

"No more questions and no more talking, or I will have no choice but to kill you." It is not a lie. I will.

A light, what little light there was, vanishes from his eyes. I wish I had lied, told him I would let him go as soon as I arrive at my destination, just so I didn't have to see that light extinguish like that. It hurt me. But this thought occurred to me too late. I press the tip of the knife between his shoulder blades once more to spur him forward and then lower the weapon. This is not how I was trained. I was trained to hold the knife in place, to make sure the prisoner knows that one move against me and his spine will be severed, but that feels silly. We are alone. There are no captains watching to ensure I follow their orders to the letter and no brothers in arms who watch to see how poorly I treat a prisoner. It is only Petros with me and he is no threat. I'm taller than him by a head's length, my arms are the size of his legs, and I've never before seen a man walk so gently, as if he were trying to spare the lives of the bugs beneath his feet. He would never do me harm even if he could, he's proven this. I walk behind him. He knows to follow the stream. We say nothing.

I like walking. I forget the pain in my body. I even, for a moment, forget the pain in my heart. While yesterday began in violence, and tomorrow will surely end in violence, this middle part is, in fact, quite beautiful. It would have been easier on the body to take the well traveled road that joins Chaeronea and Thebes, of course. There are farms on this road, with families that I know from my boyhood who would be honored to hide us for a time, but I will not put them in danger. My comfort is worth less than their safety and so we walk along the stream. She naturally stays in the valleys she created and keeps to the tree groves, lush with cypress, oaks and olive trees, that she waters. She masks our scent as we cross in and out of her deep pools as she spares us the rolling hills and the meadows that populate this land, those hills and meadows that could allow eyes to note our presence. These forests, although neighbor to the greatest city of our time, are virgin to all but the occasional travelers and the lesser gods and goddesses who reside here.

We proceed this way for a quarter of the day before a gentle song stops up. A woman's song in the old tongue, accompanying the rushing of the stream, wider and deeper in this section.

I sheath his knife. I push Petros forward with my bare hand so that, as we round the corner of the hill, he is exposed first. This too I've been trained to do. We find an old woman simmering a brew on an open fire at the foot of a waterfall. She sits on a tree stump. Mushrooms, bright red with white spots, grow between the living trees around her. She is wild, with bare feet and nails that look more like claws and her matted, jet black hair is as thick as any helmet. The pelts on her body blend with her flesh so that it is difficult to tell where she ends and her world begins. Beautiful, in her way.

"May we drink from your pot, my lady? This water is foreign to him," I say.

She shifts her eyes from me to Petros and smiles. She doesn't speak. She leans over and fills a mug with broth from her cauldron. I look to Petros and nudge him forward, trying to remember if he is friend or foe.

I watch the old woman watch me. Her eyes latch onto mine, like a dog on a bone, even as she says to Petros, "Funny, the games boys play, aren't they?"

And all at once, I feel very small.

Chapter 14: Hephaestion

Hephaestion finds himself in a dark and wet cave. He hears a shuffling before him and shouts out to warn the other of his presence, to let them know he means no harm. The being barks, not like a canine though, how a human would bark, if a human barked. He wakes up afraid. Hephaestion is not often afraid.

He leans over his cot to get a glimpse of Alexander, who would be asleep beneath him, and a new wave of fear falls upon him. Alexander is gone.

Hephaestion jumps to his feet and sparks a torch, the morning sun having not yet come, and then he sees the letter, tied to the rope that cinches the leather door closed. It's in Alexander's hand.

Dear Hephaestion,
I cannot do as my father commands, and I will not ask you to commit treason by joining me. Please be well. Please obey. I do this so that we might rule one day. I as king; you as general. Not just of Macedonia and Greece, but of the world. Until then, please keep your head.
—Alex

How dare he? How dare he? How dare he? The question consumes Hephaestion's thinking as he feels his temperature rise.

He tears the letter apart as he imagines tearing the hairs off Alexander's scalp. He has, in fact, lost his head and he does not care.

Where are my sandals?! An actionable thought finally

coming to him. “Saddle my horse!” He screams. He knows his boy is near enough, asleep in the adjacent tent.

“Sir?” a tired little voice calls back as Hephaestion puts his sandals on his feet. The boy peeks his head in.“Prince Alexander said that I should not allow—” The look on Hephaestion’s face averts him from continuing his prepared speech. “I will saddle your horse at once.”

Chapter 15: Petros

“Why don’t you just kill me?” I ask. “I’m tired of walking. We both know I’d make a shite hostage. They won’t actually care if you kill me.” But he says nothing in response.

It has only been a few ticks of the sun since we left the old woman and the waterfall and I’m not actually physically tired at all. While I could never beat my adversary in a fight, even if I cheated, I am certain I could out walk him. I wasn’t much of a soldier but I was quite good at the marching thing. There are some advantages to being slight. Truth is, I’m bored. The stream has given way to a much larger river. The Theban farmers living in the countryside have planted wheat and barely here. There are no trees or forest critters to break up the monotony of the scenery and Leksi won’t speak to me.

“Answer me,” I nudge. But he doesn’t. I’m not surprised.

“What, you want to do that to me, too? That’s why you’re keeping me, isn’t it?” I ask.

“I would never do that.” He speaks, finally.

I know. It was a rude thing to say to the man who avenged me, but in fairness he also kidnapped me and is currently leading me to what I can only assume will be a short period of enslavement followed by an unceremonious and violent death. Which would all be just fine if he would speak to me. I’m not good with silence.

“Aye. Camp full of kings and generals, and you kill him.” It’s my little way of saying thank you.

"I killed him. Yes. I killed him. I've killed many men. Be quiet now."

"I don't want to," I say.

"You should've killed me when you had the chance then," he snaps, right mad.

"I didn't want to either," I say in a pouty voice, keenly aware I'm being a child, but I can't match his fury.

"Now, I must act upon my orders," he offers as he turns away from me. *Interesting*, I think. This is the first I've heard of orders.

"What's that?" I say. He goes silent, but how important are the details, really? Whatever his orders are, it can't bode well for me.

"You don't have to, you know…we could just…go somewhere else. Get on a boat somewhere and sail off." I've thought of doing it plenty of times back home; perhaps he has, too. "There's not much of Greece left to fight over, but it's a giant world. Aren't there ferries to the south of here? A day's march, not far."

He stops, finally looks at me. I suspect he is truly considering the thought.

"No. I have orders," he says, pushing away whatever he was pondering.

It sounds like an apology.

"I cannot," he says again, without any objection from me on his first answer. But the Gods immediately let him know what they think of that.

A hound, large and brown, flies out of the brush and sinks her flashing teeth into Leksi's arm.

They tumble to the ground, and I fall into the brush from which the bitch emerged. I can't intervene here either. This man, my feelings be damned, was leading me to my grave, and so I watch as blood flows from the beast's jaws—his blood, Leksi's blood.

A moment filled with snarls and groans goes by before Scar arrives. I know him from camp, because he was always alone, like me. Early on, I thought perhaps, like me, he wanted to sit next to someone at chow, but this was not the case. He prefers solitude. He's also cruel.

As is his dog, thrashing and tearing at Leksi's arm. I guess Leksi will get his wish. Death by dog. Terrible way to go.

Scar doesn't think so, though. Scar, who doesn't see me hidden behind the bush, chuckles at the mayhem his beast is causing. But then his chuckling stops.

"Ayo!" he calls out to Leksi, who is making his way into the river, the shaking dog dangling from his bleeding arm. The river, which appeared boring and slow a moment before now reveals its depth and strength as Leksi is covered up to his neck in a few quick steps out from its bank.

"Ayo! Dog can't swim!"

I've never heard Scar speak before, and now I understand why. He slurs his words as if his own tongue is choking him.

And Leksi continues into the water, submerging the hound under the river's surface, both man and beast flowing downstream in the powerful current.

“Dogs ain’t cheap!”

But this dog’s life seems to be, as its body releases its hold on Leksi and floats downstream. Leksi’s shield, having been torn off his back by the current, goes along with the beast. It’s an odd sight, the two objects floating off, both lifeless.

“Out with you!” Scar garbles. “Out with you!”

Leksi wades back to shore. Somehow, his sandals have stayed on his feet when nothing else managed to cling to his body.

“They want you dead, boy,” Scar declares.

Leksi shrugs an *if-the-gods-insist* with his shoulders.

“Be still. I’ll make it painless,” Scar says.

Leksi doesn’t move. Scar's angry confidence bleeds a little from his eyes as he unsheathes his sword and steps forward.

A smile escapes Leksi’s lips when his eyes find mind. The angry captor who carried me from the camp and to this point is gone. The quiet soul who asked me with no malice if I was kin is back. I smile back at him, wishing that we could spend a lifetime together, even if just this one. I take comfort knowing that he’s about to get exactly what he wants. Scar thrusts his blade at Leksi’s heart, exactly the way Leksi told me to do.

But the weapon doesn't find its mark. Leksi turns to the side, dodging the blow. At once, he grabs Scar’s wrists, but the brute is strong, and he yanks his hands back, still clutching the blade. The steel edge catches Leksi’s side and opens him up deep.

Scar pulls back to deliver another blow, but then he stumbles back, holding his throat. A punch from Leksi must have landed there, although I didn't see Leksi's arm move.

Scars holds the blade out to keep Leksi at bay while he recovers his breath. But Leksi does not pursue.

His eyes find mine once more. Another smile. But I don't say goodbye. I won't be fooled again. Leksi falls to his knees, the wound on his side gushing blood, staining the earth. Still, I don't say goodbye.

Leksi's hand pats the rocky shore, as if guided by a force outside of himself. Scar stalks towards him, the blade positioned in his hand to drive down. Scar takes his time, an eternity to sniff at his wounded prey, as if honoring his deceased hound by savoring the kill. Finally, he raises his sword and plunges it down. The fool. I saw this coming. Leksi dodges the blow, and with his snake-like speed drives a stone from the river into Scar's jaw.

The snap of his teeth coming together must be the last sound he hears, for in the next moment he falls onto his back like a downed tree. His stiff legs twitch as Leksi pounces on top of him. Leksi savors nothing. There is no joy or emotion as he drives the stone into Scar's head two, three, four more times. He continues to pound, like a craftsman, until the matter from the big brute's brain comes dripping out from the top of his skull.

Leksi drops his rock and looks back to me, and I am unexpectedly overcome with guilt and shame. This kill was for me. I hadn't realized it until the deed was done. Now I can escape my execution. Now I can return with Leski, dead or alive, it won't matter. I can earn back my life.

Leksi, his naked body red with his own blood, collapses onto Scar.

What should I do? Carry Leksi's all the way back to Chaeronea? Prove my worth to kings and princes? I'm not strong enough for such a feat, but that isn't the point, is it? That's not what Leksi wants. The point is the boat. The point is a ferry to somewhere else, anywhere. It's only a day's march south. I had heard soldiers talking about it before the battle. If Macedonia lost and they escaped with their lives, that's what they would do, escape slavery, make it the ferries, leave this land. That's why Leksi made this sacrifice. To allow me to escape—not back to Macedonia, for even if they do spare my life, it is still a death. There is no life for a kin in Macedonia.

I suddenly feel very alone. The idea of the ferry, so appealing only moments before, now fills me with despair. This life of freedom had worth when the fantasy had Leksi in it. Now, I'm frozen in my solitude.

"What are you doing? Save him, little one!" A woman's voice calling from the trees pulls me from my self-pity. I look up and see the woman we met earlier in the forest staring down at me.

"Save him!" she bellows once more.

I want to shout, *How?* I want to explain why I think Leksi did this deed and ask her if I should run to the ferry, but my legs move without my command, and I'm racing to Leksi, kneeling over him.

The wound continues to bleed, and the color is gone from his cheeks, but there is still breath in him. It wheezes and lessens with every inhale, but it's still there.

"I don't know what to do," I say to myself, but the lady of the woods is right by my side.

"Bring him to mine, my medicine is strong," she says.

"How?" The word finally comes from me. We have no cart or horse.

"Carry him!" she demands. My mind shrieks in protest. *I'm small!* But all at once, Leksi is on my shoulders, and I carry him, following the witch back toward her lair.

I think about the ferry once more. Maybe one day soon I will manage passage on a boat, but not now. Now, I strain to hold him up, his blood streaming down my chest and back. I think for a moment that I am hurt, that this blood is mine. And I try to remember what it feels like to be alone.

Chapter 16: Leksi

Lay me down and let me die.

If only I had the breath to speak these words. Or the will to stop the breath I have. But I have neither.

And I am being carried, I know not where, on the shoulders of my Macedonian friend, who is proving himself a sturdy little mule, a little Hercules, but every step he takes sends blades of pain through my body, and not one will bring the death that I have earned. I would have let the big one with the scar on his face end me if I had known that Petros wouldn't have simply run off. That was the plan. One last kill so that Petros had one last chance to live a worthwhile life. Why I care, I do not know. Maybe because it would add some meaning to my death? Or because he was kind to me, perhaps? But this is not kindness, him carrying me like this. This is righteousness, a desire to be better, more generous than me. It is rude to not take a gift when it is offered to you. Do they not teach that in Macedonia? Savages. I am annoyed. Perhaps annoyance will be my final emotion. I will welcome death annoyed. Sigorin would laugh at me when I was annoyed. The blackness comes, finally. He'll have a good laugh when Hermes brings me to him like this.

A waterfall beats down on my back. I open my eyes to the night. No, that's not right. The air is damp here, cool.

"You're in a cave, Leksi. You're in her cave," Petros says as he lays me down on a stone floor. This is not Hades. Wrong cave. I live. It is that cursed witch. It is her cave. The waterfall is her doorway. I knew she was trouble when I heard her song, as beautiful as it was. I knew she was the meddling type. There she is, rummaging through an olive wood box, one of many in the room sized cave. She stands, having found what she needed, revealing an ink drawing of a serpent needled into the skin of her leg. She moves about the tiny cave as a snake would, purposeful, speed without haste. She's magic.

Let me go, goddess, I think to myself, as the lady of the forest hands Petros the treasure she recovered—a thin bone, most likely from a river fish, and hair from a donkey's tail, perhaps.

"Mend your man," she says. What is this? Mending is not a high priority for me at the present time. And *your man?*

Petros drives the point of the bone into my side, and just when I thought my body could not hurt more, it does. He punishes me for protecting him.

I try to call out, *Stop!* But all I manage is a moan.

"He's lost too much blood. I'm only hurting him."

You're correct. You're very correct. You should stop.

"Nonsense," she bellows back. "This is your work. So work," her bellows turning into a song, a spell.

"But—" he says, only her spell does its work and the doctor in Petros answers the call. That man who tended my wounds in Chaeronea comes forward and he will not let me go. He is to the work of saving men as I am to the work of killing them.

I turn then to the witch, doing work of her own. She drops pieces of her red white-spotted mushrooms into a small stone bowl and grinds them with a pestle. She pours steaming water into the bowl. I have heard of this witchcraft before. I want nothing to do with it.

Take me from this body. Take me from the world, I plead with the gods, any which one who will listen.

"What are you doing?" Petros asks the witch, the authority of his craft in his voice.

But she does not answer. She tips my head back to pour her brew down my throat. I try to resist, but my body will not play along. It wants to drink.

"He needs a reason to live," she offers.

I swallow it down.

And all at once I do leave this time and place, but I do not find myself in Hades, or afloat on the river Styx. I am home. My father's farm. I am six years old, sitting beside the cottage covered in grass and mud, built into the earth, inside a small hill, as is our custom, the chimney smoking with the promise of warm stew. A white mare, young and strong, flicks flies away with her tail. And my dolly, the little toy my mother gave me, dances in my hands. I am truly happy. My father comes marching out of his field. He is exhausted. He's always exhausted. Even at this age I know why. It is exhausting to be a man. To live up to the demands. To be the biggest, the strongest, the bravest of all. And when he sees me with dolly his exhaustion breaks. In a flash, he snatches the dolly from my hands.

"You are no kin!" he says harshly. "You are no kin!" he says it again. He hits me. The back of his hand across my face. My head snaps around. I see stars.

For a moment, I am back in the witch's lair. Back with Petros. But another wave from the brew rolls over me.

And then I'm hit again, but not by my father. This is Marcos's doing, the big, mean boy from the schoolyard. Every school, everywhere in the world, any time in the world, has its Marcos. Thebes is no different. His fists fall down on me as the chant of "kin, kin, kin" rings out from the children watching, enjoying the show.

But then they are gone, too. And I float in a space all of my own making. And for perhaps the first time in my life, it is quiet enough to think.

I've always been kin, I consider, but I forgot what it was like to be kin and not part of the Band. Even in the Band, we mocked those kin who were not of the shield and sword. Not to their faces, of course; they were still our brothers and sisters. And we would never let others say a word against them. They were ours, but we mocked them still. We were men. And we were better at being men than those who were not kin. But I forgot what it was like before all that. And now I remember what it was like. I remember the shame. Damn this witch, damn Petros. I could have left this world without remembering. I wish I could leave, but the next wave hits me.

This time, I land on the doorstep of the lodge, where my father, tears forming but not falling from his eyes, hands me over to Grogorious, the leader of the Band. I know my father's words even though he does not say them: *Only here can I be proud of you. Only here do you not bring me shame. Only here do you have worth.*

"Remember the Band. Remember." I hear her voice from outside of me. The witch. And I do. I remember. Gods help me, I remember.

I am thrust past the lodge's threshold, too young. I know it. They know it, too. Beatings, constant beatings, savage beatings, until I learn that the only way to stop a tormentor is to hurt a tormentor. And this is how I learn to fight, not by instruction, but by necessity. Every punch I throw has a purpose, to stop my pain by causing irreversible harm to the one who caused it.

Cosimo is the first to take the whip to me, lash on lash. I am too little to stop him. But I find another escape, a hole I can crawl into. In this hole, I enjoy every lash, the pain turned to pleasure. Eyes rolling into the back of my head as I ask for another, as I ask for it harder. *Please, sir. Harder.*

I remember all this as the witch pours more of her brew down my throat and Petros continues with his nagging knitting at my side. I know what they're doing, knitting me back together again, keeping my form, when all I want is to dissolve back into the earth.

With this thought, the next wave hits me, and I am thrust back into the lodge, where I meet him for the first time. Months of fighting, beatings, torture, and then I see him. My desire for love has been removed from me. He is another man to break, to scar, to deny. I attack, fists blazing, teeth snapping. I overwhelmed the last three men they sent to beat me. When I ripped into the last one, biting his cheek hard, four more had to tear me off him. He bore the scars until his death in Chaeronea. We would laugh about it in the barracks.

So who is this new man they put before me? He is different. Despite his massive size, he moves like water. I cannot get hold of him. When I finally manage to grab a wrist, he spins himself free, intertwines his fingers with mine, and pins me to the ground. I snap my teeth at his throat, but I miss, and he smiles. He pushes his member into mine. I growl. I thrust up, with my hips. He laughs as I push him into the air.

I roll, try to crawl out from under him, but he lies down on my back, wrapping his massive arms around my neck, pulling me close to him, his bicep under my chin.

"My name is Sigorin, and I've been watching you, Leksi," he says, "I choose you."

I rage, shaking, resisting with every fiber of my being. But that bicep only flexes into my throat. I cannot breathe. All goes black.

"Breathe, Leksi!" I hear Petros's voice demand and feel him jabbing his needles into my side. I do. I choose to breathe.

Then I am back with Sigorin, his arms still around my neck. "Do you choose me, Leksi?" he asks. "Choose me, Leksi."

I rage again, digging into his forearms with my nails.

"No," he says.

Once more he squeezes, and once more all goes black.

"Breathe for me, Leksi. Stay with me." I breathe because Petros says to.

I awake back in Sigorin's arms, remembering, reliving.

There's no fight left in me to resist those arms around my neck. He allows enough room for words and that is all.

"Please…"

I feel his manhood, probing at my rear.

"Please," I say again.

"Once more, hmm…?" he asks. "No," I reply. But he is not really asking.

The arms tighten and all goes black.

"Try again, Leksi," Petros says. "Try once more."

And I do. I breathe, and…

Sigorin is inside me. I feel him, all of him. I dreamed of this moment, and now it is happening for the first time. I feel him thrusting in and out. He turns my head, yanking it back, and kisses my lips, his tongue in my mouth. It hurts. All of it.

"Do you choose me?" he says.

"I do," I say. I choose to turn pain into pleasure. I have been taught to do that.

And then there's that space again, where it is quiet enough to think. So I do. There was no choice here, except the choice to surrender, surrender to him inside me, surrender to feeling safe in his arms, surrender to my lusting for his weight on top of me. Surrender to never surrendering when I fought by his side, when I held his shield in battle. Surrender to his love and only his love. Surrender to what it means to be Band.

And all goes black again, except now I breathe—shallow, weak breaths, but I feel them inside me and hear her, the witch.

"Perfect the Band was not, my son, but know this: fags they'll call our kinship when the next sun rises. Fags, after the sticks they use to burn us when there is no one there to protect us. For Greece, for Thebes, for kin, the Sacred Band has done a great service. Good or bad. Good and bad, they lived in the light. Do not let the light go out. They must not be forgotten. Our children will need stories of your strength."

Chapter 17: Alexander

For the first time in Alexander's entire life, he is alone. No servants, no mother, no tutor, no others at all.

There's a glorious novelty to this. A wonderful sense of freedom, no pressure to be a prince, no pressure to be great, to be what everyone thinks he is. All he has to do is be.

He misses no one, except Hephaestion, whose absence he always feels deeply. He wants for no one, except Hephaestion and perhaps this other who he pursues, the bandsman, sandal print by sandal print. The chase sends Alexander North, towards the temple of Delphi. This is convenient as Alexander has business here, too; and surprising. Delphi is sacred land and violence here would offend the gods. While Alexander considers himself the author of superstitions and not subject to them, this would not limit his actions, of course, but he did not suspect the Bandsman would be concerned for his own physical well being. Perhaps he does want to live after all.

This in turn makes Alexander question the prudence of his actions, this pursuit of the bandsman. While he knows this rival is most likely alone, and while there are very few men Alexander would expect to lose to in hand to hand combat, he does not assume that he would win against this man. In fact, he suspects he would lose should it come to that, especially since, as signified by his intended destination, the bandsman does seek to preserve himself. It is not a fight Alexander is looking for, however. As these sandal prints lead up the steep, northbound trail, Alexander's horse continues on, but Alexander's thoughts dig further in their investigation as to his own real motivation, which illudes him.

I do not pursue him to be his executioner, or to test my skill with a sword, so what do I want from him? What does he offer me? Why am I compelled to track him down? These are the questions Alexander asks himself.

He wants to know more about the Band, that's certain. They ruled Greece for a century, beat the Spartans when outnumbered, were unconquerable until his horses rode them down and King Philip's masses consumed them, but even then they were true to their word. They never showed fear, never thought to retreat, never showed cowardice as they fought to their end, together, an end that would not have come had the Athenians honored their promise to hold their line.

They were kin, paired off in ceremony with their lovers, married, some would even use that word, the bandman himself had confirmed this. Alexander tries to push that image out of his mind, two soldiers married, too forign to his Macedonian sensibilities to make sense, but the thought persists. *Yes, they married each other. And if they married each other, then...* His next thought is of Hephaestion, and how much he wishes Hephaestion were here. *Strange,* Alexander thinks, but he does not consider the possibility that the thought that came before led to the thought of Hephaestion and Alexander pushes the image of Hephaestion, and his own feelings of missing his friend, aside.

Alexander continues where he was before. The Sacred Band showed no fear because kin never showed fear before their beloved. While Alexander would not believe it from the kin he's seen in Macedonia, who hide away, he saw it with his own eyes on the battlefield of Chaeronea.

Aristotle, Alexander's tutor, would call these thoughts foolish, Alexander considered. A fixsation of Alexander's, Aristotle would say, but Aristotle thought most things to be foolish. It was his own rival, Plato, who postulated that an army made up of lovers would be unconquerable so of course Aristotle would call it foolish. Aristotle hated when Alexander pursued a Platonic line of thinking so Alexander did so often, if for no other reason then to get a rise out of his tutor. It was great fun to see Aristotle flustered.

It is in this moment, when Alexander realizes that he's musing about his tutor's rivalry with another philosopher, that he pulls his thoughts back to the task; follow the sandals into this thick grove of olive trees intermixed with shrubs and bushes. He dismounts and draws his sword as an ambush would be easy here and he is not interested in Hades just yet. He came here, he decides in this exact moment, to strike a deal, but the bandsman does not know that. Alexander pauses as another trail of thinking distracts him from the task. He allows for it to play itself out before continuing. *I have disobeyed my so-called father who has probably been looking for an excuse to disavow me all along and so let us fortify this new plan.*

I will take my Pythia bride, without my father's blessing. I will take on the bandsman as my second. Greece will fall behind me, not because of the force of my blade, but because of the company I keep. A Pythia in my bed. A bandsman by my side. It's a plan even my mother would approve of.

And Alexander decides in hindsight that this is the sole reason for his pursuit.

It's a good plan, I know it. He convinces himself further. *With the Bandsman by my side, I would be unconquerable, truly. And I will gladly give him anything in return.* And while Alexander enjoys reflecting and clarifying his thoughts, he does not explore what *anything* actually implies and why he would gladly give it.

With a new enthusiasm and his focus returned, Alexander follows the sandal prints until they arrive at a cliff, the prints leading right to the face where they abruptly end. And the component of his plan, that component he was most proud of, had only a moment ago conceived of, was excited to see fulfilled, takes a leap to its own sudden and unexpected death.

Alexander grips a branch from the large oak next to the cliff and leans over the side, the face too steep to climb down, even for the most fit and experienced climber, a low hanging fog masks the rocky valley far below him. He's surprised. He did not expect this man to take his own life and yet the bandsman's desire to do so does make more sense of this destination. He *was* there to find refuge, either from the Pythia of Delphi or, as it turns out, the gods in Olympus.

Alexander appreciates, should he himself want to die, to fly for the first and last time, this place is surely where he would do it. The forest sings behind you and, on the mountain top opposite the valley beneath you, the only mountain top higher than the peek you stand on, sits the towers of Delphi. The gods bathe in its sanctuary. From that high ground, on the opposite mountain, Apollo's beams kiss the marble walls and columns without assault. *The Macedonians would have built a fort there*, Alexander considers. The Greeks built a place of worship. Alexander squints and pretends he can read the engravement on the archway leading inside the temple, *know thyself*.

The place, this cliff, surely beats the end of any man's sword, even Alexander's own. As Alexander turns back, he wonders what the Bandsman would have said about his proposal and what he would have asked for in return. With the fantasy fading, Alexander can now accept that the Bandsman would never have agreed. He wonders if he would have laughed. Alexander would have liked to hear him laugh. With the fantasy all but vanished, Alexander wonders, if the situation had been different, if they would have been friends. Alexander would have liked having him as a friend.

Before Alexanders turns back to the trail he surprises himself by speaking aloud, directing his voice down into the valley.

"I salute you, my brother. Perhaps we will meet in our next life. I hope then we will be friends." He feels suddenly and unexpectedly ashamed by the use of the word brother, but there is no one here to hear him.

Only, there is. If he would only look up, he'd see a feral witch perched high above in the oak tree the Prince of Macedonia holds tight to. She smiles down upon him swaying her feet covered with the sandals of the Sacred Band of Thebes.

Chapter 18: Petros

It was a long night. I don't remember falling asleep. I meant to watch Leksi breathe through the moon's arc. Chest up, chest down, chest up, chest down. I remember doing this for hours, even as my eyelids grew heavy. But here I am, awakening in this cool damp cave. I see it for what feels like the first time. There are two large cots, filled with hay and hides, I couldn't even say which animal they at one time belonged to, but they are comfortable enough for sleeping. On the other side of the cave is her storage; shelves made of driftwood, tied together with twine, holding clay jars, drying meat, various blades and hammers. Her possessions are sparse, as if she was only borrowing them. They reveal nothing about their possessor, except that she is one who cares not for possessions.

I see that Leksi still breathes. He's sleeping beside me on the cot. We share a bed. I forget the context and smile, but my mind drifts to all the people I betrayed to make sure he stayed on this earth: myself, my captain, every Macedonian there is and ever was. I even betrayed Leksi.

It's that woman's fault. I look to find her, to tell her that we, or—let's be honest, she—needs to end his life now, that this has all been a terrible mistake. Everyone—seriously, everyone, my entire world—will be angry with us. But she's gone. If it wasn't for the small contents of her cave that seem as if they were handled within the last day, the pot, some rags that I think are meant to be clothes, the beginnings of a quilt, I might doubt that she existed at all, but she's real. And whatever happens next is entirely her fault.

And so there is only one choice I can think to make. Take Leksi back to the Macedonian camp. I can't go off on my own, to the ferry. That's a silly thought. I rely on others for my survival. Even when I'm the victim of their teasing or worse, much worse, I still survive because others agree to share their food with me and there's no sense pretending otherwise. I am not going to catch, kill and serve up a rabbit on my own. I have no choice but to go back, with Leksi in tow. It might be better that he's still alive. No harm done by his escape. Well, he did off three Macedonians, but they were a daft lot, perhaps that can be overlooked. They'll let me live. They might not like the sight of me, but they'll put bread on my plate, and that's more than I'll get on my own. So all I need to figure out now is how to carry him and which way to go.

I certainly can't carry him on my shoulders like I did before. It's too far, and I'm not entirely sure how I managed it the first time. But the answer presents itself straight off. A raft. It sits in the small pool of water that is the witch's doorway, her waterfall door showering down beside it, the morning sun focused by the falls pointing it out. It's not so much a proper raft, really, little more than several man-length logs bound together by leather strips, but it's enough. Leksi will fit on it and I can tow him along. It wasn't there last night, at least I don't remember it being there.

I prepare Leksi to be lifted, find fabric and animal pelts to cover him, less his nudity offend some river nymph, and look for his sandals, which I can't find. Funny. The image of Leksi emerging from the river in nothing but his sandals is emblazoned in my mind, and yet where are they now? No matter.

I half-carry, half-drag Leksi to the raft. Last evening he felt like a normal size man, but today he feels like a damn titan. He groans as his side meets the wooden raft. I don't mean to hurt him. I'm trying to be as gentle as I can, which is not gentle at all, but still. I jump into the cool waters and take hold of the bow. I push us through the falls, the weight of the water stirring something within me as it stirs the river beneath it. Nothing can stay the same here. It is change. And I am changed for it.

I come through on the other side as a golden oriole announces our entrance with its song and a hoopoe bird chases after the flies that sniff out Leksi's blood even as the full rays of the morning sun heal his wounds. The river is only waist deep in this place with a current that only suggests and does not demand her direction. Every tree on her shore bears a fruit, every bush a berry. No wonder men are willing to die to say this land is theirs. I see Leksi's eyes open, appreciating the beauty of this land, I hope.

"Which way?" I say in my most demanding tone. There is business to attend to.

He squints at the sun, or is that a mocking smile?

"Which way?" I demand again.

He croaks something out, but I don't understand.

"You need water." I wedge the raft against a stone trying to remember if there was anything in the cave that I can use as a cup, but Leksi doesn't wait. He takes up the river water with his unbound hand and brings it to his mouth.

This is his home, his land. He can drink the water. It's part of him. I forgot. I am the stranger here. I push that thought aside.

"Which way, tell me!?" I blat out.

"Or what?" he says. His smile falls off.

“You were either going to Athens or to Delphi,” I respond, ignoring his challenge. I just realized it now. I’ve been busy trying to save him. I know he owes me nothing, but I feel like he should at least be nice to me for the service of sewing him up.

“You are a fool,” is the response I get, though. Cruelty doesn’t suit him. He can’t look me in the eye when he says it.

“I only want to go home,” I say, remembering how that line worked before.

I see him struggle. I wait for him to look at me, and then he speaks…

“I was returning to Thebes to lead a resistance to the Macedonian occupation. Kill as many as I can until I am killed or they run home in terror. I was going south to Thebes.”

“You lie,” I say.

“I do not lie,” he responds.

For a moment I believe him, and then I’m not sure. “If I were you I’d go north, straight to Delphi, neutral ground, regroup, reach out to remaining allies, see if support is on its way or if all of Greece has really surrendered. Which means you took me north, which means I should go south, back to camp, back to Chaeronea,” I say, just a little proud of my powers of deduction.

“There is no Greece without Thebes. Thebes falls, all of Greece falls with her. Delphi was not a part of my orders.” Saying this makes him sad. I see it on his face. There is no more Thebes and he knows it. Greece then, is gone, too.

Perhaps he's realizing it for the first time. He pushes through and continues. "I went south, towards Thebes. If you want to go back to your camp, go north." "I don't believe you." I state. "The truth does not care what you believe. Don't you remember which way the river was flowing?" He continues, annoyed at how terrible I am at this.

And he's right to be annoyed. I don't remember which way the river was flowing. And he's right, it is that simple. If we were following the river in the direction of her flow, I should tow Leksi against her flow; or reverse, only I cannot recall. I have a selective memory. If I wanted to go back to camp, I would remember without issue, but I mostly just want to lie back on the riverbank and take in the beauty of this place. Enjoy the moment. Giggle about what a fool I am that I did not even notice which way the river was flowing when I was the hostage. But there's no time for that now. And Leksi will not laugh with me.

I set my eyes southward and tow Leksi in that direction. He was going to Dephi, I decide. We were traveling upstream. I will travel south, downstream, back to the Chaeronea. He's lying.

"You are terrible at this," he says.

He's right, for a variety of reasons. I am terrible at this. But I am all alone, so I will have to do.

Chapter 19: Hephaestion

Hephaestion follows the prints of Alexander's horse from Chaeronea north, towards Delphi, he assumes; opposite the direction of King Philip's orders, South, to Thebes. Prince Alexander took no time for misdirection, he is not accustomed to being pursued, and all Hephaestion has to do is simply follow behind. *Any fool could track him,* Hephaestion considers, adding to his rage. *Alexander actually thinks he's a god and that no one can hurt him. To think on it is enough to drive a man to lunacy, truly.* Hephaestion considers letting Alexander be taken down by simple bandits. This wouldn't change the conditions of his life at all. His life might even be a care easier without the load of Alexander's hubris. Now that he thinks on it, he doesn't even know why he's here. What God possessed him to follow? What curse has been placed on him? And if he finds Alexander unharmed, he'll have a thing or two to say. He might even slap him. *I will,* he thinks, his rage coming unhinged. *I will slap him right in the face. Hard.* When he finds him… If he finds him, Hephaestion considers. *If I find him...* And that thought sends an arrow through his heart. Hephaestion's anger turns to fear. And his fear gives way to loneliness. And now Hephaestion feels tears on his checks. And then he is angry again. *I am going to punch him with a closed fist,* he decides.

"Hold." he hears.

Hephaestion's hand fires to the handle of his sword as he feels gratitude for this interference to his runaway thoughts.

"I wouldn't," the voice says, with an unnerving confidence.

But it's only a stranger's voice in his ear for a lying moment. In truth, it's Alexander's voice. And now Hephaestion does cry. And he cannot speak out of fear of sobbing.

"Take your hand from your hilt or I'll put my arrow through your neck." Alexander persists.

"It's me, you twat." Hephaestion blutters out.

Alexander laughs as he maneuvers his mare outside the treeline, no arrow drawn on his short bow.

"Hephaestion, we are not exactly beloved in this land, yet. You know better than to ride out in the open, alone, unprotected. And I told you not to come. My father will strip you of your post." Alexander chides.

"What? You think you were doing me some great favor by leaving me? Do you think your father will let your most trusted man keep his post after you've run off without me?" Hephaestion says, only he cannot speak these words and call back his tears at the same time. *Without me,* is too much.

"Are you crying?" Alexander asks, honestly confused.

"You are the most vile, spoiled, inconsiderate, goat's ass." Hephaestion manages out, wishing his tears would relent.

"Goat's ass?" Alexander says, laughing.

And Hephaestion boils over. He dismounts. "Get off your horse! Now, Alex!" he demands of Alexander, intending to break his arms.

"No." Alexander says calmly, as his horse maneuvers outside of Hephaestion's reach without being told.

"Hephaestion," Alexander says his full name. "You overestimate my father. He's not that bright and will not punish you for my betrayal. He won't even think to. I'm ordering you to return."

Ordering me? Ordering me?! The thought alone doubles Hephaestion's rage. "Get down here." Hephaestion orders Alexander. "Get down here and I'll show you what you can do with your orders." There are no more tears.

"Hepha, now is not the time." Alexander begins.

But Hephaestion is lost to Aries. And Alexander's mare did not retreat as fast as she should have. Hephaestion leaps forward and grabs Alexander's arm, yanking him from his mount.

"Hepha!" Alexander calls out, laughing, as he tumbles off, knowing better than to fight back.

Hephaestion pins Alexander to the ground, grabs him by his collar and presses his fists into his chin.

"If you are so stupid, that you think marching to Delphi to marry some spored out country girl is going to get you whatever it is you think you need to be happy with this pathetic existence of yours then I am going with you. Is that perfectly clear?"

Alexander closes his eyes as Hephaestion spits more than he speaks.

"Hepha?" Alexander says calmly, smiling, like a cat who got her mouse, pleased to have been mounted.

"What?" he puffs.

"Would you like to come with me to Delphi?" Alexander asks.

"No. I'm mad at you." Hephaestion says.

And Alexander, prince of Macedonia, laughs so that the whole world can hear his mirth. And branches sway and birds sing and Hephaestion laughs, too, because, when Alexander laughs like this, Hephaestion has no feelings of his own. All is one. And Hephaestion knows why he's here now. He remembers. It's this feeling he desires. This feeling he needs.

They lay back, look up at the clouds, the mountains, the trees, and laugh. *I am so glad for him.* Hephaestion thinks to himself.

Chapter 20: Leksi

I was not lying when I said we had gone south, away from camp. I have never lied, and yet we continue to go south, the direction I had intended, down the river, towards the place of my birth, far away from Chaeronea. If I wasn't in such pain, I would laugh, but that might cause my stitches to tear. And I feel bad for Petros. He walks with such purpose.

Petros walks along the shore, with the rope tied to his waist, like a ferryman on the pier. For a man who has no hint about the direction that he walks, he has such an easy way of moving. Birds don't even take flight as he approaches. They simply watch as he gracefully tows the boat in the opposite direction of his countrymen, taking me to the place I'm meant to go. I wonder if he pretends to be my enemy, but in fact was sent by the gods to see me home. Or perhaps such a divine mission requires that the instrument be unaware of its purpose. I'm not used to entertaining such daydreams. It's not an unenjoyable pastime for me.

The surroundings are familiar. Chaeronea is not far from Thebes, and my family farm is on the path that connects the village to the city. When the Band was stationed at home we would walk the shores of this river to see plays at a theatre in Chaeronea, a beautiful spot, open air, its stadium built into the mountains. Masked actors would play out the latest tragedies to come from our Athenian rivals. Athenians made far better dramatists than soldiers. Most of these plays made fun of us Thebans. We would laugh at their jabs. We should have paid greater attention to how they valued us but none of that mattered then. I pretend for a moment that the rope I hold in my hand is Sigorin's own hand, squeezing as we watch one of these plays. I pretend that the turbulence in the river is Sigorin, jiggling with laughter with my head on his shoulder.

These fields and woods are where I played as a child. I know the man who tends the rows of barley on the opposite shore, his daughter married my cousin; and the farmer who owns those oxen, drinking from the eddy without concern, I know him, too. This is where I dreamed of being a farmer like my father. And there is the cyprus tree with the rope tied to the high branch that I would swing from as a child, landing with a splash in this very river. There it is. Right before me.

And there is my shield, lodged right there in the reeds along the shore, waiting for me, calling to me. I wish it were a dream or a memory, a vision. But it's not. It's real. The shield of the Sacred Band of Thebes has found me. And I know it's time.

"Petros," I say, and Petros turns to me.

"Petros, I need to relieve myself." This is not entirely a lie.

"Go in the river," he says, turning back away from me. I miss being his friend. I liked that. But there is no time for that now.

"This river is sacred to us. Such an act would anger her gods," I say, and this, too, is not entirely untrue. There are river gods.

"I doubt they give a piss about a little piss," says Petros, and continues on his way. I suspect he knows I have not been entirely truthful. But then Petros doubts himself; I see it in the way he bows. He feels guilt in his body like that. It starts from his belly and it causes his chest and then his head to fall forward. It slows his gate and turns his gaze apologetically to the ground. It would be endearing if it wasn't a weakness.

"Please, Petros," I say, taking advantage.

“No, the ropes. It’ll take me an hour to re-tie them,” he says. That makes sense. Except...

“Petros, look.” I show him the rope that had bound my hands, Sigorin’s hand in my mind’s eye, now unraveled and useless. I knew they wouldn’t last when he tied the knots, and it did take him an hour. They came undone a while ago. I cannot be blamed for my silence.

Petros’s bow turns into a fully realized slump. He’s defeated.

“They unraveled on their own,” I offer.

“Is that supposed to make me feel better?” he asks.

I shrug. It was not my intent to upset him. Upon second thought, I suppose I would rather be outwitted by my enemy than undone by my own ineptitude. But the truth is the truth.

“May I get up?” I ask. “Please.” I try to restore his confidence in his control of the situation.

“Just to wee,” he accepts.

I slowly drop my legs over the raft and into the shallow water.

“Easy, you’ll tear your stitches,” Petros offers, as he steps over the reeds that line the shore to help me.

Even though he’s witnessed it several times over, Petros still does not understand how thoroughly I have been trained to disconnect from pain. Nor does he have enough experience to know how shallow these wounds are or how well he himself stitched them up. All wounds of the flesh, except those that kill you, are shallow. The poor man. He has no idea what I am.

With his careful, caring hand guiding me over the plants as if I were a princess, my feet find the shore, and I feel my homeland beneath me, my ancestors, those river gods coming through the soles of my feet and into my soul. I wish they had a peaceful welcome, but they do not. They want blood.

I lean against the trunk of the tree, my tree. I see the rope from my childhood dangling from the thick branch it was tied to, the bark having grown around the twine, enclosing its history in its own flesh as we all do. I see a smaller branch underneath this one, a twig when I was a child, flimsy and flexible, green, but now it is thick and hard. Time has made it something that could be a weapon in the right hands, my hands.

I hold onto this branch as I drop my drawers and piss down into the river.

"Ayo," Petros says. "You're pissing on some nymph. You said so yourself."

It is not until Petros points this out that I realize my own unintended intention. I chuckle. Some god is working through me, too, I consider. *It is a clue for you to run, Petros,* I think to myself. *My pissing in this river after I told you there were gods here. It is a message for you to run. It's my way of saying I've lied. I don't have to piss. I intend to hurt you.* I laugh again. I did this without realizing it. I wonder if I have any freewill left or if I had any to begin with. And then I calculate the number of times Petros has refused to run when given the opportunity and I cannot. I've lost count. He too refuses to surrender. Why should this moment be any different?

I yank the branch from the trunk of the tree. It's snap echos like a war horn.

"Ayo! I don't have any more needles. You tear those stitches and then what'll we do?" Still, he doesn't get it. *Please, run. I am a dangerous man with a big stick. Run!*

Finally, he sees my face and my expression reveals his future for him. It is not anger or wrath, but regret he must see, regret burning my insides. I have never felt such regret for something I have yet to do.

"No," he says. It is not a request. It is more of a statement of disbelief, which I answer by swinging the branch, driving its far end into his chin.

Petros hits the ground with a thud. He squirms.

I should have knocked him out. I should have swung harder. I should have killed him with that swing, but my heart betrayed my training.

And now Petros lies squirming on the muddy bank of the river, whimpering, crying, and that same heart breaks for what I must do now.

I jump on him. He offers up his back almost immediately. My arms find his neck, and I lock them in place.

"No, please, you don't have to," he manages, but I do. The band is watching, and Sigorin is watching, and every Theban who has died for this land and these waters is watching, and Aries is watching and even the tree is watching and I do have to.

I squeeze. He is silent, thrashing, and then he is still.

I relent. I let myself slide off his little body. I know he will breathe again soon. I know I didn't hold him long enough to kill him. The same god, or goddess more likely, who had me piss in the river and had me swing not quite hard enough, had me let go of my murderous embrace before sending Petros off to Hades. I'm sure Aries is shouting his disdain towards this rival now for he is no longer in me. Petros will wake and pretend to sleep, because what else can he do? I will pretend not to notice. The Band will have to forgive me for that.

I take Petros's dagger. I cut the rope from which I swung as a child free from the high branch. I tie Petros's hands with a knot that will not come unbound by its own will. I know how to tie such knots. I pick up my shield. It has never felt this heavy before.

Chapter 21: Alexander

The trail leading down the mountain top, through the valley below and up the adjacent mountain towards Delphi, is boring in that terrible way dangerous things are when they do not appear dangerous. Alexander would have to spend the entire journey watching for threats, except that Hephaestion is now by his side. His eyes give Alexander's rest. Alexander can let his mind wander. He can imagine, envision. He does not have to be so vigilant against the threats of the mundane. Alexander trusts Hephaestion, and only Hephaestion, to be his guard in this way.

As far as Alexander knows, the mountain the Bandsman's sandal prints led him was deserted, other than for the oak trees and song birds that occupy this region. Not so for the valley below, the one they now transverse. It is known to be populated, however sparsely. Hephaestion insists that they mask themselves with the cloaks of common Greeks and has thought to bring these cloaks with him. Alexander accuses Hephaestion of paranoia, and pretends to comply in wearing the fabric only in that it will be easier to put it on than to argue, but he silently chides himself for not thinking of this strategy himself. It is elegant and simple.

And so as the road through the valley does indeed find inhabitants, poor locals, carrying barrels of hay and driving livestock, Alexander and Hephaestion pull their cloaks down over their eyes to disguise the Macedonian look of their faces. Their horses do have a well bred gait, Alexander realizes. These Greeks know these cloaks mask something, but they are unsure what. Fortunately, the locals here are, like Hephaestion, more paranoid than curious and keep their distance. And they are busy.

These villagers had only recently found themselves without statehood. While culturally they would not call themselves Thebans, they did live within the domain of Thebes. For several generations they had contracts with the Theban city state to participate in a more specific trade. Here, farmers grew barley and shepherds raised sheep. They journeyed with their product to the Theban market where they exchanged their goods for other grains and meats. Those contracts had vanished only days ago in Chaeronea. The promise from the state that they could trade wool for goat, or barley for wheat is now gone. Should they want variety, and life needs variety, they will have to grow it themselves. They were without a country now and were in the process of turning their economy insular. The shepherds were collecting wheat and rye seeds and the farmers gathering goats and oxens. Their ancestors told them how. They are strong. They will survive. They are determined and focused on this task. They do not have time to investigate the strange looking men in peasant clothes but riding well bred horses. Alexander will be proud to call these people his, he considers. And he will make them proud to call him King, he promises to the gods.

They ride past the point where Alexander suspects the Bandsman's remains would have fallen and tells himself that he would like to give the bandsman a proper burial, but he cannot find the body. Alexander considers circling back to give the area a more thorough look, but he had told Hephaestion that he went up the mountain next to Delphi to allow himself time to meditate on his decision to marry the pythia. He had lied. He did not want to reveal to Hephaestion that the Bandsman is still on his mind. And so, he thinks, he allows the Bandsman to remain where the Bandsman chose to fall. *Hephaestion would not understand why I followed him*, Alexander tells himself, *I do not fully understand myself.*

As the valley gives way and the road begins its ascent to the mountain temple, the path becomes more densely populated with pilgrims, not just Greeks, but Persians from the east and Africans from the south and even those that the Macedonians refer to as Northerners, with their pale skin and fair hair. The local farmers have set up stands where they sell their fare to the hungry travels, smells of roasted lamb and fowl fill the air. One merchant sells flatbread layered with honey and nut meal. Alexander's mouth waters. This is his favorite. Alexander knows Hephaestion will summon Hades himself if Alexander dismounts and engages this merchant to secure one and so he pushes down his desire. For all his privilege, Alexander excels at this. Alexander's desire to be king rules all his other desires, even those that are not in conflict are shadowed by Alexander's devotion to the crown that will be his.

Alexander finds distraction in hearing an exchange where a traveler pays for a sheepskin hat with Macedonian coin. *That did not take long*, he thinks to himself. The people recognize who mints their coin.

Hephaestion pulls his stead close and his leg rubs against Alexander's. His touch feels so natural to Alexander that he wonders if they were twins in his mother's womb, but this is impossible. They are not brothers.

The temple comes into view. It's not much from this angle, Alexander considers. He's seen fairer, but the Greeks do love their Delphi and so he's here. *It does have location going for it*, he thinks, *nestled on this mountain top as it is*. He once again considers that one day, he may turn this temple into a fort.

The pilgrims line up before a gate, beyond which begins the final, steep climb to the temple doors, so steep the incline the builders included a narrow staircase so that it can only be traversed by a group single file. Alexander considers the advantage to this in battle as he and Hephaestion command their mounts to slow their gait in response to the line of pilgrims. Alexander's steed neighs, annoyed, wanting to push forward. This horse is accustomed to man and beast parting before him, like calm waters to the hull of a well manned shipped. He has not been conditioned to waiting in lines. Either has Alexander. They're both annoyed by the custom.

Hephaestion nudges Alexander once more, and directs his gaze to a group of older men, Greek soldiers, Alexander knows at first glance, officers probably. They're seeking asylum here, he deduces, or perhaps they want to know their destiny. Most likely both. He does not suspect trouble from them, even if they do recognize their enemy. Even if he's wrong in that, Hephaestion has them in his sights and Alexander is confident they will emerge victorious if the confrontation requires steel.

"Your mother sent word?" Hephaestion asks. "They're aware of my coming." Alexander responds. Alexander knows Hephaestion wants to bypass this line, too. That's why he pointed out the Greeks. That's why he confirmed that Alexander's mother sent word.
Even so he will make a show of objecting to what Alexander is about to do, Alexander predicts. That's why he spoke around the point.

Alexander lets the cloak fall back around his neck.

"Put that back on. There are Greeks here." Hephaestion objects, to Alexander's amusement.

"And that's exactly why I have to remove it." Alexander says, watching as Hephaestion removes his cloak in turn.

The asylum seekers ahead look back to the royal Macedonian garments the cloaks had concealed. Alexander watches as they grip their blades. But it's not hatred in their eyes, he notes, it's exhaustion. They do not want to fight. They're simply obligated to show ill will.
Alexander turns quickly to Hephaestion so that he can see him puff up to twice his size, as he always does at the site of a threat to his Prince. Alexander knew he would do that. Alexander loves when he does that. Hephaestion brings his own hand to the hilt of his sword but there is no need for that now, Alexander knows. The calculations are done. This is sacred ground and there will be no violence here. This will be their rival's excuse.

With the revelation that the victors are in their midst, the pilgrims step to the side. Alexander's steed snorts. *Next time, be faster,* he says.

A cloaked figure at the foot of the stairway greets them. Small and slight, probably a lady. She takes their mounts by their reigns, a signal for them to continue on foot, which they do. They cross under an archway. Alexander does not need to imagine the words etched here any longer for here they are, not in his head, but in this the real world: *know thyself.*

And Alexander wonders, as he walks up the steps of Delphi, *do I?*

Chapter 22: Leksi

He is awake. He does not pretend not to be. He stares right into my eyes, his face broken, his will intact. He stays silent. I tie the loose end of the rope that binds his hands to the old fence, the one that held the pigs my father raised. It was at the edge of his land, out of sight from the homestead. My mother was against raising pigs. She said she did not care for the smell, but my father insisted. He considered it a great act of kindness to keep them this far away. He stopped raising them three years ago, my mother told me in a letter. She was very happy about that. The pen is overgrown now with vines and shrubs, the swines that used to live here only a memory. I hope I will not have to keep Petros here long. A voice inside me vows that *Petros will not have the same fate as those pigs*. I do not consent to this voice, but it does not ask for my consent. It simply makes the vow.

Petros pulls against the knots I tie, testing their strength. "I wish someone had taught me how to tie a proper knot," he says.

I do not laugh, but I want to. It is funny. And true. I wish he were better at this. Then I would not be here. He would have slain me or allowed me to be slain three times over.

"I am sorry," I offer. And I am. There is a quivering in my lower lip, pressure around my eyes. I do not know where it comes from, and it comes on all of a sudden. Petros tracks it, I see it on his face. He wants to ask me what's wrong. He wants to listen to what my heart has to say, to offer soothing words in return. It is his nature. But he holds it back. Even his kindness has limits.

"Sigorin does this," I explain, even though he didn't ask. "Sigorin makes these decisions. I only do what I am told. I am sorry," I offer again. Sigorin never would have apologized, let alone twice.

The look on Petros's face offers condolence, in spite of himself. It is more than I deserve. I leave it at that as I carry on with my orders and walk towards the home I grew up in.

Chapter 23: Hephaestion

Hephaestion and Alexander pride themselves on maintaining capable bodies; all cavalry men do. They train like the horses they ride. They move as well off their mounts as they do on, and, it's been said, they look good doing it. But neither man can keep pace with the tiny frame who seems to float up the steep stone steps leading to the temple above. She seems only to go faster as the air thins. And so when Alexander catches Hephaestion's eye, covered in sweat and panting, they can only laugh off their wounded pride.

They arrive. The smell of sulfur fills their lungs as the statues of the gods lining the stone platform stare upon them, unblinking, uncaring. Hephaestion can't help but wonder what man carried the marble to this point, gods fear him. And then he considers, *it was probably a donkey.*

A woman, robed in silk, her face covered, sits beside the statue of Pallas Athena.

The waif motions to her to announce the entrance of the young Macedonians. Alexander glances to Hephaestion, who reads the story on his face. Alexander is hurting. And Hephaestion is glad his friend is hurting. He pushes down any guilt he feels around his lack of sympathy. He hurts, too, and while he understands none of this he knows it is Alexander's fault so *to Hades with his pain.* Hephaestion is further injured by the ease by which Alexander masks his discomfort when he turns to the robed woman with, "My lady, you know why I'm here?"

"And much more." She responds, her voice assured and confident. "Your mother sent word."

Hephaestion resists a laugh. She said it with a tone, *your mother*. He likes this one.

"Then you are willing?" asks Alexander. "You will be my bride? My queen?"

"Queen? We can not be sure." Offers the priestess, the pythia, as they prefer to be called in Delphi.

"With you, as my wife, it's assured." Alexander counters.

"Is that so?" The pythia responds "Then I'd be so inclined."

"Fantastic" Alexander interjects.

"If my demands are met."

"My lady?"

"Nothing is free and I surely am not." She says. Alexander nods and she continues. "Dephi, will remain neutral, holy ground, safe for those seeking asylum. There will be no turning this place into a fort," she begins. "My sisters will remain protected, unharmed," she continues.

"No blood will be drawn here by my sword or hand." Alexander gives his word and his word counts for much.

"Anything else?" Alexander asks, with a side-glance to Hephaestion. He's surprised by her gall, but submits to it.

"Monuments will be raised to honor the fallen Greeks of this war. Their graves, too will be honored and remembered."

"When I am king, I will make this so." Alexander offers.

“You do not pretend to have power you do not possess. This is good.” She says, a hint of flirtation now in her voice. She appreciates his integrity.

“Is that all?” Alexander asks again.

“Yes, for now,” she says.

She unveils her face. The wind on the platform peaks to flutter her robe. Her beauty rivals the gods she serves.

“Apollo will allow you to share our bed. Let’s go.”

“Go where?” Another question from Alexander, this one nervous.

“To consummate,” She says, as if it’s obvious.

And she walks by Alexander, towards a staircase, hidden behind a column. Alexander’s internal conflict morphs into full blown terror as he looks to Hephaestion. Alexander has never been with a woman before. Neither has Hephaestion. They are virgins. They were told that withholding that moment of formal release would make them more viral in battle and that they should wait, and wait they have. In fact, they promised each other they’d wait, but wait for what?

For a moment, Hephaestion’s amused by this woman’s forwardness, the ease by which she talks of the deed. But his amusement is fleeting and replaced by an instinct to protect Alexander from this… *this whore*, His temper takes over his thoughts. *How dare she? Doesn’t she know who he is? Who he is destined to become? How many cocks has she spread her legs for? And now she’ll lie with a prince as if she’s having afternoon tea?*

But as Alexander follows the Pythia down the staircase and Hephaestion trails after, a new reality sets in on Hephaestion. *This is exactly the plan*, he remembers. *This is exactly how it's supposed to happen.* And he's right. They're men now. *We will marry and make love to our wives. One of us had to be first.* And then once again Hephaestion's temper growls. But it's not Aries who calls him to arms. It's a silly anger, a pouting anger. An anger that makes him want his mother. He is sad. Alexander has made him sad. Where is he in this marriage? Where does he fit?

The threesome continue their descent until they find, under the platform, a spacious quarters. The platform that Apollo travels over, the majesty of Delphi, is at its top. The function of that place is to take the breath of the beholder and its form is matched perfectly to that purpose. Under the platform are the pythias' quarters where form is also matched to function. It's simple, comfortable, lived in. The Pythia is proud of her world here and her beauty grows as she leads Alexander and Hephaestion down a narrow, stone hall connecting several small rooms. She opens the door to her own. Hephaestion peers in. It's void of personal effects, except for clean white sheets covering a comfortable cot, with a warm fire held in a neat miniature stove. She signals Hephaestion to wait at the doorway as she motions Alexander inside her rectory. She smiles at Hephaestion and offers her name: "Helena."

He feels as if he has lost a game of chess to her, a game she won with ease and she has no idea how much winning would have meant to him. His breeding demands that he behave with grace in this moment so Hephaestion bows his head, "Hephaestion," he says. Helena looks at him for a long moment before retiring to her chambers. Hephaestion feels seen at least. It is her gift to him.

Chapter 24: Leksi

The walk to the homestead is short and familiar, like a recurring dream. Every tree, bush, and stone is an ancestor ashamed by my presence, by my very life and breath, ashamed that I survive and walk among them. I hold up my chin anyway. I fought my fight and will find my death in this war, fear not, immobile objects of my youth. Fear not. You will not know me as an old man.

The homestead is as I remember it and nothing as I remember it at the same time. It was a marvel to me before, a testament to the strength and ingenuity of my paternal line. Now, it's a hole dug out of a mountain with grasses growing from its roof. There are no windows. Smoke floats from a stone chimney. This smoke is the only thing gentle or homely about this place. And even the smoke suggests a fire within.

I approach the door. My mother's garden, a patch next to the lodge, is bare. Color flourished there in my youth. Year round, something grew in her corner of the earth. Why is it bare? The mare neighs a friendly greeting, corralled in the pen opposite the garden. I recognize her, a filly when I left, all legs and head. She was my mother's beast. Now she is strong, proud. I would think she too would be ashamed, but her call says otherwise. It is welcoming, playful, and excited. She looks to my mother's garden and snorts, as if to say, *isn't this a pity*? I pause as I look at her and she neighs once more. She calls me home, this mare. It is her voice that gives me the strength to perform the next, simple action.

I knock on the oak door, formed by my father's own hands, his faded family seal chiseled on its facade.

I wait. And I wait, the remnants of that seal staring back at me, two swords crossed together overlaid on a dragon's tooth. My father claims to be able to trace his lineage back to the founding of Thebes, when Cadmus slayed the dragon whose teeth were transformed into the race of Theban people by the gods. *He is a tooth*, I think to myself. *He is for biting and for eating.*

I raise my hand to knock again when his voice bellows forth.

"If you are not of my cloth then prepare to meet your end."

I am of his cloth. I am of his loins, in fact. Even so, I feel foreign here, in the one place I should feel connected to, rooted in, like a tooth in the jaw of a dragon. I feel a stranger. And his words, "meet your end" chill me. I know he is only playing at toughness. I know what real strength is now. Even so, his voice sends shivers through me. He is my da, after all.

"It is me, Da."

Word of the Grecian defeat would have traveled here by now. In his mind, I am a ghost. My earth-bound voice must rip at his ears. Any pride he had felt about his kin son's sacrifice to the god of war must melt away to expose his loathing. That pride was paper thin, only a mask. I am no fool to that, not anymore, thanks to the witch's brew.

"You breathe, why?" he asks from behind the closed door.

Why do I breathe? He asks. *Because I lack the will to prevent my lungs from doing so*, I consider answering but he would not understand. The rest of the bandsmen are gone. I should be, too. He is not wrong to ask. It is the essential question.

"I was pulled from the grave before my soul crossed. I am here to…"

My voice fails me as the memory of my brothers, of Sigorin on the River Styxs floods my mind. I try again.

"I am here to keep fighting," I say. I am playing a role. I am pretending to care what he thinks. I do not. Not at all. I admit this to myself, and then my truth comes spilling out without my permission, without even my awareness until it is said.

"Is Ma there?" My real reason for being there.

The silence is eternal. I did not have to come here. I could have gone to any farm or even the citadel. Except that my mother would be here. I came here to see Ma. I do not care about a dragon's tooth.

"Da?" I ask again.

Nothing. I raise my hand to knock again, but the door opens. I step back, but it is not he who exits. It is a young lady, no older than myself. She is heavily pregnant, and immediately reveals a kind smile and a loaf of bread tucked into her apron. It is a barley loaf, with nuts and berries baked in and glazed with honey. My mouth waters despite myself and I am unable to focus on its bearer, only the bread's scent. I have not eaten since the few morsels of gruel Petros and I shared in Chaeronea.

"Leksi," she says, her voice as warm as her eyes. "Come with me."

She leads me into the barn, standing opposite my mother's garden. She tears me off a piece of bread and I bite into it. It is good, very good, but it is not like how my mother made this type of loaf. It is her own. We enter the barn, barrels of hay stacked into a corner and two stray chickens, outsiders from the flock, greet us. I took solace from my father here when I was a child, hiding from his rages. Only fitting for it to be my solace now.

My guide looks at me and smiles, too familiar.

"Leksi." She calls me by my name again, as if waiting for me to return the greeting, but she is a stranger. "Do you not recognize me?" she asks. And in that moment, I do. She is not a stranger.

"Aello," I say. My friend, my childhood friend. We would walk to the school together. She grew up on the next farm over. This is my friend from another life. But it was this life, wasn't it? Before I was turned into a weapon of war. She was a friend.

"Leksi, I'm so glad to see you. We would play together!" And it is as if her joy, long held back, is exploding out of her now and out of me, too. As if I were eight years old again.

"For hours, I remember!" And we embrace and I smile a real smile.

"I had hoped we would marry," she offers and then grows still, serious.

"You should not be working in your condition," I say, my eyes drifting to her pregnant center.

"I am the lady of the house," she says.

I understand, but I scramble that understanding. I do not understand. I push back comprehension, hoping that it will not overwhelm me if it comes a little at a time. Perhaps she had come on as a servant to my parents; with a child coming and unwed, she would have no choice but to seek work. This is the story that my mind tries to create, and my heart hurts for her. But this is not the case. She is the lady of the house. She just said it, with no jest in her voice, only sympathy, a shared sadness.

I understand. Damn the gods. I understand.

My mother is gone.

"Athena be kind, Leksi. I thought you knew."

She puts a hand on my arm, but it is not kindness I desire.

"When?" I ask, but there had to be time for the wedding, the arrangements, the conception, the pregnancy.

"Last spring," she confirms.

Enough time to send word. I was not even a half day's march from this farm. I was still in the citadel.

My blood boils and, without thought, my feet carry me outside the barn and to the yard. Aello hurriedly walks behind me. I think I hear her call my name, but that is not important now, only my feet and their direction.

Through the yard and to his door, they carry me, and then through his door, my foot doing the work of the key. Wood splinters as the door comes off its hinges and crashes in upon the hearth, no more crossed swords, no more dragon teeth.

I enter through the newly empty doorway to find him, gut dangling over his breaches, beard stained with mead, eyes dreary with sleep. This man who seemed so formidable even ten minutes ago would be nothing to walk over now. I see him for what he is. A failed soldier, his spirit broken by his own foolish, broken expectations. Expectations of me.

“How dare—" He begins, but that is all I allow him.

“I am not here as your son, so hold your tongue,” I announce. “I am here as a Theban soldier and the commanding officer of the Theban army, as there are no others left. It is my shame that I stand before you, but so it is. I will perform my duties per my orders and my orders are as follows: build a standing army in secret, recruit, train, and then await an opportunity to repeal the occupiers and return a Theban citizen to the senate floor.”

“All soldiering men are dead,” he counters.

“I was twelve when I was sent to the Band. There are children of that age amongst your neighbors?”

“They are not—”

I cut him off. ‘Like you’ is not a phrase I will allow from him right now, nor is ‘kin’, so I do not let him say it.

“Are you a loyal Theban or no?”

“I am,” he spits back.

“Then I thank you for your service and hospitality. I task you with the recruitment of your neighbors' sons. Should you fail in your duties, you will be executed as a traitor by my hand.”

I turn back to the broken door, desperate to leave his stench, but then I remember why I’m really here, what motive had truly possessed me to break down my father’s seal. I turn back, but only my head, still wanting to feel the night air against my chest and stomach.

“You could have sent a letter. She was my mother.”

I hate that I had to say it, but I had to and so there it is. I leave.

I know Aello will sleep in the barn tonight, as my mother would do when she knew my father would need his solitude. I will be grateful for her company. But it is not Alleo’s touch I crave.

I march through the field, to the pig pen where I tied Petros. He remains there, his face swollen and bruised by my hand, but his body is entirely relaxed and laid out, as if he were taking in the sun on an island beach, enjoying an afternoon nap.

He looks up at me, irritated by the disruption and remembering that he’s angry with me.

I fall at his feet. He flinches, expecting to be hit. “All I wanted was to see my mother. My mother,” I fail to withhold.

And I cry before him.

"I would hold you, but my hands are tied to this pole." He says.

I look up and catch a wry grin that he quickly extinguishes. He is making a joke. His heart of kindness is still intact, even if he is still angry with me. Perhaps it is his lack of warmth towards me that allows me to lay my head in his lap. I am not able to ask for his help directly. This pain, I do not know how to handle.

"Just breathe," he says warming. I realize I am not. "Take a breath for me," he says, sincere.

And I do. I breathe because he tells me to. I breathe for him.

Chapter 25: Alexander

By all objective reasoning she is the most beautiful woman Alexander has ever seen. She resembles the actress in the Macedonian court troop who the Cavalrymen are all entranced by. Alexander comments on her, too, from time to time, to make a point. He has even experimented with himself by fantasizing about this actress, with the auburn hair and olive skin, to some success. This Helena could be her twin, he considers, only Helena is even more enticing, as there is wisdom behind her eyes. And she's not shy either. She sits on that bed, perfectly naked, perfectly groomed, perfect. Other than the image of a serpent permanently painted, slithering up her leg, she's perfectly inviting.

"I'm lonely," she offers with a smile. "Come join me."

He knows what he is supposed to do, in theory, but his feet remain frozen to the floor with a goofy look frozen on his face. He has never, in all his life, felt so far from greatness as in this moment. He might as well be a toddler who has been tasked with climbing a rope. He understands the concept, can visualize the act, but his body will simply not comply.

"Must we do this tonight?" He manages out.

"Of course, it's our wedding night!" She responds.

His cheeks grow even redder.

"Of course, it's our wedding night." He parrots.

"Come here! I'm freezing!"

And his legs finally thaw. They carry him with purpose, but not to his wedding bed, away from it and away from it with haste. They take him out the door and straight to Hephaestion, who he finds, as he knew he would, standing at strict attention, his hand gripping the hilt of his sword, his jaw painfully locked.

"Hephaestion." Alexander begins, not entirely sure where to go from there.

"You're still dressed." Hephaestion says, sounding almost relieved.

"Yes. I do not know what I'm doing." Alexander confesses. It's a request for help. He hopes he does not have to make it any more clear.

But the relief Hephaestion displayed when he saw Alexander still dressed flies off and he returns to attention, closing the gates to the wall around his heart.

"Don't your royal instincts tell you what to do, Sir?" He says. He never calls Alexander sir.

"Are you angry with me?" Alexander asks the question despite the obvious answer. "Because it is a profoundly bad time for you to turn cold on me." Alexander continues.

"You really don't…" Hephaestion begins but stops, looks down. It's not like Hephaestion to be shy or withholding. Hephaestion is the only peer Alexander has who will speak to him directly and his withholding in this moment angers Alexander. But Alexander keeps his temper contained because it seems as if Hephaestion may cry again and

Alexander does not want this evening to grow any more strange.

"What?" Alexander carefully pries. But Hephaestion says nothing. "Speak," Alexander orders, losing interest in Hephaestion's tears. They can sort that out later, Alexander figures. He needs help now.

"Do you really not see me or are you just being unkind?" Hephaestion says. And with those words he looks up at Alexander. Alexander sees his friend's eyes do fill with tears that he won't let fall. He sees Hephaestion's lips tense at their corners holding in his breath and Alexander feels Hephaestion's heart aching or is that his own? And, without understanding why, Alexander has the distinct feeling that he has indeed been unkind to Hephaestion and to himself. All at once it's clear; it's not this perfect form of a woman who he wants on his wedding bed. It's Hephaestion. He realizes this was probably obvious to anyone in the world who had access to his inner thoughts and many who do not, but, to his own shame, it was not obvious to him. He had not let himself see it that clearly until this moment.

"Hepha… we -" Can't, was what Alexander was about to utter, but he does not have a chance. The door opens again and Helena exits out, unrobbed and unashamed of her nakedness.

"What is the problem? Did you not hear what I said? I'm freezing. I need another body to warm me. I have no more tricks to lure you to bed and my tits are about to drop off while you two yabber on -"

And then she stops her diatribe. She looks into Hephaestion's eyes, but he turns away, not daring to reveal their secret, his jaw locks once more.

And so she looks into Alexander's eyes, but he is not accustomed to looking away. That's not something he's learned how to do. And his eyes reveal all.

"I see." She says. "Come inside, then." And she swings open the door more fully.

Like a chided school boy Alexander enters back into the bedchamber, leaving Hephaestion at his post.

"You, too." Helena says to Hephaestion.

Alexander turns back to see Hephaestion standing at the strictest attention he's ever seen. If he wasn't totally unglued in this moment he would have found this wildly amusing.

"Are you deaf?" Helena snides at Hephaestion. "The bedchamber, anon!"

And Hephaestion accepts the order. Helena closes the door behind her.

"Undress." Helena orders next, to both of the young men.

Now it's Hephaestion who looks to Alexander for salvation, but again Alexander finds himself without words. Alexander is in no position to lead them through this moment.

With no aid coming from his Prince, Hephaestion speaks. "My lady, I hardly think that is appropriate on your wedding night's ... I'm not sure what to call this event, but you understand my point, I'm sure."

"Consummation is the word. And my first husband was Apollo the sun god, I'll be the judge of what's appropriate. Undress." She demands.

Hephaestion's jaw locks again. *He is impossibly attractive when he's nervous*, Alexander thinks, shocked by how freely he considers his desire for Hephaestion now. Alexander always kept eyes on Hephaestion when he knew his friend's confidence was cracked but now he finally understands why. When vulnerable, Hephaestion was much more of a man. It's when the world could see his heart. It made him irresistible.

"I'm Macedonian. Macedonian men do not -" Hephaestion tries to protest but Helena interrupts him.

"You're not in Macedonia. You're in Greece, in the house of the gods. Love is love here," she insists.

And as she speaks, as she says these words *love is love*, Alexander's eyes sink into Hephaestion and Alexander's tunic falls off his chest. He does not know what's in control of him. He doesn't act. He flows. There is no resistance. Hephaestion sees Alexander's nipples turn hard and Hephaestion's own doubts flee and his tunic flies free from his frame.

Alexander's heart warms and his stomach turns as it does every time he sees Hephaestion's bare chest but this time the turning doesn't stop at his stomach. It flows down through his center and his member grows, pointing the way. And Hephaestion's does, too.

And Alexander recognizes now that he loves Hephaestion and that he's always loved him. And this isn't a brotherly love. This is everything. This is an aged wine uncorked. He remembers his pursuit of the Bandsman, the questions he had for him, the quest for understanding. This is what he was after. This is the answer he sought. He wanted the Bandsman to explain to him the very nature of Alexander's heart because this is what the Sacred Band was, Alexander realizes. This thing inside him that's pulling him with an irresistible power towards his dearest friend was the band's lifeforce. The make believe notions that he cared to know more about the military strategy of his rivals, or desired to foster a political alliance, in this moment makes him laugh at his foolishness. Of course he did not. He wants only one thing.

"Kiss him." The goddess in her human form says. *Kiss him.*

And they do. And their legs give out as they fall to the floor because there is no bed that could contain them.

Hephaestion lands on top of Alexander, pins the Prince's hands above his head. Hephaestion is stronger than Alexander, just enough that Alexander has no choice but to blissfully surrender, as Hephaestion surrenders to Alexander's tongue pushing apart his lips to get inside.

And if Alexander could spend the rest of time right here, curled into Hephaestion, as one, listening to the goddess laughing… *oh, if I could.* He thinks.

Chapter 26: Petros

On a bed of hay, I wake up to the morning sun beaming in through the cracks of the barn's broken roof. I feel his body next to mine. I push myself closer to it. I don't know why. Well, I do know why. My member asks me to.

I'm bruised and sore, because of him, but I'm still comforted by his presence. His warmth. I am in harm's way, I know. If I were my patient, I would tell me to get away, to run off first chance I get. Leksi is bad for my health. Leksi has orders, a purpose that's been assigned to him. And those orders may very well require him to hurt me. It's true. He's already done it. It's proven. But I do not feel that Leksi, this man next to me, means me harm. I came to understand that last night, that difference between his orders and him, when he bathed me in the river. He washed himself, too. He let me watch, with my hands bound. I had to will myself to keep my prick soft, had to think about my own mum, and other ugly things. Not that my mum's ugly, but she won't make me go stiff.

He tended to my wounds when he brought me back to the barn. He said nothing, hummed softly, although I don't think he knew he was humming. It came from a place deep inside him, under the orders and the purpose imposed on him.

So where I was abandoned and tied to an abandoned paddock, now I'm in a warm barn sleeping on a bed of hay, tied to an old plow by a much longer cord than the one that bound me to the fence, so that's something. Things are getting better. I am still bound, sure. There was a young woman who slept on the hay bale across from us, but she's gone now. Leksi would not allow her to speak to me, but the two of them talked and even laughed. It was all so human. There are two chickens here also, bonded rosters. They cluck and carry on. They're not much into crowing, thankfully.

And so while I should be planning my escape, my thoughts are with Leksi and how I might pull my body even closer to his and if he would be offended by my stiff prick. He dragged me halfway across Greece, beat me to within an inch of my life, and will indeed probably be the death of me, but I only want to be closer to him. What foolish god made us kin?

And in this morning sun, my stiffness begins to hurt. So desperate I become, I consider asking Leksi for a hand—what's a reach over to him at this point? I pull hard against my binds and get close enough to Leksi to touch his thigh. I pretend I'm asleep. He cannot blame me if I've done it inadvertently, right? He inhales deeply. I open my eyes, see that he's awake and staring back at me. I cannot read his expression. It's not judgment or anger. Is it desire? His face moves closer to mine. But then the barn door creaks open and he pulls away.

A large man enters. There's no mistaking that he's Leksi's father. The same dark features, broad shoulders and stern gaze. But there's something defeated about this man. He's slovenly and unkept, only a ghost of a spark in his eyes. In that way, he's the opposite of Leksi.

Those sparkless eyes land on me, and an even greater darkness falls over him, a dangerous darkness. I turn to Leksi as my member goes soft. I'm grateful to find him matching his father's stare with his own brand of darkness. I wish I wasn't in the middle. I wish I could tip-toe out of this place, but the ropes prevent me.

“What is this?” Leksi’s father grunts, motioning to me.

“A hostage,” Leksi offers. “You can use him as a slave should you need.”

“I have no need for a slave, as I suspect you have no need for a hostage,” his father responds. I’m good at picking up insinuations, and there are plenty in his tone.

“I did as you wish,” his father continues. “My neighbor’s sons await you in my field, but I will not have you exposing them to your unnatural ways. Dispose of him. Now.”

The fat man unsheathes his dagger, flips it over, and offers the handle to Leksi.

Leksi turns a shade darker. He takes the dagger and says, “When I see fit, I will do what needs to be done. I have killed more than my share of Macedonians, but I will not do so because of what you suspect or what you think of my ways.”

Leksi’s father reaches to take back the blade. “Then I will do the deed.”

“You will not,” Leksi offers back. The look in Leksi’s eye is all the confirmation his father needs, and he retreats out the door. No matter how strong you are, it’s hard to stand your ground against your father, I think.

Leksi sits back on our bed of hay. He looks tired. He wears his injuries. I know I should keep my face shut, but I need clarity. “I thought it was different in Thebes,” I say.

"In our place, kin are respected and honored…" Leksi considers what he said and repeats, "But in our place."

In our place? And what place is that? I wonder. *Killing for them? Dying for them? Where they don't have to see you lying with your lover? What is our place?*

A chicken clucks and Leksi exits to his work. My questions remain in my throat.

Chapter 27 - Leksi

I march out of the barn with my father's words ripping at my ears. It took all my strength not to take the dagger from his hand and remove his spleen. Patience then, be my guide. I will see that man in the grave.

But he did do his bit. He did what I required. Before me stand two boys, my neighbor's sons, timid and frightened, only thirteen years old, too young for this. My first instinct is to kneel down to their height and draw them in, tell them everything will be fine. I took an oath that all children of Thebes are my children. *You are children of Thebes. I will do this work for you,* I want to tell them. *Go back home to your mothers and tell them that you love them, and let yourselves be hugged. The Band is here. Your Sacred Band of Thebes. And we will protect you from the others, those men from far-off places who would have you and your mothers as slaves.* But I resist this impulse because it is not true. The Band is not here. The Band cannot protect them. It is only me. I am alone and I cannot do this work for them. If they wish to live as freemen of Thebes, then they will have to earn that honor. They will have to protect themselves. And all I can do is teach them how. For my sake not theirs, I decide here and now to consider them as young men and not boys. As I could not, they cannot afford a proper childhood either.

All this flies through my mind as I stand there, watching them. They awkwardly stand at attention under my stare, probably something they saw at a parade.

I turn and walk to the shed. I assume they'll know to follow and they do. I feel them doubletime their tiny stride to keep pace with me and I am confronted with doubt. They are so small. If I do not introduce the notion that they might fight back, perhaps they will not conceive of the possibility themselves. Yes, they will live their lives as subjects of the Macedonian crown, but is that such a terrible fate? I do not consider that question to its conclusion before moving on to the next thought: Theban pride will someday boil over and face off against Macedonian imperialism, with or without my proding. As the eldest of their generation, these two behind me will be in the first charge of that conflict. They deserve to be trained and prepared for that moment. And yet, they will not have near the numbers to defeat their opponent and will find their death, with or without my training. If they know some tenderness from me before their untimely death, even if it means they are less prepared for that battle, is that not better in the eyes of the gods? Considering it won't change the outcome? *No,* I hear Aries say within me. *Teach them to fight. Teach them to kill. These are my orders for you and you are not the keeper of their destiny.*

I am good at following orders.

We arrive at the shed. I hand them both hoes.

"Time to till," I offer.

I see them relax. They have lived their short lives on farms and tilling they know. They are comfortable with tools of the earth, but we will not be tilling for long.

In the field now, under the cover of barley stalks, my two apprentices use their tools as they have been taught, to tend the earth. I watch them work. They are efficient, smooth and strong. They are born farmers. This is good. Farmers are strong. Farmers work. Farmers are clever. Farmers will fight. Farmers protect their land.

I keep my words to myself and watch as they grow accustomed to my strange silence. It is not long before they begin to talk to each other. Deimos and Phobos are their names. Good Grecian names. They are brothers, twins but not reflections of each other. They speak like I do, or like I did before I moved to the citadel and was taught differently. These boys speak Greek in the Theban dialect with a country accent. They laugh easily. They amuse each other. I wait for their previous anxiety to become a distant memory. I wait for them to be completely at ease.

And then I kick the hoe out from Deimos and take him off his feet. I drop my shin across his throat. Phobos looks up from his work, confused.

"Do something," I suggest to him, speaking for the first time. Phobos's confusion turns to fear. His brother is hurting. He feels it, too.

Phobos attacks, throwing a promising punch right at my face, but the blow is easily deflected, and I toss him aside.

"Do something else. He can't breathe."

Phobos looks to his brother, wheezing, unable to fill his lungs with my leg over his throat.

Phobos figures it out. He grabs the hoe, swings it at my face. I catch the tool in my hands, protecting myself, and step off Deimos. He coughs his first two breaths.

To my delight, Phobos yanks the hoe back and takes another swing at me. I pull it from him this time, and point the metal part at him as a warning. He freezes, still engaged in the fight.

“Excellent,” I say.

Deimos jumps to his feet, angry, and joins his brother, ready to fight. They’re game, these two.

“Stand down,” I demand. They do not. “Stand down,” I say more kindly. “That was lesson one. Are you not curious to find out about lesson two? It’s far more fun.”

They check in with each other with a sideways glance and then lower their arms. I lower to my knees and signal them to do the same. I put my hands on their shoulders and pull them closer to me. I whisper.

“They will not let you train. They will not let you have weapons," I say as I hand the rake back to Phobos. "But everything—your brain, your heart, your soul, this thing you till the earth with—everything is a weapon. And with weapons, we will take Thebes back.”

From the determination now etched across their brows, they understand. These young men were indoctrinated well, as all young men of Thebes are. They have grown up watching parades of Theban soldiers and have been fed on the stories of their forefathers’ victories against the Spartans. In school, they have tracked the great families of Thebes back to Cadmos and the teeth of his dragons, from before the time of the man-god Hercules, who was born on this very soil. They were raised to believe that to be born a free Theban farmer is the greatest honor a soul could aspire to. The notion that

Thebes is under forign rule is in opposition to everything they know to be true and good of the world. They will give every drop of their own blood to restore their homeland's independence. They cannot comprehend an alternative. Aries was right.

Chapter 28: Petros

I never would have expected being a captive, a prisoner of war, a hostage to the loathed Sacred Band of Thebes, to be so thoroughly boring. But that's exactly what it is. I'm bored. I'm tied to this plow, at least I think that's what this thing is, in this old barn, with these two chickens to keep me company. And the odd mouse. There's nothing I can do. I'm grateful for the occasional bout of hunger because it's more interesting than dullness. I have make-believe friends. Aries comes to speak to me from time to time. He tells me to pull against my binds, to gnaw off my hand if I have to. But the bind holds. And let's be honest, I'm not the type to bite into my own flesh. Aries isn't really my god. Aphrodite swings by from time to time; things get more exciting then, but it's all just fantasy. And it's only been three days. This can go on for years, but I try to push that thought out of my mind.

I've run out of scenarios to think over by which I could die here. My favorite is the one where I'm murdered by a mob of Theban farmers. Leksi tries to intervene, but they hold him back, even make him watch. He cries while my head is split open like a melon. I'm very brave in that one. My last words are *it's not your fault.* My least favorite is Leksi releasing me to the Macedonians. They kill me for sport and for my generally being useless. There are other, less likely scenarios, too: starvation, infection, being mauled by some terrible beast. As I meditate on the possibilities, the door opens, and she walks in.

"Hello," she says. It's a defiant hello. The first night we were here, she slept in the barn with us and was told not to speak with me because I was very dangerous. She was very polite not to laugh.

“Hello,” I respond. I don’t know how I didn’t notice the first time I saw her, there was a lot going on I suppose, but she’s the most pregnant woman I’ve ever seen. It’s as if she carries the world in her womb. I want to help her to a chair and bring her water, but I’m tied to the plow, or whatever it is. She looks behind her to make sure she hasn’t been followed or seen.

“I’m not supposed to be in here,” she confides, with a smile. She’s a kind heart, I knew that right off. I would gamble that she sees the same heart in me.

“I would tell on you, but no one would believe me.” That was a stupid joke, I’m immediately aware, but she’s kind enough to chuckle. “I wouldn’t do that. By the gods I swear,” I feel the need to add, fearing that my humor will send her away.

“I brought some bread,” she says, as she removes a chunk of dense loaf from her apron.

If I weren’t starving, it wouldn’t be particularly delicious fare, I’m aware of this. But in this moment, it is of divine origin.

“You have kind eyes,” she offers. “You don’t go for all this warring business, do you?”

“Correct,” I say. I show her my binds. “Nor am I particularly good at it. I’m mostly here waiting to be killed.”

“I’m sure you have much more to offer,” she offers.

"I was a doctor's apprentice before the military scooped me up. I'm much better at putting people back together than I am ripping them apart," I say, beyond grateful to have someone to talk to.

She chuckles again. She sees something outside that makes her grow still. I look through the slits between the wooden planks and see it too.

By the well, next to the mare's corral and the abandoned garden, Leksi is holding a sword by the blade, not the hilt. There are those two boys with him, doing the same, I saw them there two days ago, through the same slit in the planks. *They'll hurt themselves, that sword is sharp,* I think, knowing better than to say it allowed. I see Leksi's muttering something now, but it's inaudible from this distance, but the boys are saying something back to him, in unison. I see their mouths moving. Then I understand. It's an oath, a blood oath.

"What difference does it make who you pay your taxes to?" Aello asks as she stares at the scene.

"I don't know," I say. "I've never thought of it that way before." I haven't. And I don't know what difference it makes.

"Don't mind us ladies. You boys go ahead and kill each other. We'll keep making more," she says as she rubs her pregnant belly. Then, she winces in pain.

Chapter 29: Hephaestion

It took Hephaestion, Alexander, and Helena days to reach the walls of Arcadia, where Alexander's mother, Olympia, fled her husband's wrath. Her brother is ruler here. And while King Philip technically ruled all of Greece he could not kill his wife and son under this roof. She is revered everywhere, but here even more so. She knows this and so does King Philip. In other lands, perhaps he would have more leeway, but he could not cross the Arcadians. Arcadia is a major political and commercial power in the Southern part of Greece. Should they be riled to revolt they may bring aboard their neighbors, the Spartans. A revolution by the Arcadians would not be unmanageable, but the Spartans, who sat out The Battle of Chaeronea under the condition that Philip would not tax their state, might be less likely to allow the Macedonians to flex their muscles unchallenged so close to their ancestral lands. Still all the might of Macedonia might be able to crush even the Spartans, but it would cost time and many lives. A feud against them would mean King Philip would not in his lifetime see the great Macedonian empire extend into Persia. By going into exile here, Hephaestion considered, Olympia and Alexander presented King Philip with a choice that is no choice at all. Kill Olympia and Alexander to preserve the crown for his favored, younger son or keep focused on the lands to the east. And for King Philip, like Alexander, Persia is everything.

When they set forth from Delphi towards Arcadia, Hephaestion had ill feelings about the journey. He knew the path was treacherous and had expected Helena to slow their pace. He was wrong. She had a natural ease on horseback and was delighted to see the world from outside the temple's walls. She explained to Hephaestion that the Pythia are recruited as girls no older than thirteen and for the whole of their lives stay within the sacred city's boundaries, devoted to serving Apollo. That her journey would take her all the way to the Southern Isle of Greece, was an unexpected treasure for her. As she delighted in these new sights and experiences, it allowed Hephaestion to establish a new normal with Alexander. On the first day, it was as if they didn't know each other. Every movement Alexander made, every word he spoke, suddenly had a new meaning. The attraction Hephaestion felt towards Alexander had been corralled into the dark corners of his mind, unrealized and unsatisfied. But now Hephaestion could touch Alexander's shoulder, hands, the small of this back. He could kiss Alexander's cheek. He could go as far as to rub his cock into Alexander's leg if he desired, and Alexander responded in kind. As the week ticked towards an end, this was commonplace. This was their new normal.

And so in this moment, as statues of the gods greet the company as their horses gallop into the main entrance of the Arcadian palace, Hephaestion looks to Alexander by his side and sees his friend, his prince, and now his lover. So much has changed.

The palace is as beautiful as any other palace Hephaestion has seen in his life and, young as he is, he has seen his fair share. Several stories tall, it was painted in bright, striking colors with the requisite marble columns.

Hephaestion assists Helena out of a carriage. They had bought one in a nearby village to make an appropriate entrance. It is suitable, he considers, but he still finds himself wishing he had made a greater effort to find more lavish arrangements. Not that Helena was bothered by the carriage they used, nor Alexander. Helena would have preferred to travel the entire distance on horseback. But, for Olympia, perception is far more important than preference. And she's right. While this carriage that they purchased is more appropriate than the back of a horse, it is not suitable for the future King and Queen of the world. It does not support the image that will lead Alexander to the crown. Hephaestion takes a calming breath, *I will be judged, no sense judging myself,* he thinks. He reminds himself that he has delivered Alexander and Alexander's bride, and this was not made easy for him. He considers his mission a success.

A trumpeter boldly announces Queen Olympia's arrival as she and her entourage make their way down a staircase. And Hephaestion finds himself nervous once more, forgetting his previous mantra. He simply fears Olympia, all wisemen do.

Alexander anxiously poses Helena for his mother's inspection. Helena giggles at the gesture. Alexander's not laughing.

Olympia arrives before them and the carriage is indeed the target of a distorted glance.

Even when disapproving, Olympia's beauty is unsurpassed. It's an icey beauty, untouchable, but it warms for Alexander, and only for Alexander. She waltzes to him and takes him in her arms.

"Alex. Your father is so angry with us," she says, more than delighted.

"You know I always preferred you to him, mother." Alexander offers. Olympia giggles.

“May I introduce you to my wife?” He asks, as they turn to Helena, who delicately bows her deference.

“Helena, of Delphi.” Alexander proclaims.

“Helena of Delphi,” Olympia repeats. “Olympia of Greece.” She adds. Not Macedonia, Hephaestion notes to myself.

“It’s an honor,” Helena offers, continuing the delicate dance.

“The honor’s mine,” Olympia offers back. “Had my life unfolded differently I would have liked to be in the ranks of the pythia, not that I have the talent for it, of course.”

“I doubt that’s true.” Helena flatters her.

“Perhaps. Nonetheless, I’m glad to have one in the family now, daughter.”

But then the dance sours as Olympia sniffs. Helena instinctually looks to the floor as if she knows what’s coming.

“But why haven’t you consummated?” Olympia says, proving her aptitude for second site.

Even Helena is without words as her eyes dart to Alexander, looking for an answer, but he too looks to his shoes and is without speech.

Standing off to the side, as he considers his place to be, all his life force rushes to Hephaestion’s face, turning him the color of crimson blood. It’s an irresistible beacon for Olympia, as if the story of Alexander’s and Hephaestion’s attraction for each other, their life long friendship, their night of passion, their intimate journey to Arcadia, is spelled out in his skin tone. Gods save him.

He remembers that she had always treated him kindly, even though he suspects she did not always like him. *She knows I would kill and die for her son, she at least must respect me for that,* he considers, but he follows the thought to its natural conclusion: *But she also knows I am kin and love Alexander, and not as a brother. This is probably the reason for her distance.*

In truth, he isn't far off. Olympia's discomfort is not with the idea of Hephaestion and Alexander being lovers. Olympia is Greecian, originally, not Macedonian. Like Helena, she is more open to matters of the flesh. But she's lived in Macedonia long enough to understand the circumstances. To understand, unlike Helena, that this could never be, at least not for the Macedonian court to see.

But whatever she knew before, with Hephaestion's face the color of his heart, she knows all now.

"Hephaestion, what is the nature of your relationship with my son?" She asks, not one to speak around the point, but unable to fully repress her cat like nature.

Hephaestion speaks a near truth in a clear and honest voice. "I am Prince Alexander's loyal friend and servant."

"Really?" She fires back. "Let me rephrase. Who is the swordsman and who the shield boy?"

While Hephaestion feels trapped, he does not feel shame. His chest swells. *We haven't done that yet. We pleasure one another with our mouths and hands. One day soon, I hope, we will. And I suspect we'll take turns, giving and taking each other as the gods dictate.* He wants to say, but he doesn't. Alexander cuts off his chain of thought.

"Mother, please, don't be crude." He says.

At which point he's promptly slapped. Hephaestion's heart breaks for him, even as he resists the impulse to cut off her hand.

Helena jumps in "Apollo, my husband, himself approves their holy union."

"Shut up, little girl." Olympia says, raising her voice. "I've been spinning tales about Gods and their approval since before you were a seed in father's cock."

But Helena bravely counters. "Your son is kin."

Olympia laughs.

"My son is to be king not kin and he will be king because he is a great man, battle proven and beloved by his men and the masses of men who occupy the land he will rule. He will be king because Zeus himself is his father and his mother a great sorceress and he shares a bride with the sun god, Apollo. He will be king because he appears, to the Macedonians, as a king, not kin."

Hephaestion has no choice, but to push back. He loves her son, He can't stay silent.

"But these are stories," he says. It even sounds stupid to his own ears as the words come out but it's too late to call them back.

"Myths, Hephaestion, the most powerful weapon in the world." She says and then takes a step closer to him.

"And he will be king or he will by killed by those who will be. So perhaps, if you love him, and I believe you do, you should not stand so close. She is Greecian. She doesn't understand. You have no such excuse."

Hephaestion's heart breaks all over again. Not because of her cruelty but because of the truth it contains. He can't deny it. He glances to Alexander for a kind word, a look of sympathy perhaps, but his lover has turned cold.

"Dismissed, Hephaestion," Alexander says. At least for this moment, Hephaestion ceases to be. He is destroyed. He grabs up a trunk and carries it inside. If he cannot be Alexander's lover, he will be his mule.

He hears, as he hauls off the luggage, Olympia say to Helena…

"And you, make me a grandson."

Chapter 30: Leksi

We hear her screaming from the barn all night. Nothing from my father. Not a call for help, not a cry of sympathy, nothing.

I went over when her wailing first began, and my father refused me. He did not want me there during the birth of his son. "Me and my way," he said. As if the infant would catch *my way*.

There is another harrowing scream, and Petros tugs against his binds.

"That's not normal. It's been going on for too long. She needs help. If you're not going to go, then I am," he says to me as if he isn't bound to the bed.

He tugs hard again, but my knot holds tight, unyielding. I cannot let him go. I cannot.

"By the gods, Leksi, do something. Now. You'll let mother and child die with that brute? That's your brother or your sister in there," he continues. "And...all children of Thebes are your children. All of Thebes. In the eyes of the gods, that babe is as much your own child as your brother or sister," he says, remembering my vow, whipping it at me like he would a stubborn mule. And it works. I go. I make a note that Petros has deduced how to control me, but he is not making me do something I don't want to do either, at least not in this moment.

I do not have to kick my father's door down again as it was never fixed. I enter. My father, in his chair, his beard stained, rises to stop me. He lunges, but I side-step, and he stumbles against a table. He could have chosen to recover himself, but he does not and falls to the ground where he lies still. I've seen that before with drunks, not just my father. It is their form of surrender: lie still and blame it on the mead. We both know it has not made him do something he does not want to do.

I hurry through the musty air, guided by only the light of the single fire, burning in the fireplace, the stone mantle, formed from a single piece of granite, above it. I avoid the furniture by memory, it has not changed since my youth: the olive wood table, to my left, used to prepare meals; my mother's stool and loom on my right. The space felt vast in my childhood, like the entire universe, but I travel its length in a few steps to stand before Aello, her face flush with fear and pain, laying on the bed of my parents, its straw soaked with Aello's sweat, urine, blood and the fluid of birth. This is the same bed where I was born.

"Something's not right. This can't be right," she says, echoing Petros's words.

I look down between her legs, and my stomach threatens to toss up its contents. I have seen men have their heads separated from their necks and I have not blinked, but that is violence. I can comprehend violence. This is something else and it confuses me and makes me ill. I had no idea that creation caused this much gore and I am unprepared. I force myself to look again and I see a tiny foot. My legs will not hold my weight and I fall to my knees. Even as my vision fogs I am aware that, indeed, something is very wrong. I do not know much about how babes make their way from their mother's, but I do know that we enter the world head first.

“What is it? What do you see?” Aello calls out. I do not have the words to explain it and my voice will not answer her call, but my legs do and I find myself on my feet, even if my eyes will not look again.

“Leksi!” She calls my name, ripe with desperation, but her shout only drives me out the door with more haste.

I run back the way I came. The cool night air licks my face, calling me back to alertness. I hear Aello yelling for me, “Leksi! Don’t leave! Leksi!” The horror in her voice is as if Hades himself were upon her, and he is. I know it, but this is not a sphere where I have power. I know not what to do. I push into the barn.

“What’s happening?” Petros asks, his concern palpable.

I grab up my blade, and fear flashes across his face. “What are you—”

I cannot fight this enemy. Perhaps you can, is what I would like to say, but I do not respond. I still lack language.

I cut his binds. He springs from the bed, questions gone from his lips; he knows my intent. Words are not necessary. He hurries out the door with the speed of a predator on the hunt. For an instant, I’m frightened he'll flee; I wonder if every instinct I had about this man was wrong.

I race after him, but he does not run into the darkness of the night; he enters the lodge. I feel foolish for having the doubt.

I make it to the lodge in time to see my father climbing off the floor growling, “You, get away from her!”

Petros ignores him, sees me out of the corner of his eye. He knows there will be no danger from my father with me there. "Leksi, the stove, get me some hot water," he commands. He's in charge now.

"You will not touch her!" My father says as he moves towards Petros. Petros doesn't react, only continues towards Aello.

I grab my father around his enlarged waist. I pick him up—he is the size of a cow, but I manage. I drop him back into his chair. It is an act of strength that even surprises me, but I was ordered to do this and I really do take orders well.

"You will sit here and say nothing," I say, my words forming on their own.

I am surprised again to see him nod his head in surrender, and then I see that my blade is at his throat. And I understand why my hand drew on my own father without my command. I understand his surrender, too. I would kill my father to protect my brother or sister. And he knows it, so he sits there.

With my father submitted, I hurry to the fire, lift up the ever simmering kettle of water, its weight massive, and run it to Petros.

Petros dips a rag into it, wipes down his hands with the scalding liquid and does the same to Aello's leg. He dips the rag again, lays it under Aello. She winces as she feels its heat.

"Oh, these men, Petros!" Aello yells. "Let this one be a girl," she says. *How does she know his name?* I consider, but my concerns pass over me. For this fleeting moment in time, Petros is my captain and I cannot question my captain.

“Come on, now,” Petros offers back to Aello. “We’re not all that bad,” he adds with a smile, throwing a guilty glance back to me.

“If it is a boy, let him be kin,” she says.

“Very well.” Petros smiles back, as he digs his hands into her body as if he’s done this countless times. She winces, moans in pain.

“I’m sorry,” he says. He pulls as gently as possible, I imagine, which is not gentle at all. He is slow and smooth, however. *He is not trying to kill her*, I remind myself. My stomach turns once more and I feel my legs weaken. I have no choice but to turn away. I am useless. I turn back, forcing myself to watch. It is demanded of me by some cursed god.

Aello is seized, every muscle in her body firing, her back arched and her jaw locked. Petros shoulders are around his ears as he too is tense as a rock. He pulls but there is no movement. Maybe a second passes, maybe an eternity. I feel a gurgling from deep below. My insides find their way out through my mouth and I fall to my knees.

“Leksi, I need your knife.” Petros finally says, as he bows his head down. Aello cries. He has given me an order again. I crawl the blade to him and hand it over. I do not question my captain. I see Petros look up to Aello and she nods her head. She gives her permission. He dips the knife in the hot water before bringing it between her legs. *A mercy killing*, I think. I can think of no other reason why he would want my knife. I know it as a weapon of destruction. But his slices are short and precise, however, not intended to kill. Aello winces, but does not call out.

Petros puts the knife down and resumes his position. He pulls again and a form emerges from Aello: a foot, a leg, slowly at first, but then there's a flood of flesh and fluid. I expect to hear the cry of new life but nothing comes. It's silent.

The look on Petros's face tells the tale, and he hurries the lifeless lump out past the broken down door with my family seal, rubbing its back.

"I ask for sons, and she brings them cold as stone." That is my father's contribution to all this.

I return to Aello's side and recover my blade.

"Not another word from you!" I demand. As the sound of a loud slap echoes from outside.

"Or what?" he fires back, as another slap sounds out.

I don't make idle threats. My father's challenge is tantamount to willful suicide. I'm happy to put him out of his misery, happy to return my blade to its intended use and have it remove his insides, except there's another slap followed by…

… a baby's cry. A loud, healthy, booming cry.

"It's a girl! A beautiful girl! Five fingers and five toes!" Petros says with a hearty laugh as he hurries back inside.

Thank the gods indeed.

As Petros puts the infant into Aello's arms, my father stirs and says, “Dead things should stay dead.”

I wonder if he realizes how close to death he has come tonight—twice. Perhaps he’s the one who should have stayed dead.

At least he has the good sense this time to curl himself into a ball in his chair and fall asleep. He can do no more damage tonight.

I glance up at Aello, nursing her newborn at her breast. She looks to Petros with a quiet dread on her face. She is scared she’s going to die, I realize. I have seen enough men breathe their last breaths to recognize the similarity of expression on Aello’s face, only she is not afraid for her life. She is afraid for what will happen to her daughter if she does not survive this night.

Petros turns to me. “Did your mother sew?” He asks and immediately I know the plan. I go to her lum and the small cabinet of supplies she kept beside it. I find the fish bone needles and search for thread, but I can only find yarn. I see Petros watching me. “The horse,” he says. “A strand from its tail.”

Another order from my captain and I race back out into the cool night. A hear the beast neigh, calling to me and I feel my mother’s spirit urging me forward. The mare does not ask me to chase her down. She greets me with a snort at the border of her corral. I cut several strands of hair from her tail. Knowing the chore is complete, she walks back into the moon lit night and I run back to the lodge.

As I enter, I hear Aello speaking to Petros in her soft, calm tone that defies the blood pooling between her legs. The straw from the bed has drunk its full and will absorb no more. "Lura," she tells him.

"Lura," Petros repeats.

"You gave her life, Petros," Aello says to him. "You must be like a father to her now." And then she falls into a slumber. Petros scoops up little Lura and brings her to me, trading for the horse's hair. I hold my sister to my chest. I pray that the gods show me how to be warm and kind, teach me how to be something other than a warrior because I understand how little Aries has to offer this tiny creature.

Petros looks over and smiles at me. Petros positions his face between Aello's legs and does what he does best, heal wounds, one stitch at a time.

Chapter 31: Petros

My hands still covered in drying blood, fluids, and bits of human, Leksi guides me to the old well. I don't know what he's thinking. He's not all that good at using his words. And by not good I mean to say that he doesn't use them. He mostly just stands there and looks strong and threatening. I did see another side of him tonight though. He listened to me. He did what I asked. He trusted me. He held an infant and didn't break her so that's something, granted she is his sister.

As I reel in the water bucket, he finally speaks. "Thank you. I can never repay you for that," he says. It's an impressive string of words considering.

"You're welcome. And you don't have to repay me. It wasn't a transaction." It wasn't. "Helping people was what I was trained to do." I offer. I loved my work before joining the army. That's what the gods meant for me to do with my life. Heal people. I know it. Tonight proved it to me.

I offer up my hands to Leksi, showing him that they're clean, and he guides me back to the barn.

Inside, I put my wrists against the crossbeams, waiting to be tied back up. When the rope doesn't come, I look to Leksi. I'm confused. Leksi seems almost disappointed; perhaps he'd prefer me to fight in this moment? But surely he knows that I could never beat him in a fair brawl. Perhaps he wants me to run? I really wish he'd say something, but he has gone mute once more.

After a long moment in which I grow perfectly comfortable with the loaded silence, he says, “I can’t do this.”

“Thank the Gods. My wrists are killing me. Don’t worry. I won’t run off,” I say and curl into the bed, hoping he lies down next to me. I won’t run. It was not a lie. But, in this moment where I wish he would do what he’s been doing all along and say nothing, I know there’s more that needs to be said. I sense it. It’s not as simple as me promising not to run.

“You must,” he responds. And that’s all he says. It’s a complete thought. I understand his meaning, but I pretend not to. “Leave,” he adds. I continue to feign a lack of understanding hoping it’ll allow him to change his mind. “Run from here,” he continues.

“Are you telling me to go?” I ask plainly.

“Yes, man, go, please! You gave me a sister. You saved my dear friend. I can no longer hold you as my captive,” Leksi spits out, as if he’s accustomed to speaking in full sentences.

“But where will I go?” I inquire.

“Home. It’s what you want.”

The fool, I think. *The fool!* “I can’t! My punishment for your escape will be death. Unless you go with me, I’ll be killed on sight,” I respond, realizing Leksi hasn’t thought this through, at least not from my point of view.

His eyes twitch, and his jaw tenses. He had pushed out of mind the part where I die when the Macedonians find me. But now I've shattered his vision of me comfortably alive with my own tribe.

“I can’t keep you here,” he finally comes out with.

“Why not? I respond. I know he can. He can do whatever he wants.

“Once the other Thebans know you’re here, they’ll kill you,” he says.

“You think, but you don’t know that for sure. You might be able to talk them out of it. Or I might prove myself useful to them, or they might kill me or who knows what else might happen. I know the Macedonians will cut off my head. I know it. I would rather take the road where at least my living is a possibility.”

I see him considering what I’ve said. His brow gets wrinkly when he thinks. If I wasn’t fighting for my life here, I’d find it attractive.

“Then go to an island—Lesbos, Sicily, Crete maybe. Leave here, start a new life somewhere else. You said you can always do that, right? Go to the ports. I’ll give you coin.”

It’s a good suggestion. It is the solution, in fact, but my mind spins off on all the things that could go wrong.

“I’m not like you,” I finally say, coming to understand my resistance for the first time myself. “I don’t survive outside the pack. I don’t just go out on my own to some strange island.” I don’t know why, but I begin to cry. What kind of man am I? So afraid to be alone that I’ll even stay with my captor before I face the world as I am.

"Of course you can, Petros. You just birthed a child and you saved me. And you will not be alone for long. You'll find a new pack," Leksi says. There's a kindness in his voice that I have not heard since Chaeronea when we were in the tent. And then he adds, "You're easy to love."

Leksi turns away from my tears, but he is not embarrassed for me. I know that look on other men, I've seen it enough. He turns away because if he watches me cry, he'll cry too and he thinks he is fighting for my life. He cares too much to give me hope in the form of his tears.

Now I question the cause of my own tears. Is it my shame for being afraid to face the world on my own? Or do I cry because I'm saying goodbye? I might never see Leksi again. Am I crying for the two of us not being together? And is that why tears threaten him, too?

Whatever it was that threatened to draw water from Leksi's eyes, he shoves it back and the hard, unmoved soldier returns. He draws his dagger, holds the point towards me. "If you would prefer it be my blade than someone else's, simply say so," he says.

"Leksi, please," is all I can think of to respond.

"Go." I would bet all the coins of Macedonia that he would not use that blade on me now. I even have an instinct to knock the stupid knife aside and kiss him. But I do not. I do not want my kiss to be a weapon to save myself. And now there's only one other option available to me.

I leave.

Chapter 32: Leksi

I watch Petros walk alone into the night. I tell myself that the world needs Petros in it and not in this farm in the countryside and absolutely not dead. He is good. He fixes people and there is a whole world filled with people who need to be fixed. I watch as he bumps into a tree and trips on a root. He returns to his feet and turns back to me. I hold my dagger out, pointing it after him, afraid that if I lower it, it will signal him to return. He continues away.

A nagging point occurs to me, while the world needs Petros, so too does Petros need the world. He's right. While his chances of a long life are better this way, the odds will not favor him on his own either. And I am overcome with sadness. All roads seem to end with his death.

I was sad at the loss of the battle. I was devastated by the loss of Sigorin and the rest of the Band. I grieve my mother, but that is not the source of this sorrow. These things are in the past. I mourn their having left. I mourned what we had. But now, I mourn Petros, but not what he was or even what he is. I mourn what he could have been. I mourn a possible future, a vision that had somehow slipped into my mind without my permission.

I am usually comfortable holding onto my thoughts. As much as I loved Sigorin, and I did, we didn't speak much. Our communication was based on touch—his hand on my back, my head on his chest, our fingers intertwined. But this thought, a future with Petros destroyed, demands that I find another soul to confide in.

I go back to the lodge to find Aello. I am grateful to find her nursing Lura, while my father mercifully sleeps, leaving them their peace.

I sit by Aello's side. "How are you?" I ask.

"It all hurts, every part of me, parts I did not even know I had. But I will live. We both will. Thanks to you. Thanks to Petros. More, Petros, though. He saved us tonight," she says.

"He sends his heart to you," I offer, not knowing quite how to tell her that he's gone.

"Where is he? Resting, I hope?"

I smile at her question, still unsure.

"You didn't tie him up again, did you?" she continues. "I think he's earned better treatment than that."

"He does," I respond, grateful that she led me to the thing. "I let him go."

"Oh?" Sadness registers across her face. "Did he want to go?"

"No… no," I confess. "He wanted to stay."

"So then why is he not here?" she fires back, her good nature failing her.

"He is not safe here," I retort.

"He is safe on the roads, alone? And even if he makes it back to Macedonia, it is not safe for kin there, even I know that."

"Perhaps safer than he is here. And he does not have to go to Macedonia," I offer in my most comforting voice.

"Nonsense." There is nothing comforting about her tone. "And who is going to help me while I recover? I cannot do this alone. I'm split open, Leksi."

"I will," I say.

"You?" She responds, shocked that I would suggest it. "I'm sorry, Leksi, but you are not the motherly type."

She's right. I had not considered her recovery, but it is too late.

"I'm sorry." I say. "I should not have disturbed you." I stand, preparing to leave. She closes her eyes. I know what she's doing. She's summoning up a new tactic. I turn to go before she has a chance.

"Petros is your love," she blurts out. I return.

"I had a love. His name was Sigorin," I say.

"You may have loved Sigorin, but he was not your love," she says. "I know it. I see it. You love Petros."

I do not want to hear this.

"You need your rest." I hope this will appease her. I should not have thought to burden her with my mourning a future with Petros. I need this conversation to end, but, I see it in her eyes, she knows this tactic is working and has no intention of surrendering now.

“Just because some general says, 'Love this Sigorin,' does not mean it is so. The gods decide on love. The gods. And the gods gave you a great gift, Leksi. Do not discard it. You were given love, so love. Love!”

I smile at her, masking my great annoyance. She does not understand. How could she? She married my father, granted she had no choice in that, but that is her limited understanding in matters of the heart. And she has no idea what Sigorin meant to me, and she has no idea how I feel about Petros. None whatsoever. How dare she? She is making me angry and I am even more angry that I am not allowed to be angry with her. I have no idea why I came to speak with her. None at all. I don’t even remember what I wanted to say. But I keep the smile on my face. I let the sight of my sister nursing calm me.

“I am sorry if I upset you,” I offer.

“Fools. You boys. You’ll be the death of us all,” she spits.

I lower to kiss her forehead but she turns away from me. She must read the irritation on my face but it does not stop her. “You will care for us… you,” her tone is not sincere and I do not have a response.

The world does need Petros. My world needs Petros, but Petros is gone. No bother. I can tend wounds, and cuddle babies, too, at least I think I can. But I do not offer that insight to Aello. I do not want to hear her response. I quietly steal past my sleeping father towards the door. I don’t know how much longer I can hold up this mask. *You love Petros.* I push her words away. What does she know?

Chapter 33: Alexander

Alexander walks the breezeways of the palace, unable to sleep. Or that's what he tells himself. It's not entirely true. He can't sleep but he walks because he's looking for Hephaestion, hoping, restless and hungry, that Hephaestion's here searching for Alexander, too. He looks down upon the moonlit garden below, succulents and blooming cacti staring back at him but he cares not for their staring. Alexander is not one to hope for things or to send wishes to the gods. He takes action. But there is no action here he feels that he can take. So he does hope and send wishes to the gods, wishing that Hephaestion will find him and take him to the shadows and have him there, perhaps in that very garden. And that Hephaestion will forgive Alexander for not being able to take action, and for the shadows Alexander cast over them.

One by one he transverses the stone steps, feeling their cool, polished texture under his feet. Alexander is not accustomed to his mind allowing his body this kind of idle activity, but it is all that he can think to do. It is the only thing available to him, walking the stones, and thinking about Hephaestion.

A night watchman, old and seasoned, turns the corner. Alexander stays in the torch light to not startle him. Even so, the watchman squints to make out Alexander's face and his hand instinctively moves to the hilt of his sword.

"Oh, your majesty." He says, surprised and concerned to see anyone, let alone a forign prince, at such a late hour. He moves his hand from the handle of his weapon.

"Good evening." Alexander offers back.

“May I be of service?” He continues with the pleasantries, but it’s not his service Alexander desires.

“No, thank you, sir.” Alexander says, “Just enjoying the night breeze.” He lies.

“Very good, your majesty.”

The watchman waits, staring at Alexander as servants tend to do when they’re unsure of the appropriate course of action. Alexander wants him to leave so bad, but he fears to give the order. This feeling of being caught at something is so original for the Prince that he does not know how to proceed. His mind spins in its search for the appropriate course of action, the right word that will reveal an exit to the maze.

“Dismissed.” Alexander decides upon.

“Very well, your majesty.”

And Alexander watches the watchman go, relief spilling over him.

Alexander laughs at himself. *Why am I behaving as a child?* He remembers in this moment that, yes, he is a prince and, yes, he can’t be known to be kin, but that he can certainly be kin still. In fact, that is simply a fact made so by the gods and to deny it would be to offend them. He also considers that the current king has his public and private lives and if that is so why couldn’t he have a private life of his own? *That’s what monarchs do*, he affirms to himself. *It is part of the deal we strike with the people and the gods.* Empowered with this thought, he hurries towards Hephaestion's room.

Looking over his shoulder to make sure he's unseen, to make sure his private life stays private, he slowly creeks open the large olive wood door, making as little noise as possible.

He shuts it behind him with equal care, trying to make sure that the mound sleeping in the bed before him in a pool of moonlight stays asleep, at least for now.

But this mound is Hephaestion and Hephaestion does not stay asleep when the door to his bedroom opens unexpectedly. He shoots up and rolls off the bed. Alexander knows what he's doing, he's arming himself, and if Alexander doesn't introduce himself he'll end up with a throwing knife lodged in his chest.

"It's me," he whispers.

It's a long moment before Alexander hears the dropping of the blade and a defeated sigh.

Hephaestion stands naked in that moonlight and all at once, like a soldier called to attention, Alexander's member is hard, and his jaw slack.

Hephaestion pulls a pillow over his crotch, suddenly modest, and sits back on the bed.

"Does your mother know you're here?" He jabs.

"That's not fair." Alexander replies, as he sits on the bed besides his wounded friend, aware that he hasn't been invited to do so.

"You let her eviscerate me, Alex, and you said nothing."

He's right. Alexander knows it. It's also not lost on him that in another time he would've forgave that of Alexander immediately, but things are different now. Now, they are more than friends. And Hephaestion is still in pain and his forgiveness is less free flowing. Alexander puts his arm around Hephaestion's shoulder to comfort him, but also to steal a touch. Hephaestion shrugs him off.

"Do you know how much I love you?" He asks.

"I do." Alexander replies.

"And do you not love me the same?" He counters.

"Of course I do." Alexander offers back.

"Of course? You have a cruel way of showing it." His voice rising in volume.

"Shhh…" Alexander knows that his hush might incite him, but what else is he to do?

"I will not… shhh. You shh." If Alexander wasn't terrified that he'd be caught, he'd find this amusing and adorable, but the stakes are too high to enjoy it. And Hephaestion is only beginning. "Contrary to what your mother thinks I am of noble blood, not some stable boy who you can sneak off to when you fancy a plow."

And an unfortunate thought sneaks its way into Alexander's mind. He can have his private life, but perhaps not with this man because Hephaestion shines too brightly, but Alexander pushes that thought away and pretends that it never existed.

“I know you’re not, but Hepha, she’s not wrong and you know it. If I’m found out to be kin it will be the death of me.” Alexander says.

Hephaestion turns away. He does not want to allow Alexander his talking points, but Alexander does not ask permission to be heard.

“You are the most noble man I’ve ever met and you do deserve more than these shadows but, and I’m sorry, this is all I have to offer you right now. Please.” Alexander pleads as he puts his hand back on Hephaestion’s shoulder.

It’s all true. For all his power, for all his access to wealth and knowledge and servants, for all of it, this moment is all Alexander has, this secret exchange in a dark room with his closest friend who is so much more than a friend.

And Hephaestion sees this, truly sees it. He sees Alexander’s love, his fear, his lust. Alexander recognizes the expression on Hephaestion’s face, he’s seen it before. It’s realization, the moment Hephaestion comes to an understanding that he didn’t have before. His jaw opens ever so slightly, parting his lips, his hard eyes soften and his shoulders roll forward. There’s a quiet softness to him when he’s like this. All his blustering armor gone, just the man Alexander loves, deep in thought.

But I can’t ask him to reduce himself so that he can be with me. It’s unfair what I’ve done. This thought invades Alexander’s thinking next. He’s not used to having to think of the wellbeing of others but there it is and this time it won’t be dismissed.

"It's not enough for you. You're right. You should marry, start a family, have children of your own."

And Alexander tries to will himself to go, but fails. His legs won't carry him off.

"You really do deserve more." Alexander continues, but still can't leave.

"I should go -" He blutters on.

"Stop talking, you mule." Hephaestion says, mercifully.

And Hephaestion pushes his shoulders back and tightens his jaw. He focuses his eyes into sharp orbs. This is the Hephaestion of action, Hephaestion the warrior, and he's in charge. Alexander would not dare lean in for a kiss, or leave without permission now that this man's here.

Hephaestion springs to his feet. Alexander catches a glimpse of his bulge before Hephaestion closes the curtains of the open window to ward off the moonlight.

Other windows across the courtyard have a view of this room and no one must see what's about to transpire here. Alexander prays to the gods to allow him to see Hephaestion in this moment, but the darkness does not permit this. Only feelings are allowed here as hands rip off clothes and lips find flesh.

Hephaestion's hands wrap around Alexander's throat. He's still angry. His fingers squeeze, but not enough that Alexander cannot breathe, only enough so that Alexander knows…

"You're mine. In this moment, you're mine." Hephaestion whispers.

And Alexander is overcome with relief once more as Hephaestion takes on the burden of Alexander's greatness, pushing him onto his back, throwing Alexander's legs onto his strong shoulders.

Alexander wants to tell Hephaestion to be gentle. *We have enjoyed each other before, but we've never done this*. He thinks. But Alexander says nothing. *It's his right to take me as he pleases,* Alexander decides. *And I am nothing right now, only his thing.* Hephaestion spits on their point of union. He aims and positions and pushes. It hurts Alexander when Hephaestion enters him. But his body wants Hephaestion inside, needs him inside, and the pain gives way soon enough.

Alexander squints to try to pull in enough light to at least see the outline of Hephaestion's face, but he cannot. They are in darkness, but he feels him all the more. Hephaestion's hand, still around Alexander's throat, tightens as he pulses into him.

It doesn't take long. And when they culminate it happens in unison. As if they were one, their bodies in sync, one responding to the other.

And when it's done, they hold each other. They'll have to get cleaned up soon. Alexander will sneak back to his room. He'll have to be great again. But for now, he's in Hephaestion's arm. And Alexander is nothing but his.

Chapter 34: Petros

And now I am free, free to be alone, free to freeze my rear off, free to die. And I use the word *free* not to imply that I have some personal choice in these matters. I don't. It's more like, these things are free to happen to me, if they so choose.

I remember the river, and I remember the lady of the forest. The only plan I have, besides curling up and hoping a wolf comes for me—somehow in this moment that sounds like the most pleasant possible death—is to find that river and start the march home, the long march home. I know the direction of the river now, if only I had an idea where home is. The army would have cleaned up and cleared out of Chaeronea days ago. I could find them. They're probably heading north back to Macedonia, but they really will kill me. This isn't paranoia or an overly dramatic mind. I admit to having both but I know when they're acting on me, the wolf being a pleasant death for example is me being dramatic, there are no wolves in these woods. Death by copatriots is a purely rational thought. Traveling alone, I might be able to arrive back in Macedonia before the army. But eventually, someone will discover my identity. They may offer a trial—that would be nice and humiliating—but trial or no, I will be sentenced to death.

Perhaps that is the best I can ask for. A brutal, donkeyless walk home followed by the relative comfort of a prison cell and a quick and easy death. I've certainly seen worse lives lived. Perhaps I'm even lucky. I suspect it would beat death by wolf. There is also the chance that no one will identify me as the little kin man who let the last surviving member of the Sacred Band of Thebes escape. Then, I can live out my life as a fugitive, avoiding my family and friends from my former life, trying to muster a living working odd jobs. But there is only a chance of that. A very small chance.

The sound of the river's rush breaks my musings. Tall reeds hide the water, but its sound is unmistakable.

With the path to Macedonia clear—north along the river—I take my first step, and immediately my plan unfolds. *Greece is a giant place! I can go anywhere!* A little voice cries out inside my head. *And the world doesn't end with Greece. There are plenty of places I could travel.* These are thoughts from the best part of me, the part I can only hear when the paranoia has to take an inhale. *Go to the ports!* This optimist calls out. *You will find a life!*

The worst part of me, paranoia, finds her breath and she has something to say about that. *Alone. You'll be all alone. We've been over this and over this. You're little and weak, and the world will consume you.*

That's the tricky part. Paranoia is not often wrong. I don't do alone too well, but the gods must hear my despair. Up ahead, almost out of a dream: wagons, large—three of them—with horses, donkeys and oxen, travelers. Perhaps a tribe, a Grecian tribe. They'll understand. I'm Macedonian, but I'm also kin. I'll tell them if they don't see it at once. They'll think that's why I don't want to go back. *But they'll kill me at once, kin or not. We Macedonians are mortal enemy*, that worst part of me sounds off. But I steady myself. This tribe is a gift from the gods. I won't squander it. I will trust.

The dangerous part comes next. I must approach. These wagons probably containThebans fleeing their city instead of risking their luck with the Macedonians. I've practiced the

Theban accent well enough, perhaps I can pass, even if it's just long enough to avoid their spears so that I can tell them my story: *the last Bandsman of Thebes would not kill me because we became friends. He let me go. Give me a chance to show you why.* Because that's what happened, Leksi and I became friends. The thought makes me smile, brings tears to my eyes, too, but I can't think of Leksi. I force him out of my mind, out of my heart.

I approach. I tip-toe my way through the thick brush; best I see them before they see me.

"Ayo," I hear behind me, and my heart stops. These are not Greeks, these are Macedonians. But this specific Macedonian may not know me. I do not recognize his voice. Perhaps I should still pretend to be Greek, perhaps then he'll simply send me on my way. But no, he will hear the familiar sounds in my tongue even if I try to mask them. I am not that good an actor.

"Ayo, friend," I respond, leaning into my natural Macedonain speech. I slowly turn.

"Hands," he says. This isn't starting off well. I raise my hands, showing him I'm unarmed, and face him.

He's a squat, ill-tempered looking fellow, older, with suspicious 'I die last' eyes. While I do not know him specifically, I know plenty just like him. When Greeks poke fun at Macedonians, he's who they impersonate.

"Explain yourself," he says and now I see the blade he's holding.

"No need for that, I'm a countryman," I say.

“Explain yourself,” he repeats, not lowering the blade.

“Is this the brigade to Thebes?” I ask.

The stout man grabs my shirt, pulls me in, presses the blade point to my neck.

“Yes, yes, alright, I’m a doctor. Officers thought you were short medical staff. After I pieced together the last of the wounded at Chaeronea, I was sent along to join you.”

I amaze myself by how easily the lie comes, and I wait for a response. The point of the stout one’s blade falls away from my neck instead of through it, so that’s something.

“Who’s your officer in charge?" he asks.

“Gregarious, of course,” I say. That would be the chief doctor of the army, the one who said I cared too much.

The stout one relaxes even more. His expression turns pained. “I have a sore,” he says. “By the gods, it hurts.”

He has a sore, thank the gods, I think. He wants to trust me, maybe I can keep up this lie long enough to escape.

I look to the campfire starting up near the main carriage, and hear the baying of a sheep. I imagine a dinner of mutton that’s perhaps to come, might as well pick up a meal before I run off, and then I see him. Captain Tam gets out of the wagon. My heart sinks, and every shred of my newfound hope puffs away with his smug grin.

I turn back to the stout one, who is already showing me the pussy mess on his foot.

"What do you think? There an ointment or something you can give me?"

"Right, put your boot on, go on back to camp. I'll have a look after dinner, aye?" I respond, my eyes locked on Tam.

"Just have a look now, please?" he pushes back, sounding as desperate for relief as I am for escape.

Captain Tam scans the area and all I can think is, *Run. Run fast. Anywhere.*

"After dinner." I try to not sound like I'm begging.

"And why not now?" He's in pain, I hear it. Such a small thing can cause such chaos. And then something else comes over him. Doubt. "You're awfully young to be a doctor," he says.

"Not so young," I muster. "Go on back to your watch now. I'm about to relieve myself. I'll be back in a moment."

"I'll escort you to our captain, I think." He unknowingly says the worst possible thing.

"No, no," I push back promptly, and promptly the knife returns.

"Something's not right with you. Only snakes hide in grass."

He has a point. I was hiding in the grass. And while I'm not usually a violent man, I do appreciate that this moment calls for it. With my all, I kick his man spheres. It's rude and cheap, I know, but I'm small, and I have few options. And it does the trick.

The stout one groans, and I bolt towards the river, down the bank. I only get a second head start before the call of "Intruder!" sounds out. It's a pained, high pitched voice but loud and true.

I hear the clanging of swords as he shouts, "Down the bank!"

As I realize that's exactly where I am and I should move, I make a dive for the river, expecting to land headfirst in deep water, like a dolphin in the sea, but instead I plop down in mud and tall reeds, still a distance from the waterline.

The reeds are like prison walls, surrounding me, blocking my escape. I hear the voices of men coming down the hill, calling out orders and I see my cover of darkness being chipped away at by approaching torch light. The unsheathing of a sword nearby sounds out. I brace for the end as a long blade swings wildly by my head, but misses, cutting back the tall grass instead. I cover my neck with my hands and drop to the ground, awaiting the second blow. This one will not miss, but instead of the swish of the sword I hear a violent exhale, as if the swordbearer was kicked by a horse in the stomach and lost his wind.

I peek up from my defensive position to see what happened to my would be executioner when impossibly strong hands grab my shoulders and pull me up. This is, for certain, the end. But instead of being tossed back to the muddy banks to face Macedonian steel, I'm hurled across space and land in the open water of the river. I gasp for air and thrash. I hear a

Macedonian scream "That way!" right before a hand covers my mouth and pulls me under.

What is this, some river nymph come to take me away? To save me or to escort me to Hades? Whatever it is, it pulls me into the deeper water at the river's center, and dunks me under. We're carried down by the current in a blackness. My guide kicks us towards the opposite shore. No sense fighting; its arms are strong and sure. There's even something comforting about its hold.

Except that my lungs are bursting, nothing comfortable about that. In my last moments before passing out, we finally resurface. I cough as I suck in air, but a voice tells me, "Shhh…" And the identity of this river nymph reveals itself.

"Leksi," I say. "Shhh…" he repeats.

I do my best to quiet my breath as our feet find the shallow bottom. Leski rises out of the water, a stone in his hand.

In the distance the Macedonian search torches approach us, but Leksi hurls the stone past them. They hear the rock splash into the water behind their position, and all at once the torches turn and head off in the opposite direction. Perhaps these are not the cleverest persons my people have to offer.

On the muddy bank, I'm suddenly aware of my racing heart. Leksi comes back to me, lowering himself back into the mud. It's then I realize we're both naked, our clothes ripped off by the river's current. I want to laugh when I see Leksi smiling in the moonlight. I've never seen that smile on him before, like a little boy who just escaped the kitchen with something delicious.

Our pursuers remain too close. We hear them. Leksi wraps me in his arms as he moves our two bodies further into the reeds, masking us. We lay there, covered in darkness, mud, and river creatures. I feel his arm, wrapped around my chest, travel down my stomach and to my crotch.

I'm stiff as a sword. Who would have thought that moral danger could be such a turn on? Or perhaps it was his heroics. Or simply his touch? I blush, and I feel grateful that he can't see my shame in the night.

And then I feel him against the back of my leg. He's as stiff as I am. And then I feel his lips against my ear, gently sucking, and then he whispers, "May I?"

I know what he's asking, what he wants. I've only had that done to me once before. It hurt. It was an attack. And I'm scared.

"We don't have to," he whispers. "But if this is our last moment, we might as well make the most of it."

I want to with him. I know, I'm his hostage… am I still? He did let me go and then he saved me, so…

"I want to." I don't recall giving permission for the words to come out, but there they are. And it's not untrue. I'm scared. I want to experience him inside me before I die. "I want to."

That paranoid part of me says no, it tries to remember what it felt like the first time, the last time, but I can't bring the memory forward in its entirety. I do remember flexing and clenching, trying to stop the other from entering. And pain, I remember that, too.

But here, under the moon, in the music of our river, There is no pain; and every muscle of my body wants him inside. Instead of clenching, my body absorbs him, takes him in. I gasp, shocked by the sensation of unity. Leksi covers my mouth with his hand.

“Are you alright?” he whispers.

I nod, yes. He pulses into me slowly, then faster. He squeezes my body into his, and I hold onto his arms. I hope that we’ll sink into the mud entirely, that we’ll stay locked in this moment forever.

I think we just might, until, with our enemies searching for us in the distance, with the stars and the moon as our witnesses, in the mud of Thebes…we implode, together, as one.

We stay there until the sun rises, kissing our faces, chasing away the shadows.

Three Years Later

Chapter 35: Alexander

For the last three years, Alexander has slept with his head on Hephaestion's chest. No one has known, other than Alexander, Hephaestion, and Helena, but so it has been for three full years. And so it is now, Alexander's head on Hephaestion's chest, when there's a loud, assertive and unashamed knock on the door. When in Alexander's presence, most everyone and everything apologizes for not being enough. This knock does not. There is no resistance to it. It will be answered.

Hephaestion and Alexander both have blades in their hands by the next second, this knock demands that kind of response.

The knock sounds again. Hephaestion rolls off the bed towards the door and Alexander hides, *like a frightened child,* he thinks, chiding himself. He does not fear bloodshed, of course. He fears what may happen when those who spread the news learn the nature of his heart. In the short moments it takes Hephaestion to walk from the bed to the door, Alexander reminds himself of that outcome. The news spreaders will speak of it to others, who will in turn tell others, until the entirety of Macedonia knows that Alexander, the man to be their king, keeps the company of other men in his bed. Surely, the son of Zeus would not have such an affliction, the Macedonians will think, and it would follow that Alexander is not, as his mother suggested, the son of Zeus. They will stop loving him. And those in the elite who would see the crown on another's head will no longer fear popular revolt should they assassinate Alexander. And so they will do just that. Thinking this logic through to its conclusion, Alexander's own death, is his most familiar pastime. He does it often to remind himself that, while he can lie his head on Hephaestion's chest, it must not be known.

Hephaestion opens the door to reveal Helena and Alexander knows at once what has happened. It was not in her nature to knock like Hades himself. Some god had acted through her.

"There's a message." She says. Meaning, there is a messenger. Alexander knows the story she told this messenger. "Alexander was on a walk. He couldn't sleep. I'll fetch him for you," she said to him, meaning, *I'll fetch him and bring him back so you can tell him this news yourself. Tell him that his father, King Philip, is gone, murdered in some petty plot to gain power.* Alexander is unsure how he could be so certain that this is the news that will be delivered, but he is sure.

Alexander leaves his hiding spot and sits, quitely, Hephaestion and Helena watching him, waiting for him to make the short walk back to his assigned room before the rest of the castle is roused. Alexander rehearses, in his mind, his reaction when he hears the news: *I'll beat my chest and carry on allowing all to believe that I mourn the King of Macedonia.* In truth he does not, but he does mourn his own life as he currently lives it. From this moment onward, all eyes will be on him always. There will be no moments when he can lie his head on Hephaestion's chest.

With King Philip gone, Alexander begins his final ascent to the throne. He will either find the crown on his head or be killed pursuing it. There are too many powerful men hoping for the latter for there to be a misstep. The risk for Alexander to continue relations with Hephaestion now, and even more so when he is actually king, is too great for both of them.

Surviving Chaeronea was King Philip's gift to Alexander. It allowed Alexander this time with Hephaestion. *That time is through now,* Alexander thinks.

Alexander throws on his sash and continues out the door. He wonders if Hephaestion has followed the logic of this moment to its conclusion in the way he has. He suspects Hephaestion has not.

Alexander lets Helena lead the way. It's too dangerous for him now. He lets her act as his shield. Already he behaves with the expectation that some rogue is waiting in the shadows to end his ascent. *Kinghood is affecting my manhood,* he thinks to himself.

Helena manages through the maze of halls until they arrive back at their room, where a Macedonian messenger kneels upon seeing Alexander. He's his mother's spy, this brings Alexander relief, and the kneeling is an effort to appear honorable, something which spies are, by occupational necessity, not. But at least this man tries.

"The King, your father, is dead."

Alexander sees the difficulty in delivering this news in the man's eyes. *He lost his father and he loved his father. The loss of his father still hurts him*, Alexander decides while wondering what that must feel like. He has no way of knowing. Alexander sees the empathy in Helena's face as she takes his hand. Alexander wants to tell her, shout to the world, that he does not feel grief. This was not the man who raised him, that would be Aristotle. This was not even the man who sired him. King Philip was practically a stranger and, what Alexander knew of him, Alexander didn't much care for, nor did Alexander care much for his approval. He's only upset by this death in that it'll pull him further and not closer to Hephaestion.

Alexander lowers into a chair nonetheless. He bows his head in feigned grief for the fallen King. It's not the performance that he had hoped for, but it serves the point. He will sit here now and wait for his mother to arrive. Her decisions will largely dictate what happens next.

Alexander does dare to glance at Hephaestion, who is in his protect mode, thinking of nothing else but destroy all threats to my beloved. *He is so handsome in that state*, Alexander thinks. as a burning hot flame, ignited from within his chest, burns Alexander's heart. It hurts. Alexander is not accustomed to feeling emotion in this way. He considers it, discovers its source, a thought: His mother will insist that Hephaestion be separated from Alexander in fear that all those with any instinct for the hearts of men will be able to see their feelings for each other. She would not be wrong to do so. It would protect both Alexander and Hephaestion. And destroy them at the same time.

A moment ago, Alexander's fear was that he would never be able to place his head against Hephaestion's chest and that was bad enough. Now, he's imagined a future where he would never see Hephaestion again. He considers an alternative course of action. The world is a large place and this path to the crown is one he is choosing to follow. He can as easily choose to settle a far off island. He's certain Hephaestion would go with him, and Helena, too. They might not have the wealth their titles grant them, and certainly not the power, but they will make a life for themselves, a very happy one.

He asks himself, in this moment, does he want to be king, not only of Macedonia, but of the world? It's an honest question and the answer is one to be heard from inside, and not deduced. So Alexander listens for a long time. *Does my devotion still lie towards power?*

Yes, is the answer he hears. "Yes," he says aloud to no one but himself. "It does."

Chapter 36: Leksi

I have not dreamed of him in three years, to my great shame. I have thought of him often, prayed to him, but he has kept clear of my dreams since Lura was born. But I dreamed of Sigorin tonight. He was in his armor, but it fell off him. I tried to put it back on, to tighten the leather straps around his thighs and chest, but they would not hold. Over and over again, the armor would fall off and I would put it back on, only to have it fall off once more. I was embarrassed and frustrated, this was my task and I had once excelled at it. He was not angry. He only smiled at me, smiled as his armor fell away, smiled at the sound of hooves thundering towards us, that terrible sound of the Macedonian cavalry riding into our ranks, that moment only I survived.

That is the sound I awake to, hooves pounding the earth, but not a full cavalry, only two. Still, when I awake I'm already on my feet with a blade in my hand, before I even understand why. Horses approach.

As Petros wakes, I signal him to stay quiet as I gaze through the planks of the barn. Two riders come through the tree line, Deimos and Phobos.

I stand down, blade sheathed for now. The danger is not immediate. These are my men. My captains, in fact. They are too young for that responsibility, but they are the oldest in my band of soldiers, Teeth of the Dragon, they call themselves, and they have been with me the longest. And, most importantly, they are brave.

Over the last three years, Phobos and Deimos have come to love me, to love what we do and the hope we will bring to

Thebes. They want to live and die as Thebans. They want their sons to be free Theban men. They do not want life under tyranny. That is the rhetoric we preached when we recruited the others who have joined our ranks, fifteen in total now. Most are the children of farmers, like myself, Phobos and Deimos, but the other trades are represented too. The children of blacksmiths, carpenters and masons, a silkweaver, and even a son of a high priestess fight by our side. We have used my family's farm as our gathering point. This is where we train. The Macedonian convoy have took notice of our gathering, but we had a story. We gathered to construct a new barn and made that our excuse for our numbers. To my shame, I feigned a severe limp and took to wearing a hood. On the occasions when the Macedonians inspected our farm, I would moan and allow droll to drip down onto the fabric that draped me, so that the Macedonians believed I was touched and perhaps cursed. They stayed away and never questioned my age and whether I served in the Theban army or not.

Petros found my disguise amusing and took to calling me Droolius as a tease. As he had ingratiated himself to my men by healing their blisters and training wounds, they too had adopted the tease during our more casual moments. I made believe I was bothered by it and would roar and chase them. I have never been teased in love and kindness before. It warmed me. And it warmed me to see these boys grow into young men. They were strong and noble. They knew what Petros and I were to each other, lovers, we didn't hide it. They looked up to me still.

Aello was like a mother to all of us, seeing to the preparation of meals and offering a kind ear when it was needed. As payment for our being there, she negotiated the actual construction of the new barn, using the young soldiers as labor. She turned the story into something real. She made believe that was their primary purpose as she did not approve of our mission. She chose every dimension, every stone, every angel to the sun for the new structure. Most importantly to me, she revived my mother's garden. Everything she planted grew into nourishment. Lura grew strong, nimble, and fierce as Artemis. The only other person who she would go to besides Aello without protest was Petros. He was her father. This was good, as her real father was all but missing. Occasionally we would see him, stirring from his drunken sleep. He would look to the newly built barn and restored garden with confusion, as if it were a dream, and then stumble back into the lodge.

Sometimes, this life felt like a dream to me, too. Except that it was more than I could dream possible. A life with a lover that was not based on war and violence, to be able to treat Theban children as if they were truly my own, not only to die for them, but to teach them and love them and see them grow into bright, strong capable men. To see the land of my ancestors flourish and my mother's garden re-born. To live in a kind of peace.

So it was that the thunder of these horses woke me from this dream. Like an early frost, this visit was not scheduled or planned for. It feels too much like the forming of a storm, and I have grown to quite enjoy the sun. I consider laying back down, telling Petros to lie next to me, let the world continue on without us in this fight. But I dreamed of Sigorin. I know not the meaning of the dream, why I could not armor him the way I always did, why he only smiled when his response should have been rage. I wonder if he would forgive me if I gave up this fight. If I paid my taxes to the Macedonians and told my men to stand down. That was all these foreigners dared to ask for, taxes, nothing more than the Theban ruling class asked for. Perhaps they will ask us to educate our children in their language. Perhaps they will ask us to bow to the gods in the manner that they are accustomed to. Perhaps they will ask us to grow food and raise livestock that better suit their palate. Perhaps these things matter, I don't know. I wonder. All I can do is wonder.

I am a Theban, I remember. And not just a Theban but the descendant of Theban warrior-farmers, tooth of the dragon. This land has been ours since before the time of hercules. We bow to our gods in our own way. We teach our children as we see fit. Pay our taxes only to those of our own blood. As these thoughts swell my chest and prepare me for battle, a part of me, a small, powerless part, becomes aware that it is only rhetoric. It is only the things powerful men shout so that the masses will die for them. I know this. I'm awake now, I think, but I am not free. These thoughts are still stronger than my awareness. My chest still swells with this: I am tooth of the dragon; I am a soldier of the Sacred Band of Thebes. I am the last soldier of the Sacred Band of Thebes. For Thebes. To the death.

I leave the barn.

I approach Phobos and Deimos as they still their horses and quickly descend, falling at attention, awaiting my order to "speak" which I offer at once.

And they do. And I know what's to come.

"King Philip of Macedonia, sir. He's dead. Killed."

Aries seizes us with that mixture of fear and anticipation. Our hearts race. The time is now.

Chapter 37: Hephaestion

Hephaestions follows a step behind as Olympia, Helena and Alexander walk with haste towards the carriage yard, unsure if he would be allowed to go along with them on their journey to Macedonia and King Philip's funeral. In this moment, he understands what it feels like to be a puppy. *I need a purpose*, he thinks. He needs his manhood back.

His brain races, trying to figure out a plan to position himself in a more meaningful way. He knows they are not going to Macedonia to bury the king. They are going to seize the throne. There will be competition from King Philip's other sons. The winner will be king. The losers will die. From this understanding, his calculations begin.

"The people are more behind us than ever before." Olympia offers. "They've always loved stories of Alexander and the stories of his heroics at Chaeronea have spread. My sources tell me that the children sing songs of his courage."

"It's the old Macedonian ruling families." Helena utters, much to Olympia's delight. Olympia loves it when Helena speaks her words. Olympia has trained Helena into the queen she wants her to be and Helena plays the role perfectly, knowing exactly what to say and when, despite keeping her own true heart.

"The full blooded heir from the King's third wife." Olympia lets out, and she ever so quickly glances behind her to Hephaestion. *Everyone in the party already knows this*, Hephaestion considers. *Olympia does not waste words. She's tossing me a carrot.* And he catches it. He does not need to do any more calculation. Olympia had a purpose for him all along and with that glance, coupled with those words that provided no new information, *the full blooded heir from the King's third wife,* she gave Hephaestion's his orders. And while he wants to hate her for it, he knows she's right.

"He's six, mother." Alexander says, ahead of everyone, interrupting Hephaestion's thought.

"And a half wit." She fires back. "According to the reports." She says, pulling up on her own ruthless reigns and glancing back at Hephaestion once more, this time with a sly smile across her lips. *I know what you want,* Hephaestion thinks, *but must you enjoy this?*

Even as he thinks this thought, Aries fills his chest with an unwanted pride. Much to Olympia's credit, she knows that Hephaestion can do this thing when others cannot. And it is his pride that she's playing with, he knows it.

"He and his mother were hidden in the countryside after the assassination," Olympia explains, watching Hephaestion's reaction from the corner of his eye. She continues, "They'll be returning for the funeral, of course. Should they arrive in Pelo before we-"

"Allow me this task," Hephaestion interupts, denying Olympia the pleasure of a slow manipulation. Alexander will protest, Hephaestion knows, but this will only be a performance. The deed is already done the moment the words are uttered.

"No," Alexander says, predictably. But to Hephaestion's surprise it's not a performance. Alexander used his commanding tone. It's a dismissive tone, almost casual. It's intended to humiliate whoever asked the question so that they will not protest, *your question is stupid and you should never speak again,* is the tone. Alexander meant it. He does not want that purpose for Hephaestion and Hephaestion loves him all the more for that.

Hephaestion stops walking, stops following. The company stops. They turn back to Hephaestion. He is no longer the puppy at their heels. He is a man once more.

Hephaestion turns to his beloved. "I will, my lord," Hephaestion insists. "I will not ask you to command it of me. The gods will forgive my protecting my future king. No more needs to be said," Hephaestion concludes.

"Except that I specifically command you not to." Alexander declares, not one to have his will dismissed. His jaw set, summoning every ounce of greatness within him to stop Hephaestion from taking this upon himself. But Hephaestion is unwavering. He turns to Olympia as if to say, *your turn.*

"You will allow him to play this role, Alexander." Olympia insists. She is probably the only being who can command Alexander in this way, Hephaestion knows it, and she has. And it is done.

In victory, the cat-like smile falls off Olympia as an authentic appreciation for Hephaestion is born inside her. An understanding flows from Olympia to Hephaestion as they stand in the uncomfortable, urgent silence: *I'm sorry I have not seen you before. I am sorry for the games. I need you now because should this child arrive in Macedonia before Alexander, Alexander will die, killed before he passes into the city's gates.*

It's the first time Olympia has truly looked at Hephaestion in three years. And as much as Hephaestions hates himself for it, he feels good to be seen by her.

"Thank you, Hephaestion." She says it. And this doesn't come from Olympia the strategist. This comes from Olympia, the mother. Hephaestion will save her son's life. She knows it.

Alexander looks away, but Hephaestion does not care about Alexander's shame. He has his purpose and won't give it back.

"He won't make it to Macedonia." He says to Olympia, and leaves without another word or glance to Alexander. This isn't on him. Hephaestion offers a silent prayer. *This wound is on my soul and mine alone, may the gods forgive me.*

Chapter 38: Petros

Three years that were supposed to be agony, horror, living as a captive, have turned into three years of life, bliss, home. A little girl, barely three years old, who's practically my own, a great love in Leksi, and the beauty that is the Theban countryside. And I have explored it all as a free man, maybe not in title, but freer than I have ever been.

It should not have been this way, I know, but turns out I am far more useful than I thought. The delivery was hard on Aello and it took her several weeks to be able to attend to little Lura by herself. Leksi, while well intentioned, lacks maternal instinct of any kind and Leksi's father is unbearable when sober so we kept his goblet full and the man barely conscious. This meant that I alone got to rear little Lura. Aello joked that if she could simply give me her breasts Lura wouldn't need her at all. Even so, Aello was on her feet eventually, and was a fine mother to little Lura, but by this time I was closer to the babe than anyone else.

Even the teeth boys, as I called them, grew to rely on me. In the first year, I was confident that Macedonia would never have to worry about the Thebans revolting if this was the lot they were up against. They kept hurting themselves. Cuts here, broken bones there, infections and rashes that I've never even seen before. It was on me to mend them. I didn't need Leksi's threats to get them to respect me. I earned that from them on my own.

By year three, they had grown into a competent fighting unit. It made my stomach turn to see them. They might have a shot against the band of Macedonians who were stationed in Thebes. They would take their losses, sure, but they might win. But they would be slaughtered against the Macedonian elite, against the cavalry. They are good young men, the teeth boys are. Handsome and strong, they cared for their elderly neighbors, brought food to those in need, planted the fields for the widows of the war. I hoped to see them grow old. To Hades with a free Thebes. I want to know their sons and grandsons. I want us to be friends as old men.

Leksi, of course, would hear none of this. For three years we shared our bed as lovers, and every morning, I would whisper to him about what life would be like in ten year, in twenty years. How Aello might have another child or two, maybe even a son. We could raise them as our own as we are Lura. How we might find a stud to breed the mare to, and sell the colt. How we might build another lodge so that when Lura was old enough to marry perhaps her and her husband could begin their family right beside us. That we would have nephews and nieces. Every morning I created this future for Leksi. The future is so clear in my mind! Leksi would smile at the images as I shared them with him and the morning sun. He would hum a little as I talked, although I don't know that he knew he was humming. This is always how Leksi hummed.

But now Phobos and Diemos ride and their horses threaten it all.

I know what's happening.

The king, my king, is dead. They were waiting for their moment, and this will be it, the undeniable, but completely deniable, moment when action is required. So stupid. So stupid. So stupid.

Leksi comes back inside after having greeted them, and I have to stop myself from screaming at him. I have a bad habit of screaming at him when he goes against my wishes. It usually just makes him condescend to me in this voice that makes me even more angry and gets me no closer to my goal. But I've learned. So I calm myself, and instead of screaming, I beg.

"Don't do this," I say.

"There is nothing to fear," he lies.

"I'm not stupid," I remind him. "I was a soldier, too."

"I know," he says, closing his eyes.

He wants to tell me everything, but he can't. He wants to tell me that he's scared too, but he won't. And as much as I want to hear it, he doesn't have to say it because, by the gods, I know: he doesn't want to lose what we have, what we can have, either.

"What difference does it make who you pay your taxes to? Some Theban rat in a high tower or some Macedonian fool up north, who cares?" I say, Aello's words flooding into my memory.

"I'm Theban. This is Thebes. It matters," he says. Sacred Band jargon. I recognize it immediately; even the pitch of his voice is different when he's repeating what he learned from them. I need to ground him in what's real.

"I'm Petros, you're Leksi, what about that?" I ask, but it's not really a question.

He pulls out his armor from where he's stashed it, behind a hay bale. At least he's past pretending that nothing's going on.

"This has been the plan all along. You've known it," he says while he straps on a chest plate.

He's not wrong. I have known it. I have known this moment was inevitable. That doesn't mean I won't fight for us.

"You weren't afraid before." It wasn't fair of me to say that, but this is not the time to fight fair. His look shows the wound I've made. Leksi doesn't like to acknowledge his own fear, but I see it on his face. It's all over him.

"You have something to lose now," I say. Again, I'm being cruel, I've set this up over years, but I'm fighting for his life, and mine too.

"What would you have me do, Petros? The Thebans will never submit, with or without me. There will be war," he says.

"Then without you," I say, even as he straps leather guards to his legs. I know what he wants. He wants me to kneel down and take over this task of prepping him for battle. He wants me to send him off with a strong word, *with your shield or on it,* like some brain dead Spartan wife, but to Hades with all that.

"It's a huge world, Leksi, we'll go settle an island, we'll run off to Crete or Sicily, we'll go to the ports and take the first ferry out, the destination does not matter," I blurt out, and I win a battle here somehow. I see the fantasy of that playing out in his mind's eye. That future might be real to him. But I also see him fighting it back, wrestling, willing it away, not letting it gain enough momentum to take over his fate.

“Please.” *You stubborn mule.* “Please,” is all I can think to say.

“I owe him. I owe all of them,” he says, as he shakes his head no. I know he means Sigorin, the Band.

“You love me now,” I come back with. I know how it sounds, petty and juvenile, but he teased me with the look of hope in his eyes, and to see it slip away burns even more.

“You love me. I know you do. Don’t do this,” I continue, but I know it’s hopeless now; perhaps it always was. His armor’s on now. He put it on by himself. My words bounce off it.

He kisses me on the forehead and leaves my side.

Chapter 39: Leksi

I know Petros is right. I know it. But that is a new knowing, a surface knowing. It has not buried itself into my soul yet. Down there, deep down there, I am Theban. I am Band. And I am oath-bound to defend this land, not just for Lura, but for all children of Thebes. I cannot stop my legs from moving me closer to battle, even if I must tow this new truth along with me.

Deimos and Phobos lead me to the lodge. My father is having one of his rare moments of sobriety, Dionysus has not seized him yet today, and he is there, too. We all know the plan; we wrote the script a year ago and we know the roles we play. It ends with a Theban civilian in the speaker's office. This is a review.

Deimos and Phobos, steam coming from their nostrils like angry bulls, set up the model of the Theban citadel: clay bowls and mugs for the buildings, a spare piece of wood for the great gate, string to mark out the outer wall.

"There's no movement from the north, sir," Deimos spits out.

"And they haven't changed their shifts," his brother adds.

"Twenty men are always in the city; twenty men outside," says Phobos.

"Forty," my father adds, as if we cannot do the math. I am tempted to pour his wine myself in the hopes that it will quiet him.

"But they are using civilians now, Thebans, to man the gate," Phobos says with enthusiasm. "If they are loyal, and we suspect they are, they shut the gate once our force is through."

"We will keep them at twenty," I interrupt, leading him to his conclusion.

"They'll still have the numbers." *Thank you, Father,* I think to stop myself from punching him in the throat.

"Yes, but we're men defending our home, fighting for our future," Deimos counters. "One of us is as good as every three of them," he continues, looking to me, these are my words, offered to them after every drill we completed. He's learned them well.

"You are boys. Boys who are still outnumbered by six. This is foolhardy."

My father, again, is not wrong with his calculation, and this gives me pause, but I know how these boys fight. I know because I have trained them. I also know how Macedonians fight because I have fought against them. Deimos is not wrong in his assessment that our men are worth three of theirs but it is not because of our reasons for fighting. I only told them that to build their confidence. It is how we fight that gives us advantage. The Macedonians are organized, strategic. They fight in phalanxes and with rows of mounted elites, on an agreed upon field. This battle will look nothing like that. We will be fighting within a city's walls. Mostly within a single building, if the plan plays out. Not knowing our numbers, the Macedonians will barricade themselves inside the capitol building to buy time and strategize a plan, executing us to wait to meet them on a field of battle, but we will not. The largest space is directly behind the front entrance, where the Theban senate would assemble. The room is large, but banked, like an outdoor amphitheatre. We will break down the door and this miniscule stage is where our battle will unfold. This battle will be contained, quick and brutal. My men, while boys, will have an advantage in that they know no better. I have trained them exactly for this.

I can see my captains growing uneasy with my silence.

"If not now, when?" Deimos pushes. He is tired of living in Macedonian shadows.

Never, I want to say. It is not that I don't think we can win, but I know what the costs will be, and they will be great. While I see us winning this battle, men younger than myself will die, and unlike the Macedonians we do not have men to spare here in Thebes. I almost say the word. *Never. It is not worth it.* But I don't. I hear Sigorin speak from the underworld. *If you wait any longer, Thebes will stop being Thebes.* And he's right. The world revolves around the Theban citadel, where the dragon teeth were buried. The sun and moon orbits this spot. If we do not fight now, that center of the world moves north to Macedonia. *This matters. It matters*, I hear Sigorin say. *It must stop.*

I nod my head. It needs to stop.

"Now," I say, to my father's guffaw. "Deimos, alert the thirteen," I command.

"Phobos, rally the civilians," I say. "By the end of this day, a Theban speaker will sit in this office." I point to the senate building. This is the mission.

Aries seizes them; fire appears in their eyes as they race out the door, leaving me to face my father.

"This is a fool's battle," the old goat says again. He likes that word…fool.

I stay silent. Sigorin used to chide me about that silence. He said others found it intimidating to be on the other side of, but he knew that all it meant was that I knew not what to say next. Here and now, however, I know it serves both purposes. My father pours himself his first drink, and I think it safe to leave him. He will not be able to interfere once Dionysus has him.

But as I turn to leave, upon seeing the door, all at once, I know I cannot leave my father here like this. I see the future clearly. My plan—not my plan for Thebes or my plan for battle, but my plan, the plan for my life, for myself—comes into sharp focus.

My father cannot stay here. Should I die in this campaign—and the gods will probably ask for my life before this day is out—he cannot be here. He will never let Aello and Petros flee with Lura, but that is exactly what must happen. With or without me, Petros, Aello, and Lura need to be free to go, free of him. This is a fool's battle, he says, and perhaps he is right. I am choosing to be a fool. And now I have something to say.

"Then come be a fool with your son."

He guffaws at that, too.

"You were a soldier," I push back. If his fatherhood doesn't compel him, then perhaps his manhood will.

"Aye, a good one, a great one," he bites.

"Then come show me. Come fight with me," I tempt him.

He narrows his eyes, but does not look away. He is playing with his bait.

"Are you still ashamed that I am kin? Or are you simply ashamed that I did not die with the others?" I say. He looks up at me. I see that both are true.

"Then come with me. Watch me today. Fight with me today. I will earn your pride, or I will die trying." I'm not so bad at jargon myself; perhaps I have a way with words after all. I could give a donkey's ass about his pride, but I need him gone. The thought that I might actually care about his approval finally draws him in.

He nods his head in agreement.

May the gods forgive this crime.

Chapter 40: Petros

I stare through the planks of the barn, while I cradle Lura.

For three years every moment has been occupied with chores, chores I've delighted in: caring for Lura, tending the fields and the flocks, doctoring the teeth boys. I remember how suspicious of me and my accent they were at first and how within weeks they were treating me as one of their own. Time builds unlikely bridges. I am loved. And, perhaps more importantly, I am never without a list of chores that need to be done. I am always needed. It feels so good to be needed.

But now, of course, in this moment when I am desperate for something to occupy my mind and body, I have nothing to do. Aello is here. She ran in with Lura just as Leksi had left. We sat quietly to try and hear what was being said. We heard nothing, but we did not need to hear to understand. In most times, Aello and I chatter endlessly, we talk about the weather, gossip about neighbors, imagine silly songs. And we laugh. We laugh until our insides hurt. But not now. As there is nothing that needs to be heard, there is nothing that needs to be said. And there is nothing to laugh about.

Through the planks, we see Leksi walking back towards the barn. Aello takes Lura from me. She takes my hand in hers and squeezes it, her eyes closed in prayer. I know what she wants from me. *Fight for our family, Petros. If he will listen to anyone, he will listen to you.* She does not need to say it.

She releases my hand and takes Lura from the barn as Leksi comes back in. He smiles at me, as if that's what I want from him, a smile.

“Should I not return by the moon’s height, you are to take the coins, all of them, bring Aello and Lura to the piers, and go settle on an island,” he says, as if he were telling me what to pick up from the neighbors. That casual. That’s his plan, but that’s not a plan.

“Oh, that’s all? Just go start over in a far away land?” I offer. He can read my tone; it’s not hard.

“I did not say it would be easy but that is all. Yes,” he says, without any tone at all. This is Leksi the general. I don’t much care for Leksi the general.

“Your father will just let me take his wife and daughter?" This isn’t the obstacle that’s really holding me up, but General Leksi thinks in logistics, details. If I can disrupt his thinking at that level, I may have a chance here.

“He is already handled,” General Leksi says.

What does that mean? I wonder. I suspect I can untangle his meaning, but I’m scared off by a shadow. Perhaps this wasn’t the best tactic after all. Better to be direct, appeal to his emotions.

“Come with us,” I say.

“We’ve been over this,” he responds.

We have. We’ve been over it and over it. The fantasy of us growing old together, either here or on an island, is one we shared, but Leksi never let himself believe in it. I never broke through completely with that image. He was never so unkind that he let me believe so either. Still, I hope. My heart cracks with hope. He takes my head in his hands and kisses my lips, the general fading, my Leksi returning. And my heart cracks some more.

“I want nothing more than to return to you,” he says.

“Or to return to him,” I say. I mean Sigorin, of course, and he knows it. It was a mean thing for me to say. I know it. Again, not the words he wants me to send him off to battle with. But I have a mission and I will not so easily surrender.

“I miss him. I love him, too, but I do this for us,” he says.

“Don’t lie,” I push back, still plenty of fight left in me.

“If we win Thebes, we have a life. We live here, this is our city, a city for all, for kin,” he says.

“A city where we’re put on the front line? Where we’re the first to go? Where they’ll let us die for them?” I blast back.

“At least we die in the light,” he says, calmly. I’m not introducing a new idea to him and he lets me know it.

“I’d rather live in the shadows with you,” I say and I mean it. It’s not a tactic. I’m only speaking truth.

He pulls me in. He kisses me once more. I melt. He gently pushes me away. I try to pull him back, to hold onto him, but his embrace has taken the fight from me. He removes his hand and gently breaks his hold on me. He’s always had the power to do this, I remember, to crush me like this.

I never use my kiss as a weapon, I think, as I watch him leave me.

Chapter 41: Hephaestion

Hephaestion pushes the future action out of his head as he rides towards the Macedonian outpost, just south of Delphi. Cavalry officers are trained to see the battle in their mind's eye before the event itself. It's part of their preparation. But not this deed. That would do more harm than good. Should he imagine it fully, he may decide not to do it at all, but it must be done. He pushes the image of it away again.

He wears the black cloak. It's the cavalry uniform when they perform deeds that may anger the gods, but the needs of man demand. It's so the gods don't recognize them. It's a silly tradition, he's aware of this.

And he knows the shadows who he travels towards care not about offending the gods. That's what Alexander would call them in private, shadows. They are cavalry, by title, but Alexander and Hephaestion made it a point to conceal them as best they could. They lack not only a noble title, but a noble character as well. That's why the nickname, shadow. They are, in fact, the cavalry's shadow. They are unknown but by a few. They are tolerated and loved in those moments when shadows are needed which is not infrequent in violent times, but in all other moments, they are hidden. They themselves prefer it that way.

Since Alexander and Hephaestion were no longer in command of the cavalry, these shadows were banished by Captain Tam, perhaps by King Philip himself, when it was realized they were impossible to contain without the charisma of Alexander or Hephaestion to keep them in heel. Because cavalrymen are fiercely loyal to their own, without question, had King Phillip tried to kill them off or discharge them, he'd risk mutiny from his most elite. Instead, the shadows were assigned to this most remote outpost. Reserves are kept here, stockpiles of weapons and armor should they be needed. This is exactly where the shadows belong. This place does not govern over a territory. There is no need to maintain appropriate optics on behalf of a conquered people. What's here is here to be kept out of the way until the business of the day calls it into action.

As Hephaestion arrives at the camp, he sees an untethered, uncarroled, stallion. The beast huffs at his approach, warning that it is not the kind of animal that flees from strangers. This tells Hephaestion that he is in the right place. It is not the cavalry way to give horses this much berth, but this is a cavalry stallion.

The stallion gallops forward, teeth gnashing. Hephaestion's mare is not one to submit either and she pounds her hooves, ready to do battle, but, once they get closer, they recognize each other. These two have fought beside and not against one another in the past. They are friends, allies. The stallion's fierceness melts away. Hephaestion smiles.

A man emerges from a simple tent, naked and hairy, thick muscled, scarred, taller than most with an impossibly large cock to match a massive broadsword in his hand. He too greets all who approach as potential foes until they prove otherwise. The old bear's eyes won't allow him to see Hephaestion's face from this distance, but he can see how Hephaestion rides and that's all he needs to unveil who approaches. He smiles as Hephaestion dismounts, and the horses kiss.

Hephaestion drops one of the two extra cloaks he carries at the bear's feet and the bear's smile magnifies. He knows he's about to do work, work that would make most ill to think of, but work that pleases him. This is why he's a shadow.

"Where's Tullik?" Hephaestion asks.

"Having his way with Aphrodite." The bear growls.

"We must make haste." Hephaestion says.

"He knows no other way." The bear says with a laugh. "Ahhi!" He shouts out to the heavens. "Time to ride!"

Time for dark deeds.

Chapter 42: Leksi

We ride towards the Theban citadel, my father and me. I never thought I would see this in my lifetime, my father and me, with a joint cause. I look over at him, and I see him sitting tall on our cart, the reins in his hands, his eyes clear and bright. I have not seen him like this since returning, perhaps I have never seen him like this before. I know not to admire him or to be proud of him, but the shadow of pride is there, like a framework inside me where pride could go if I chose to put it there. But I do not. He has done too much and not enough all at the same time for me to allow for pride.

The mare strains against the weight of the cart, loaded with armor and swords and covered with pelts to mask our stash from the possibility of a Macedonian inspection.

My father says nothing. I say nothing. It is that beautiful moment, quiet and still. I know what is to come. The storm. The sounds of war with their own melodies, my ears trained to respect their beauty, too, but right now, on this cart pulled by the mare, beside my father, in my countryside...this is beauty.

But then the thought wiggles up. I did not invite my father here for atonement. He is here so that if I die, he dies with me. And not for any honorable reason in the eyes of the gods, but to allow for the escape of those I love, a mostly selfish cause. And with that thought come the sounds of war. Quiet, at first. The groans of young men, the clashing of swords, the war cry of a horse, and the galloping of hooves, diminishing, as the beast runs away and not towards us.

My father pulls hard on the reins, guiding the mare to the right, off the path and into a dense tree grove, knotted with thorny shrubs and feral olive trees. I find myself off the cart and sprinting up the hill, my legs and feet again moving on their own command. I know where they take me, although I do not control their movements. They take me to the statue of Hercules that sits atop this hill, overlooking our citadel. The place where Phobos and I agreed to meet.

I arrive to find Phobos there, but not how I hoped to find him. He lies at the feet of the statue of the man-god, his hands pressing into his middle and covered with his blood, holding in his insides.

I have seen that wound before. It is a terrible way to die. And all die who have it.

I hurry to his side.

“I told him nothing. He knows nothing,” Phobos mutters as I put his head in my lap.

“Did I do good?” he asks.

I could never train the boy out of this one, as hard as I tried. He always wanted my approval, as if what I thought was more important than what he knew inside to be true. As long as I approve of him, he approves of himself. I did not want that for him. I want him to love and trust himself above all else. But in this last moment, I am grateful I can offer him this final gift.

“Yes, very,” I say, forcing a smile out of my lips. “You did very good. You’re very good.”

He groans, as Hades reaches up for him.

"The Thebans at the gate?" I ask.

"They are with us. True Thebans," he manages a smile now, as his exhales expel out droplets of his own blood.

"Good," I say. "Good. Close your eyes, now."

He coughs, trying to say his last words. They will have to remain unspoken, but I can hear them. He speaks of his brother, his family, his country. He hopes to know me in his next life. He hopes his life and his death have meant something to someone. I have heard it before.

I take his jaw in one hand, his forehead in the other. "You are good now," I offer. "A good Theban. A good man." And I twist, hard and fast. There's a sharp crunch and a final spasm of his legs. His pain ends. He dies by my hand and not the Macedonian's. Not that Hades cares either way, I know, but it brings me some solace.

I look up, and I see my father watching. The shame of having not seen him before washes over me. Had he been an enemy, I would have been slain.

But my error does not stop me from seeing what's behind his look. I see his fear, his shock, and it occurs to me that this is not the look of a man who has seen death like this before. My father has never killed a man himself. For all his blistering spit, he was a soldier only in title. He has never done the work. And in this moment, he does the thing that I have always wanted, without even knowing it, the point of all my training and warring, the reason I did not flee from my training, I see it in his eyes, in the way his shoulders press up around his neck: he forgets that I am kin. It no longer matters to him. And I am sad for myself, because I understand how much that desire controlled me but how little it mattered. All he sees now is that I'm a killer. And, to his and my own surprise, he is scared of me. Terrified. I preferred it when he was ashamed.

This thought comes and goes in a flash. No time for that now. I let Phobos's body slump to the ground and jump to my feet, we will attend to the dead after the battle. Phobos will not journey alone, I know.

I pull the looking glass from my bag. I hurry past the statue of Hercules and I set my gaze in the direction he points his club, the city of Thebes, where Hercules was born, the center of the world, until the Macedonians decided they were the center of the world and proved their point with might.

Walls jut up around her, walls that have long been infiltrated, the infection inside her—that is my failure, and the failure of my brothers. A wounded man makes his way to the wall, I see. By the way he rides, he is Macedonian and hurt; he must be the man who took his blade to Phobos.

Three other men exit through the lowered gate. A quick exchange between them, and at once these three are riding towards our position.

One down, three more headed our way. If I slay these newcomers, that will be four down, but they have war horns, and others know of their mission. If I take down two and the other has a chance to blow his horn, the Macedonians away from the city will be alerted, and our mission foiled. The risks to an encounter are too great, I decide.

But if we can lead them away, if they think this incident does not require their full numbers, perhaps Phobos's sacrifice will not have been for naught.

I turn to my father, fear of me still emblazoned in his eyes.

"What is it? What do you see?" he asks.

"Three approach," I say.

"We return. They know of our plans. There's no point going through with it now," he says, quick to retreat, wanting no more to do with the fighting business.

"They know nothing, and our numbers have improved. The gods bless this mission" I respond as my father's attention drifts to Phobos's body.

I grab him with more force than necessary and force him to look at me. He steals himself, to his credit. I pull him back down the hill, towards our cart.

"Take the mare back to the farm. They will follow you. Tell Petros what has happened, he will know what to do."

"Then what?" he asks. I remember my intention for him.

"Then, do as your heart demands. Flee with your wife and babe," I say, trying to rekindle his fighting spirit.

"Never, I am a Theban," he says, chomping down on the hook.

"Then fight like a Theban," I offer. *Die like a Theban* is what I truly mean, what I truly hope, too, gods forgive me. "Feed your fields with their innards," I say.

His chest wells up, his eyes moisten, he is moved. I realize that with this new fear of me comes pride and respect, authority even. Why my killing another man causes him to respect me when my loving one causes him shame is a riddle for another time.

My father unhitches the mare, mounts her, and charges down the hill, back the way we came, back to our ancestral farm. *Pride and respect are useful weapons*, I consider.

I slip behind the tree line and count the seconds before the Macedonians ride by me.

They dismount at the cart, see the hides that we used to mask our true intention. They do not look closer to find the swords that hide beneath.

"Fur traders, pelts," one presumes aloud.

"Shame to die to avoid a tax," one of the other says, with a glance towards Phobos's remains.

"Foolish pride," the first comments. "Tracks, fresh ones," he says next, discovering the mare's hoof prints.

I listen as they mount up and continue down the trail, following my father towards the farm. They make less haste than he does. He will have time to warn Petros. Petros will run off with Aello and Lura while my father is slain by these men after exchanging foul words. This is my prayer. *Aries make it so.*

Chapter 43 - Hephaestion

They ride, cloaked in black, these three, to do the work of Hades for even Aries would not take on this deed.

They stay silent. The mission has been reviewed, each know their roles in it. The shadows don't have much to say beyond the necessary, not to Hephaestion, not to each other. This lot is not much for speaking. They've picked up the caravan's tracks miles ago in the unpopulated terrarian of the countryside south of Pelo. They could have overtaken them hours before, but they linger far enough away so their presence remains unknown. They know the location where the deed is to take place, a small cliff out cropping that will seal their prey in on one side, hindering their escape. No sense alerting them of danger until then. The whole party must be silenced, especially the cowards who try to race away. It's not enough to kill the child, the half wit, as Olympia calls him. They all must die.

Hephaestion remembers the moments in which he's slain men in the past, steel into flesh, the look of disbelief in their eyes, a sudden understanding that what they were fighting for was not worth this, that nothing was worth this. And the gore of it. Hephaestion was not raised on a farm where young men are conditioned to the sight of blood pouring from the death wounds of beasts. He's only done this deed twice, both times in the chaos of battle. Both times against men who would have slain him had he not done them the service first. Even so, *there was so much blood,* he remembers.

This is different, he considers, and he can't seem to stop hearing that in his head, *this is different, this is not the same, this is not right.* The more he pulls out this weed of a thought the more pervasive it becomes.

But he made his choice, he reminds himself. If this child lives, Alexander will die. For Alexander to live this child must die. The plebians, the farmers and craftsmen, the soldiers in the army, even the artists, love Alexander. They want him as their King. Their old king never publicly denied that he was Alexander's father and so these plebeians consider it the way of things that their hero would be next in line. *But be it for these others*, Hephaestion considers about the noble families, of which Hephaestion himself belongs, the bankers and rule makers, they fear Olympia. They know she's the wisdom behind the persona that is Alexander and she is not one of them. She's Greek. It was these families that spread rumors questioning Alexander's parentage, true as they might be, and built up the reputation of the son born of Philip's third wife, the full Macedonian heir, that son for whom Hephaestion had plans for now. And yet, the only way the populace will accept this young boy as their King is if they are able to bury Alexander first. They need a corpse. The elites, Hephaestion's own birth tribe, will do just that, provide the populace with Alexander's corpse. That is, unless Hephaestion can provide them the corpse of their boy King first.

And so there is no choice at all for Hephaestion, not really. He considers that perhaps it did not have to be him to do the deed, perhaps Olympia could have found another. But Hephaestion would not have trusted another with this task. There is too much at stake. He could have one of the shadows perform the final deed. He does trust them to succeed. They will not suffer from the guilt of murdering a child. But this option does not sit well with Hephaestion. The shadows will kill for their country or for simply their own perverse pleasure in the act. Hephaestion will kill for his heart, for his love. *If a child is to die today*, he considers, *let it be for this*. And so he proceeds.

And now the time has come. The cliffs are in view, the caravan in their sights. The three Cavalrymen pull black hoods over their heads and charge.

The first ax is thrown by the bear and it finds its mark, the soldier at the reins, one man down before the enemies' eyes fall upon the shadows. The carriage horses stop their advance as their downed driver tumbles from his post. And another ax flies, removing the ear of their flank guard, the man screams out a warning.

Archers hidden behind the canvas of the wagon reveal themselves and pull back on their bows, but the shadows are too fast and have closed in. They pull the archers from their perches and hack away with broadswords. Arrows fall from quivers without realizing their purpose as limbs are removed from torsos.

The child comes forth from the carriage, well fed and bright eyed, waving a wooden sword. He's delighted. He thinks this a game. Hephaestion chooses to take comfort in this. This boy's last thought will not be one of horror, but rather merriment. Up until the end, he lived such a life of privilege that he even thought his execution an act of theatre designed for his amusement. *This is proof*, Hephaestion thinks, *that King Philip was not Alexander's father as there is no way this child is Alexander's brother.* Alexander never knew privilege like this. Not because he was not born into it, he was, but because his own mind constantly sought out the truth of things. He was born like that and has always been like that. A King's son or not, it is why he is destined to rule.

A woman comes out of the carriage, young, beautiful, Macedonian, King Philip's youngest bride. Hephaestion recognizes her from the wedding. She was even more beautiful then. She pulls at her would be king, trying to get him back into the carriage, not that this will help, *but it is heroic*, Hephaestion thinks.

The little boy resists with a giggle, certain this charade ends with him as the champion.

Tullik, the shadow, swoops in, grabs the young queen off the carriage and onto his saddle. He rides off into the timber as she shrieks. He gets what he wants from this ordeal.

Hephaestion kicks his horse forward as he sees the fantasy unraveling in the young prince's eyes. Hephaestion pulls his sword hoping it finds the prince's neck before the last bit of yarn is gone from his mind, hoping to take him while he is still innocent to the ways of man.

Chapter 44: Petros

Even though I know the gods do not intend for me to stay here forever, there are moments when my heart feels locked in the Theban countryside. It is a beautiful place for certain—hills, but not too many, trees, but just enough. An obedient river, fields that grow food in abundance, barley, rye, vegetables of every kind. And there is no livestock that will not thrive here. The gods have indeed kissed this land.

But now I stand ready to leave at the chirp of a strange bird and I must unlock myself. My family, and we would never deny that's what we are to each other, stand beside me: Aello and Lura. It is my task to protect them. Not because Leksi has asked me to, but because the gods demand it. I do not remember swearing this oath, but I must have. It must have been made in blood, too, because I feel it flowing inside me. *I will protect my family.* Even Leksi, especially Leksi. He's all that's missing now. My love, Leksi. He's who I watch the countryside for. I know his return is unlikely. Should he succeed in battle, he will remain at the citadel and send word back. If he doesn't succeed, he will find death. There is no probable outcome where he returns to me now. Still, I watch the trail that leads into the citadel and pray that he does because he is the only missing piece.

And so we wait, and we watch. And when a horse and rider appear in the trees my heart leaps with the possibility that it's Leksi, and that together we'll flee to find another place as beautiful as this, but without the ghosts. But as quickly as my heart rises it falls again. It's not him, it's *him*.

The mare froths under his weight and the speed that he demands of her.

We leave the safety of the barn to greet him, to hear news of what's happened. It's too soon for the battle to have been fought.

"Aello, in the lodge, now," he bellows while the mare is still in full stride.

Aello looks to me for courage. I know not what to say.

"What's happening?" she asks.

"Just do as I say," he demands.

"Kin. On your knees," he adds as he dismounts. I'm confused by the request.

"If something's gone wrong, we flee," Aellos insists.

"I will not abandon my land," he says. "I am Theban, you are Theban!" He continues. "I said on your knees, kin!" He shouts, turning to me.

"Petros, let's go," Aello pushes back, as she reaches for my hand, but I am distracted, watching the hillside, praying for Leksi, but fearing something else. This man was being chased. Aello tugs at my hand, more true to my oath than I am, but, before she can pull me away, his hand grabs my hair and pulls me towards him. All at once his blade is at my throat.

Aello screams, but he doesn't react. I see him focus on the hillside. I was right. Someone's coming, and it's not Leksi. More than one person. Three of them. They ride like Macedonians.

“Aello, go to the lodge, now,” he repeats. “Barricade yourself and the babe inside. Don’t come out no matter what.” The fire is gone from his voice. He’s scared.

Aello's eyes meet mine. I nod my approval. It’s too late for her to run. They will only chase her down. She hurries towards the lodge.

“Sir,” I say, “if you would let me know what happened, perhaps I can talk our way out of this. I’m very good at talking.”

But he only stomps down on the back of my leg, driving me down to my knees. “And if we can’t talk then we’ll fight. Two have a better chance than one,” I say.

“You, sir,” he says, with a tone suggesting I don't deserve the title, “are now, as you have always been, a hostage.” He hates me. I’ve always known it. Perhaps I could have tried to win him over. I doubt it would have made a difference, but it’s a regret. I should have smiled at him, offered good mornings. Raindrops tear down mountains over time and I had time. Our being able to stop these men is Aello and Lura’s only chance at survival. But me and this man are not friends.

And I don’t have an opportunity to build a bridge now as the Macedonian riders are within earshot, having slowed their horses from a trot to a walk. These are not men who are expecting a mortal battle. Macedonians don’t walk horses into battle. They charge without thought. Their hands only move to their swords when they see my predicament. If this escalates to bloodshed, they will not be to blame.

"I have a hostage. He's of Macedonian blood. Get off my land or I spill it here and now," Leksi's father yells.

The first rider comes in close.

"I recognize him, aye!" he calls back to the other. "From the drawing. The kin prison guard, let free the Band, bounty on him."

He steps even closer. I can see his yellowed teeth and the dirt on his brow.

"Get back!" Leksi's father bellows again.

"No, I don't think I will," the intruder says, only feet away now. And in a flash the Macedonian pulls his sword and drives it towards me. I twist, but not fast enough, and an impossible pain shoots through my entire body. I look down to see the blade point in my shoulder. He was aiming for my heart.

I don't cry out. I hold it in. I don't know why it matters.

"For Zeus's sake," I hear the other say, as I try to fight off the blackness.

"What?" says the sword bearer. "He's worth as much dead." I'm worth something, I think, almost amusing myself with the thought. I was worth so little to them as a guard, less as a healer, but as a traitor, I'm actually worth something.

I look to Leksi's father. His eyes go wide with the realization that whatever asinine plan he had is collapsing around him. Collapsing because I do have value, though not the value he expected me to have. It's all so silly, I actually do let out a chuckle. In place of the hope he had, I see a lifetime of regrets take its place. I wonder if our never sharing a kind word is among them? This thought amuses me, too, but I suspect I'm in a state of shock. I shake it away and return my attention to Leksi's father in time to see what must be a tremendously novel idea wash over him—perhaps something that will bring redemption? Tough to say.

He roars, and releases me. The Macedonian swordsman removes his blade from my person with such force that it yanks me to the ground, but the man's too late. Leksi's father is in full battle mode as his blade finds the Macedonian's stomach, throat, chest. His thrusts are fast and true and send the man into death spasms before his body hits the earth. I look to Leksi's father, and he's just as shocked by his actions as anyone else. I only have a moment to appreciate the sheer spectacle of the act when my body reminds me of my own mortality as a geyser of blood shoots from the empty wound in my shoulder. I cover it with my hand, sticking a finger in the hole. I imagine there would be pain if I had the time to experience it but I do not.

"Fuck Aries!" screams out the Macedonian as he and his comrade jump off their steeds and wrestle Leksi's father to the hard ground.

They work quickly and efficiently, as Macedonians are trained to do, pulling him up and driving him against the big oak. One blade is driven into his hand, pinning him to the tree, and the other into his gut, ensuring a slow death.

"We were here about taxes, you dumb mule!" the leader shouts.

“This is not your land!” Leksi’s father shouts back, through his own pained groans.

“That right? You’re stabbed to a tree, so it is my land now,” the leader says as he turns to his remaining fellow. It’s a valid point, I consider, as my body finally registers the searing pain in my shoulder.

“Burn it. Burn it and let him watch.”

The fellow grabs a torch from his saddle bag and douses it with a liquid from his canteen. These are Macedonians. As light as they travel, they come prepared to destroy. The man strikes the torch with a flint and a flame catches on the stick. He walks towards the lodge.

I think of the stash of wood. The dry straw. The humps of dung and what else is inside, and I silently wail as the blackness comes.

Chapter 45 - Leksi

I am at the gate. Thebans walk in and out with no questions from the Macedonian occupiers. The Thebans continue with their lives and their work. They bring their wares—wheat and barley; pelts; livestock, oxen and goats; strung fish from the river, clothing stitched by their own hands with yarn from the wool of their own sheep. They ignore the Macedonians; some even offer friendly smiles. It has been three years, I remember. They have adjusted to this. I pull the hood of my cloak further over my face. A full-grown Theban man of battle age has not been seen inside this city since before Chaeronea.

Still, this is my city, and I will not stay cloaked for long. At this very moment there's a Macedonian on top of the wall, dead, poisoned by Thebans loyal to our cause. That is, of course, if our plan is unfolding as we planned.

I continue towards the city center and see two of my infantry, wearing matching gray cloaks, fall in behind me. They do not need to wear their hoods; they are too young to be proper soldiers, but I can hear the clank of their swords and armor under the cloaks, those weapons transported by my father and me and smuggled inside to them by the widows of fallen soldiers who also support our cause.

I feel two more of my men fall in behind them. We five march in formation, five strong now. I let my cloak fall away and to the ground. I let the Thebans around me see the shield, the shield of their Sacred Band. I let them see my face, my beard. They had heard rumors that there was a survivor, but these were only rumors until now. Now, I'm real. Their business stops, some run to their homes, wanting nothing to do with what's to come, others join our ranks, out of curiosity or support, I know not. It doesn't matter.

More of my trained men fall in behind. There are now thirteen, all present except Phobos, and he surely marches with us. I feel him there.

Our march brings us past the market and up Epaminondas Way, named for the founder of the Band, our great leader, the last Theban who had to expel an occupier. His foe was Sparta.

My Band continues forward along the stone road until we arrive at the capitol building, as tall and majestic as any in Greece. Ours is not a poor city. We were the leading power in Greece for three hundred years and have the optics to prove it. Our capitol building is several stories tall and assembled from huge marble blocks, put together to make it appear seamless, as if it was chiseled from one giant continuous piece of marble. The building reminds me that I am right to do this. Athenian minds may have invented democracy but Theban might protected it. Ours is a legacy that should not be overrun and controlled by a small group of soldiers considered too inferior for Macedonia's future campaigns.

With this thought, the mighty doors slam shut. Those Macedonians who were not killed or kept outside by the city's walls lock themselves into the capitol building. It is fortified for such an event. We had planned for this. Deimos and three farmer women, mothers of the very men in my small brigade, run towards us with a giant battle axe, that instrument that will bring down the door. This was smuggled into the city this morning. Two more civilians, old men with sons who gave their lives in Chaeronea, roll a giant crate forward. There's a monster inside. This was Phobos's idea. It's a clever trick from a young mind. The Macedonians will have no counter attack for this.

We arrive at the barred door, the dragon tooth emblem on the left side, a cousin to my family's seal, the one I broke down three years ago. Hercules club, the same emblem on my shield, adorns the right. I squeeze that very shield and look up to the balcony, prepared for an arrow attack from above that does not come.

A man in Macedonian attire, strapping armor to himself, steps out. He squints his eyes, focuses on me. His mood is casual, as if he does this on most mornings. As if this is inevitable.

"Is that you, Band? Thought I'd see you again."

It's the captain from the tent. I thought I'd see him again, too. Captain Tam, I believe his name is. I'm glad it's him, no matter what his name.

"Your king is dead," I proclaim "Thebes is once again to be ruled by Thebans."

"Macedonia will have a new king, kin," the captain says. "And I'd rather face you than him." Captain Tam laughs. His laugh unnerves me, but I don't show it. There's terror in this laugh. It's a laugh of truth. This man would rather die at my hand than face off against his new king.

"No harm will come to you or your men if you choose to leave. It need not end in bloodshed," I say, committing to my planned words.

Captain Tam chuckles at that. "It always ends in bloodshed," he says.

He is not wrong. Any hatred I had for him evaporates in that moment. This was always going to be how it ended, with or without me. This is not my doing. I am simply playing the role I have been assigned. So is he. And so it is.

The captain returns to the interior. I look back to the door. I will destroy these emblems today.

I look to my right, where a farmer woman stands with the axe. I take it from her. Its weight shocks even me. I imagine Sigorin next to me, laughing, daring me to try and swing it, challenging my fitness. I approach the door. I swing the axe back and drive it into the thick wooden planks. It lands with a thud, splintering the emblem of the dragon tooth. I surprise even myself. I am not a boy anymore.

I turn back as Diemos pulls the axe from the door and drives it in again. His body is not fully developed, but he swings this axe for his brother. He swings with purpose and fury. His revenge lies within. The crowd watches silently as their sons, their future, take their turns driving the weapon into the door of their capital building.

And I wait. I know the Macedonian strategy. They're waiting, too, waiting for us to come. They'll hold the phalanx in the foyer of the building. It's the only space big enough to allow them to meet us with full numbers. It's where the Theban senate would meet when they were all to be present. The Macedonians will let us charge into their spears in this very space that is sacred to our democracy and then chop us down in the name of their king. The Sacred Band employed a similar strategy, waiting for our enemy to charge, but we did not understand the strength of horses, the advantage their height and their hooves lend their riders. I cannot ride into the senate to overcome the Macedonian line, but I will not have to. I have a monster. As the door is all but hacked through now, I let out a whistle of my own.

A dozen farmers, the strong widows and the old men with fight left in them, with the ghosts of their long dead husbands and sons by their side—gather around the crate and heave it towards the door. I hop on top of the box. I can hear the beast snorting and groaning inside. I turn to my men and see courage screwed to their faces.

"You are the children of farmers. You know where to cut. Slaughter them like pigs," It's not my voice that screams this, but the voice of Sigorin and the rest of the band, using my lungs, throat, lips and tongue to let the world hear them one last time.

And it works. War cries fill the air, and I feel the creature terrorized into a frenzy clang against the crate. I pull up on the planks facing the door, and I stick my sword into its rear.

It bellows, terror turns to rage, and he finishes the work of the axe, taking down the door and charging into the senate floor. Who needs a horse when you have a bull? Aries do your worst.

The crate blocks our view, but the sounds tell the tale: cries of horror, shrieks of pain. Chaos is the goal here. And the sounds of chaos are impossible to mimic. This is chaos.

I turn to my men, temporarily unnerved by the sounds, but they hold their ground. They do not flee. We are all farmers, we Thebans. We are not unfamiliar with the sounds of death.

In the end, a bull, a sheep, a goat, a pig, a man, do not sound all that different. My men remember themselves and I feel a bloodthirst come into them. I know that feeling well. It is what comes when the soldier waits out his fear. It's delicious. I jump down off the crate, and the plan moves forward like a well-rehearsed play.

Two men sweep in and remove the crate, revealing the carnage. The bull lies on its side, still spasming in death. The Macedonian phalanx, already unsuited for combat inside this tight space, is broken and in disarray. One man is bleeding out, a victim of the bull's horns, another lies under the dying beast. Two more are without their long spears, embedded now in our monster's side. Marble statues lie shattered on the floor, their white inners mixing with the red of the bleeding men. There are more to be dealt with, however. They're angry and bruised but not yet defeated. They have nothing to lose and they know it.

I find the foe with the most rage on his face and I charge. He's mine, that one.

Chapter 46: Petros

It’s all so stupid. A proud man pinned to a tree by a knife through his hand. Another proud man, spit flying from his mouth screaming, “Watch! Watch!” Forcing the proud man to do just that, holding his jaw in place so that he has no choice but to watch his house be burned to the ground by yet a third proud man.

That’s the image I wake up to. I assume I passed out from the pain. I’ve done that before; it’s a reasonable response. Now I wonder if I’ve died, and this is some death dream. Am I a ghost now, destined to relive this horror for eternity? I would question my existence on this plane except for the pain in my body is so real. I look to my hand, still covering the puncture wound in my shoulder, the finger embedded in the hole itself. Blood has caked around it, the bleeding is slower than the geyser it was but it has not stopped. I wonder how much life I have inside me still.

I smell the smoke wafting up from the lodge. I know who’s in there, but my heart doesn’t break like I thought it would. Instead, I feel what blood is left in my body, that which hasn’t spilled onto the ground, boil and flow into my legs. They want to run to the flames, but I hold them still. *Now is not the time*, a wise inside voice tells me. It’s not fear that stops me. It’s wisdom. *Just wait another moment*, I tell my legs.

My eyes find Leksi’s father.

“Watch!” the Macedonian screams out again, but Leksi's father's eyes dart off to the side and find mine. He sees that I’m awake.

"Petros!" Leksi's father begs not for his own salvation, I know. He calls out to me in hopes of saving the part of him that might still live. His child, his young wife. The wise voice inside me says, *stand up now*. And I stand. I wobble, the world spins around me, but my perception doesn't matter. The gods don't care how I experience what's to come, only that I play my role.

The Macedonian leader sees me awake. He heads towards me, readying his sword for my death blow.

I freeze. He stands between me and my destination, and I'm not sure how to get around him. The wise voice inside says, *wait, watch*. Leksi's father yanks his hand free from the mighty oak with a blood-curdling battle cry and charges. He drops his oversized frame onto the Macedonian and collapses him to the ground, holding him there.

"Petros, go!" he hollers. My wise voice goes silent. There is no need for words now. My legs take over for my mind, and I run. I run faster than I've ever run before, towards the smoke, towards the lodge. Had all my blood been inside my skin, I would still not have believed I could run this fast.

I hear the cries of the Macedonian behind me: "Get off me, you fool!" My legs continue to propel me forward as I offer a silent thank you to Leksi's father. If it matters, let the gods know that this man who found no honor in his life, found it in his death.

But his eulogy is for another day. I see the Macedonian in front of me, the fire starter. He sees me coming and pulls his blade. I won't outrun him. I draw back my fists, small as they are, and I charge him head on. I strike. My knuckles find their target, before his blade finds my neck. I'm sure he's well enough, but I don't need him dead, even if I wish him dead. I only need him out of the way, and he is. He won't follow where I'm going.

I continue towards the door to the lodge. The teeth boys had put up a new and mighty door of solid oak to replace the one Leksi had broken down. They had not meant to turn the lodge into a tomb but all the Macedonian had to do was wedge a large branch against the ground and the massive door to keep anyone inside there while they roasted. I pull the stick away and kick at the door. I'm sickened by how easily the wood crumbles. I move aside to let the flame's vanguard charge across the threshold. It subsides only slightly before I venture inside the crucible.

The heat burns my eyes, throat, and skin. I push into the inferno. I see only the red of flame, a storm of flame.

"Aello!" I call out. "Aello!"

Nothing.

"Aello!" I scream once more, not sure if sound works in this oven. I want to close my eyes, the heat's unbearable, but I keep them open. And I search for signs of life.

"Petros?" I hear ever so faintly. "Here. I'm here," the voice continues amidst the cracking and splintering of wood and stone. It's Aello, her voice calling out from behind a pile of debri, the remnants of Leksi's mother's loom, covering where the stone fireplace used to be. I scrape aside the smoking pile to find Aello, inside the fire pit, the stone mantle that hung above the cooking pit has collapsed onto her legs, pinning her in place. She holds a bundle to her breast. It's Lura, I pray she's still alive. Aello looks to me then up towards the chimney, where a single ray of sunlight beams down on her.

"Aello, let's go now." It's a stupid thing to say. I know. I push at the stone even though I know we both lack the strength to heave it, no two men would be able to move this piece. It's a performance on my part, one Aello refuses to participate in.

"Take her," she says. She unfolds her charred arms, already blistered to the point where it seems something other than human, but there's Lura inside, untouched by the flame, but listless and still. She's unconscious. I take her. It's the second time I've taken her lifeless form from Aello's torn body. I'm unsure if she's breathing and I don't have time to check.

I turn back to the door, only to see the walls collapse in around it, sealing us in this coffin.

But Lura's in my arms now, and there is still one more option left to escape the flames.

I climb over Aello and into the chimney. I feel Aello's hands pushing me upward. My whole life I've cursed being small, been mocked and teased for it, kept off the field of play, but the gods have their ways. I fit.

"I'll come back for you," I say to Aello. I look down but I can't see her through the smoke. I imagine her smiling at my lie, telling her daughter how much she loves her, telling me to watch over her as I would my own. *I will, my friend, or may Artemis's arrow strike me dead, I will.*

I once heard a philosopher say that while we experience time moving forward, the gods move about time as they please. They care not for our ideas of past, present, future. It's this moment where I made my blood oath. I imagine Aello's eyes drifting closed. She too dies with honor, I think, only she lived that way, too.

I continue up the chimney, holding Lura in my arms, pressing my feet against the opposite side as I press my back against the jagged stones behind me. The progress is slow. I feel my back bleed and the leather from my sandals melt off. I see the blood from my shoulder cover Lura's face and I pray to any god who will listen to see her through this. I continue until the black smoke gives way to blue sky.

Then I'm on the roof, flames still licking around me, trying to draw me back into their depths. But I'm out of the oven. I hope to feel Lura's grip around my neck or to hear a cough, but I am not offered that mercy.

I look down from the roof, two men's length high, and see the Macedonians, my own countrymen, watching the blaze. They don't see me in the smoke, the blaze's one gift to me. I remember that this lodge is built into a mountain and I turn towards the upward slope and walk until I feel cool, wet grass beneath me.

I look up to the sky as the blue turns to black, but not the black of smoke, a different black. A black that comes from within. I'm familiar with this black but it has never been this dark before. *This is my end,* I think. I hear a gentle cough, an inhale, a quiet moan from the little bundle I hold to me. *She's breathing*, I think. I wonder if saving her was a gift or a curse. What do the gods have planned for her? I force an image of her as an adult into my mind's eye, happy and strong, loved and loving, living a full proud life. She has Leksi's eyes and his unbreakable will. I feel her grip my finger. She's strong like him. She fights like him. The gods conspire in favor of those who fight, I consider. How I wish I could see her grow old.

Chapter 47 - Leksi

Macedonian infantry are well trained and disciplined—brave, too, or perhaps fearless is a better way to describe them. They do not quit. And on a proper field of combat, my men would not have made it past the first charge. Each one would have been promptly slain. But we trained and planned for this one fight, in these close quarters. We waited until the conditions were right. Not days or months, but years. We waited until we knew we could make the most of this moment. And we did.

The battle was fast and violent, as most battles are. In shock and disorganized from the bull's charge, the Macedonians barely had the opportunity to unsheathe their swords before my men swept in to confront them. For all of my men, these were their first human kills, but Aries was with them and guided their blades around armor to stomachs, chests, and throats. He stripped them of any impulse towards mercy, and the Macedonians asked for none. There were no prisoners taken.

And now this new version of the Sacred Band, Teeth of the Dragon, stands victorious on the blood-drenched senate floor. My eyes scan the room for the captain, or what's left of him, but I do not see his cape. He is not here, which means he now lies in hiding.

Deimos finds me, his eyes still wide, his mind unable to process what transpired a moment ago. He simply awaits my orders, and he will follow them without question. I have seen it all before. Entranced by battle, his mind unwilling to question any task given by his commander. I could tell him to walk on his hands and juggle the body parts that lie about the room, and he would do just that without question.

"Find the speaker. Bring him to his office," I say. Deimos is off to the task. That was the mission. A Theban civilian ruling the senate. But for the Macedonian captain, the building is cleared, all we need is the new master.

I head into the halls to complete the latest bloody task. I call not a man to be my second. I know this is wrong, against my training, but it is not pride that drives me to go alone. It is Sigorin and the Band, it is their voices inside me that direct my actions. I take my orders from them without question, and they say to hunt this man alone.

I walk the halls. I am unfamiliar with this part of the building. I only know the plans we had reviewed. These are all separate rooms, doored, not connecting to any other hall. They are offices where men of power sit and decide the fates of other men. I pause at the first door and leave it untouched. I go to the second, feel the instinct to crack it open, and do. I peer inside.

This is the Speaker's office, adorned with statues of the great Thebans who came before us. There are Epaminondas and Pelopidas, the Sacred lovers who founded the Band. Hercules is here, too; Kadmus, our founder, slayer of dragons, stares back at me as well. They say there is another room where there are statues of Oedipus, the blinded Theban King, gifted by foreign dignitaries, but he is only a silly story made up by an Athenian. He is not on display.

I look on the Epaminondas and Pelopidas statues and imagine Petros and myself immortalized in their place. I hear Sigorin's voice inside me raging, and I beg him to silence his jealous fit. But it is not jealousy that makes him call out to me.

The moment I realize this, I spin to catch the captain's blade in my shoulder instead of my neck. This wound will heal. I have had worse. The pain I feel is a source of information, telling me how hard my opponent can strike, the type of weapon he's using, whether or not I can use this body part in the battle to come. There is no emotion attached to pain anymore, not even discomfort.

I kick him back and take two steps away to regroup. The old goat charges, silent to not give away our position. If I do not call out, he certainly will not, and I feel no need to call out. At some point, he chose life, that is why he fled the battle. I care not for life. That was trained out of me years ago. I hear Petros voice inside my head, *please live for me,* but, in this moment, Sigorin's voice is louder, *you will fight to the death.* And I cannot deny my first love. I will give this Captain what he fears, not for occupying my city, but for the cruelty he showed in the tent, for what he said of the band, for what he said of kin. This is my revenge. My blade is out. My body assumes its stance. I will allow this old fool the next move, let him choose the way he dies.

He surges forward. I dodge left, tripping his feet under him. He falls to the floor. Old and armored, he is slow to return to his feet. I pounce. He thrusts up with his sword, but my shield takes the point, deep in its wood. The captain abandons his weapon, covers his throat with his armored forearm. He moves on instinct now.

The character of a man emerges in the moment before a violent death. I remember this as I drive my sword into his chest plate.

"They will forget you," he spits out, the venom of his words all he has left.

I drive my sword again into his chest plate, denting it this time; sparks fly off.

Take his heart, I hear Sigorin say.

"Let them forget all kin," he manages, his voice cracking.

I drive my blade in again. The top snaps off, but his armor fails.

"Die in the shadows," he laughs.

"You first," I say. Because I still live,

And I drive my broken sword through the cracks in his armor and push. I feel his heartbeat vibrate through the blade and into my hilt and into my hands. I push until the vibration stops. I listen to my own heart, still thumping in my chest.

Chapter 48: Alexander

Alexander is not entirely sure where this chariot came from. He knows there's a cult whose followers worship his mother, her having convinced them that she is the mortal concubine to Zeus. They reside outside Pella, the Macedonian Capital. Probability would have it that they arranged for the cubersom thing. He's always found them to be more trouble than they're worth. *Put me atop the horse where I can thrust my sword downward. Also, I appear taller atop the horse and I like that.*

But Olympia insisted on chariots and so this threesome rode on chariots. Alexander, son of Zeus, in front. Olympia, wife to Zeus, behind and to Alexander's right. Helena, whom Alexander shares with Apollo, a Pythia of Delphi, behind and to the prince's left. In this procession they ride into Pella.

The people line the road. Those on the chariots are their gods, Olympia ensured that, weaving her mythic fabric through the countryside for over twenty years now. For this reason, the people want the crown on Alexander's head. And, thanks to this, and thanks to Olympia for this forethought, the people are their shield. Fear of rioting will cause their rivals to hesitate before firing their arrows.

And still, there are others in the court, who would rather find their death by plebeian mob than give over the crown to Alexander. They know the cavalry would be loyal to Alexander and that the cavalry would make short work of their own household guards. But they are clever so they used their contacts in the military to arrange for the cavalry to be elsewhere today, the day of deceased King Philip's funeral.

They also control the inner workings of the city. In the time before a new King is crowned, they are the ones paying the administrators, hiring and firing the workers. They decide if the walls are open or closed.

But Alexander is not unarmed. Even in the stunted perspective of this chariot, he sees past the crowds, beyond the roads, to horse bound riders on the field. There are three on either side, six total. They ride with the grace only caverly riders possess. Six stayed. Six broke with orders to honor him, to protect him if they're able. He knows the play. He would have made it himself. The captain put in charge of the cavalry after Alexander abandoned the post was not promoted from the cavalry's own ranks. He is not one of them and would not notice that six of the riders he sent off on this decoy mission had only the skill of stable boys. It's how many the cavalry could spare without their insubordination being known.

Alexander sends a silent prayer to Hermes, the messenger, to tell them of his gratitude. At the cost of their treason, at least his passage into the citadel will be safe.

Alexander's chariot arrives at the walls, his mother and wife behind him in relative safety. There are too many witnesses for him to use them as shields here and these witnesses may judge his manhood should he do so. The gates, however, do remain closed. Olympia had managed to arrange for chariots and finely bred horses but failed to bribe the guards to unlock the door and Alexander can't help but be annoyed with her. But he had failed to consider it too.

A storm of doubt floods over Alexander and he is not accustomed to doubting himself. *It's a useless sensation*, he thinks, but he is unable to stop the sensation from turning into words. *Those in power don't want me in power. I have a chariot and quite a few fans, but powerless fans. In all probability I will be murdered today.* And he envisions the possible ways that death may occur: An arrow from a man on the gate; or, if he makes it through the gate, a sword in the back as he prays over his father's body; a swig of poison dropped into his goblet handed to him as an offering of peace. And all this because his mother was born on the other side of a mountain and another child's mother was born on this side of the mountain, and there are a few chubby noblemen, also born on this side of the mountain, who would prefer this other child to be king. Where he should be scared for his life, the logic makes Alexander chuckle.

As if he had a choice in the matter of his death, Alexander chooses the arrow. It seems the most dynamic. The most seen. He imagines the paintings artists would create of the moment, his arms tossed in the air as the arrow enters his chest, or perhaps it would be of his newly deceased form at the feet of a wailing Olympia and Helena. Either way, death by arrow allows that the archer not be in the frame of the painting. *More attention on my image*, Alexander considers.

But then Alexander sees two horses atop the wall and he laughs again. It's a sight that takes a moment for his mind to process. Horses do not belong up there. They're too big. Most horses, even well trained horses with moderately skilled riders, would refuse to traverse onto the narrow stretch of planks that make up that walkway. And yet these two horses are calm and confident, their riders unflinching. Which means they are not well trained, they're exceptionally trained, and their riders are the best the world has to offer. These are cavalry horses with cavalry riders. And they have made their way up on this wall to make sure the gates open and that Alexander and his company are allowed through.

Eight cavalrymen stayed behind, enough for someone to notice. The cavalry has mutinied. All their coins and their necks are on Alexander.

Olympia didn't arrange for this. She would not have known how. Hephaestion arranged for this. *Hepha did this deed,* Alexander thinks. And for only a very short moment, the mission of the day flies from Alexander and all he feels is love for Hephaestion. But he pushes it away. There's work to be done.

As the gates open, that feeling is replaced with another, an odd emotion, regret. He won't be killed by arrow, poison or sword, not on this day anyway. At least it's doubtful, too much has gone in his favor, but he will die, in a matter of thinking. He will surrender himself the moment the crown is propped on his head. He will surrender his will, his life to the glory of Macedonia. It will be death by crown.

And thoughts of Hephaestion once again flood his heart. *Will I be able to lay my head upon his chest, to kiss his lips? To feel him inside me?* Perhaps in his imagination, maybe in the darkest corners. Alexander's strength as a king, his shield, is the people. *The people must love him and these people do not love kin,* Alexander thinks. Alexander always held to the hope that he and Hephaestion would emerge from their secretiveness, but that hope is fading. This is his death, he considers once more.

Alexander lingers too long in these thoughts for Olympia clears her throat and Olympia never has need to clear her throat. Alexander taps gently on the reigns and his chariot lurches forward, into the shadows of Pella.

The journey from the gate to the temple where King Philip's remains rest, awaiting their final burial, is a brief one. Where the plebeians packed the roads for a glance of Alexander or Olympia, the streets inside the city are bare. Those wealthy enough to reside inside its walls are too aware of the potential for violence in this moment and kept inside. The streets are quiet and still.

The quiet does not unnerve Alexander, however. He listens to the sound of hooves hitting the stone street. He counts the three horses reigned to the chariots and hopes for more, but he hears none. He considers stopping, allowing the cavalry men to catch up to him, to protect him, but he does not know their orders. He does not know if they are eliminating still other threats that he may not see coming. The threats that lie ahead in the temple of the King's funeral are his to handle alone.

Alexander enters the space first. Here again he cannot use his mother or his wife as shields. This moment is about optics and that would look most unmanly. He does not waste his time gauging the reactions of those four dozen or so men already in the room. He knows his mother will do that work for him as she's much more suited to it. She will have a list when this concludes of who is to be terminated on account that they were surprised or disappointed by Alexander's entrance. These are the ones, she'll conclude, who had sooner expected news of his death. Alexander's task in this moment is to feign sadness at the death of his father, but not so much sadness as to be perceived as weak. It's a delicate balance. He relies on his stride to accomplish the task, purposeful but slow, keeping his eyes trained to the open coffin.

Once arrived, Alexander kneels over the coffin, coins over the King's eyes. He continues to pretend to feel sad. While not totally authentic, he is surprised when an unexpected sensation of actual sadness does well up within him, as if he cares.

While Alexander barely knew the man and considered him more of an obstacle than anything else, he did admire his strength. He was a warrior. And these are Alexander's parting thoughts for the man he called father and the source of this sadness, however small and fleeting the sensation may be.

Had King Philip been alive, there is no way Alexander would have made it from the gate to the coffin. There's no way Alexander would have made it out of Greece, had Alexander himself been in charge. But here he is. This is a dangerous truth for the state of Macedonia. *These people who want me dead, need me.* Alexander reasons. His presence, his breath, his living is proof of that.

With this thought, Alexander turns his attention to the others in the room. Most are old men, senators, and noblemen of enough note. They would be happy to tell anyone why they are notable, too. They are of no threat. The only real threat is a line of twelve soldiers eying Alexander, The King's Guard, a select group of purebred Macedonians from Macedonian noble families. They're a silly lot. Too privileged to be good with a blade, less they would have been recruited into the actual army. They've been conditioned to believe that their lives matter so they won't risk their lives, it's a silly riddle and one that amuses Alexander. They know him. They know his mother is Grecian. While Alexander may be the rightful heir to the throne, in accordance to some law or another, they are of the group who believe Alexander's ascent is an offense to their breeding. Alexander will take down several of them before they can slay him and his mother and so they hesitate to attack. *Let my army be filled with plebeians,* he thinks.

Olympia kneels at King Philip's coffin next. She stands a little too quickly before reaching for the crown, sitting upon a mantle beside the coffin. *A misstep, surely. She should have bided her time*, Alexander thinks, *or is it?* Olympia is not one to lose at these games.

"My lady, stop." A fat senator strides forward and puts his hand on the crown.

"This crown does not belong to you." He continues.

Olympia will make short work of the fat man, Alexander knows. He keeps his attention on the king's guard and there's still no movement from them. *Cowards,* Alexander thinks. When he's king he'll want to kill them for simply being inept. He begins to wonder if he simply started killing them off one by one in this very moment if they would think to attack him in mass. They may not. He considers it.

"I bring the crown to he who it does belong to." Olympia says with a glance in Alexander's direction, pretending that she did not fully understand the senator's meaning.

"We wait for the heir, a full blooded Macedonian heir." He says, a reminder to the King's Guard that this Greecian woman before them is the mother of Alexander, who is not full blooded.

"Foolishness, Alexander is the eldest." And with a gentle tug, she pulls the crown clean from his chubby fingers.

“Guards.” The fat man yells, giving up on hints and reminders. “Defend the throne.”

Alexander watches, silent and still, as half the guards pull their swords. He knows his stillness unnerves them and if he’s concerned, he does not show it.

“Now!” The fat senator demands.

And with that demand, Alexander does grow concerned. The remaining six pull their swords and step forward in formation, as a unit. Alexander did not expect them capable of this. His mind had edited out the possibility; and for good reason, unhinged bravery was his only defense against them. Had he thought them capable of collective action he would not have been able to muster his performance.

But the moment his courageous mask falls away the doors slam open and three cloaked men stomp in, the center man as if he owns the universe. They’re followed by six more on horseback, the cavalrymen. And all at once Alexander is brave again and this time there is no editing out of possible outcomes in Alexander’s mind. There is no performance. He is brave again because he has won. Only one man walks like this. Hephaestion has arrived.

Hephaestion takes off his black hood to reveal himself. There’s a darkness to him where there wasn’t before. It makes Alexander desire him even more.

“We have the numbers! For Macedonia! For the crown!” The fat man hollers.

Alexander fights back a laugh to think these twelve have a chance against his eight, but he's not wrong about having the numbers. Twelve is more than eight. *At least he can count*, Alexander thinks.

"There is a Macedonian heir!" The senator continues.

At this Hephaestion reaches into a satchel and removes a grizzly, undersized head. He rolls it down the aisle and it lands at the senator's feet.

Alexander watches as the guards resheeth their swords and try to blend back into the ornate curtains dangling against the walls, but their fate is already sealed. Their faces are imprisoned in the new King's mind, and his mother's.

"Are there any questions now as to who is our rightful king?" Hephaestion says in his tone.

No one responds. Alexander wonders if the rest of the room is as aroused by Hephaestion's voice as he is. But he takes this moment to will the flow of his own blood from his member back into his torso, where all of Macedonia can benefit from it. *I can only admire him from afar now.* Alexander thinks to himself and promises to *love him from a place so deep, that the world will not see.*

With this thought in his head and before the dead eyes of his half-brother and father, Olympia of Greece puts the Macedonian crown on Alexander's head.

Chapter 49: Leksi

I ride through the mountains towards the farm as fast as Deimos's steed will take me. A smokestack looms ahead, mocking me as it blacks out the sun.

The memories of what just happened flash before me. The battle for the senate; the fight with Captain Tam; the warning from Deimos that the base was burning (my men call it base; for me it is home); seeing the other garrison of Macedonians locked outside the city walls retreat; promising my men I would return.

But these are only flashes that tell me where I have been so I know where I am going, back home, back to the farm, back to Petros, Lura, Aello, and even my father. Back to my family. My family!

For so many years, the Band was the only family I knew, and our purpose was to fight and die for Thebes, but I have a family now, a real one, and our purpose is to live. Oh, Athena, what have I done? What have I given up for this crusade?

The tree line finally gives way to the field, and now I see it clearly. The lodge is nothing more than a pile of embers. Two Macedonians try to subdue my mother's bucking mare. Two bodies, dead most likely, lay not far from her. One is in the uniform of a Macedonian, the other is my father, no doubt.

My heart sinks; his death is on me. Although I prayed to them for this result, the gods will punish me as they see fit. I push that thought aside for now as I have been trained to do.

There is no sign of Petros, Lura, or Aello, and so let the gods do their worst. I still have hope.

One of the two living Macedonians sees my hasty approach. He puts his hand in the air, signaling me to slow. He should have reached for steel, not that it would change the outcome of events. I rear up, dismount.

“State your business here,” he demands. This man is not a warrior, it is not in him.

“Where are the others who live here?” I ask of the dead man while he can still speak. Then, his hand goes to his sword.

“I ask the questions,” he demands. “State your—” *Business, yes, I remember the question*, but my hand acts with its own will. It draws my blade and slashes his throat. Perhaps he had answers for my question but my hand did not care and his body acknowledges his inevitable fate as he drops down dead.

The other Macedonian, his nerve already lost, fumbles for his blade.

“Where are the others? The young man, woman, and child?” I ask. This one has a chance at life, I decide. I keep my hand within my control.

“I don’t know. I don’t know. I don’t—”

But he is too far gone. He cannot fight. He cannot speak. He has enough experience to recognize what I have just done. He’s at least seen trained men fight. He knows what that means. He cannot beat me in a fight, his body concludes for him, but perhaps it can in a foot race. He turns to run, but he's not fast enough. My legs turn over, and I catch him in two quick steps, and just like that, he too is no more, my hand and mind working in partnership now, agreeing and delivering him to his fate.

Again I find myself in a mass grave. Again I find myself the only survivor. I beg the gods, *Not this, not this again. I was a good soldier, a good son, what more do you want?*

Then he moves, my father. I hurry to his side; these are his last breaths. He still has that same look in his eye. The one I first saw in him when I put down Phobos: shock and disgust, perhaps a little bit of pride.

"You're so strong," he says, as if he's realizing it for the first time and cannot decide how to feel about it. "You're so strong," he repeats.

"Petros?" I ask. "Was he here?"

He smiles at that.

"Little monkey. He's here. He's strong, too," he says. My father turns his gaze towards what was the lodge with his last moment of life. And then my father leaves me, and I know sorrow.

I search my pockets for a coin but find none.

I hear my mother's voice. *We are farmers. He will pay his way with wheat and barley.*

I lay his head back on the earth, realizing that I have been cradling him in my arms this entire time.

With heavy heart, I remember his last words and gesture. Could Petros have survived? Did he flee with Aello and Lura?

I go to the place where the lodge once jutted out from the mountain that contained it. The wood that molded it into a home has lost its shape and crumbled to the ground in a pile of glowing red embers and drifting black smoke. I enter this voided space. I recognize nothing, except the chimney. It alone stands. Inside it, I find a human form, deceased, burned beyond recognition. I smell the flesh. I know this smell from battle. Why human flesh smells different from other beasts, I do not know. I do not need sight to confirm this but I look anyway: a head, hip bones, feet. I don't linger here. I don't imagine who this person is or how they spent their final moments. There will be time for that later. I know I loved them. That's enough.

I step back and look to the hill, searching to find hope in this mound my ancestors decided to settle. It's been charred too and I search the black until I find red. Red? Blood. A trail of. It tracks down to my mother's garden right next to the lodge, the one Aello revived.

I follow the grim marker, and it leads me to Petros. I fall before his lifeless body. Lura sits beside him, staring out. The gods have blessed her silent with shock, saving her from Macedonian captors.

Petros, covered in soot and blood, his face perfectly still and serious, looks like he is in Macedonian formal attire. Within a moment his head is in my hands. He is still. He is gone. I feel nothing but I know that for him, I need coins. He is not a farmer. There will be coins on the bodies of the Macedonians I slayed, I think. I'll get coins from them. To which my mother's voice calls back: *It's not time for coins. Act quickly.* And then I feel his heart beating. I scan his body. He's intact, but for a wound in his shoulder, a sword thrust. I tear a strip off my cloak and wrap it around his chest. He would have done better for me, but I do not have the skill for this work. My arms grip him around his chest, and I hoist him onto my shoulders. He is so light, like his insides are all air. I hear him groan. I am scared for him, but the sound gives me strength.

I grab up Lura with my other arm and hurry towards the mare.

I dodge the corpses around me, and I leave this place.

Chapter 50: Hephaestion

The King of Macedonia, of Greece and soon to be king of the known world, should all go according to his plan, lies peacefully with his head on Hephaestion's chest. The same head where the crown resides in more formal moments. The head that was a moment ago around Hephaestion's manhood. Hephaestion caresses the small of the King's back.

Alexander called Hephaestion to his chamber earlier this evening to tell his captain that this exact thing could not happen, that what they had before must be put behind them. Hephaestion must find a wife and he must leave Alexander to his. And then the King threw himself into Hephaestion's arms and his lips attacked Hephaetion's body. And so it is.

And still, they lie in the shadows, *for now anyway,* Hephaestion considers. *One day, soon, I hope, I'll get more.* Despite his objections to his own desire, Alexander is the king now and it makes perfect sense to Hephaestion that should two men or two women choose to love each other the King can allow for that to happen in the light. What better way to allow for this then by living in the light himself? Alexander simply needs to understand the power he holds. *And he will. Alexander has the capacity for this, I know.* Only Hephaestion does not say any of this aloud.

Helena sits in her chair and sews together her quilt. This is her function now. She prays and she quilts, her memory quilt, she calls it.

There's a knock on the door. Alexander is up in a start, Hephaestion does not move from his position.

“Hephaestion.” Alexander says. Hephaestion does not respond. He knows what Alexander wants, what’s implied by the use of his full name. He wants Hephaestion to hide, to conveniently vanish. But he will not. *If he wants me gone, he’ll need to say the words*, the newly named Captain of the cavalry resolves to himself.

“Hephaestion.” Alexander has stopped calling him Hepha since being crowned. Upon the second utterance of his full name, Hephaestion kisses Alexander’s rib.

“Hephaestion, behind the curtain. Now.”

Hephaestion gets up. He sees Helena, her jaw locks in anger. Where she’s from, this would be unnecessary. She hates this practice, but lacks a voice in the matter, at least for now.

She rises from her chair, slips into the bed, where Hephaestion once laid.

“Enter.” Alexander calls out as he ties off his robe.

Hephaestion hears the door open from his hiding place. From the sounds of their swords clanging against armor, he determines there are two of them. They both kneel, Hephaestion deduces by the sound of the armor that covers their legs hitting the floor.

“My majesty.” One says.

“Speak.” Alexander responds.

“The Thebans, my majesty, have rebelled.”

“Have they been assisted?” Alexander asks.

“Reports say no, sir. The combatants were youths. Theban born. Lead by a bandsman, sir. A survivor of the Sacred Band of Thebes.”

“Thank you. Wait outside for my orders.” Alexander commands and it is done.

I know the orders to come. I know he can’t stop himself. I know. Hephaestion thinks to himself and he’s sad for it.

She is lost, Thebes, and all she stands for is lost with her. From behind Hephaestion’s curtain, he knows. *The loathing Alexander has for his own heart will be projected onto Thebes, that city, that place that promised more for us kin.*

Chapter 51: Leksi

I ride as fast as I dare. Petros is balanced before me, lying across the mare face down. Her coat is stained with his blood, so much blood. I watch as his back continues to rise and fall with his breath. He continues to breathe, at least. "Breathe for me, Petros." I say aloud. "Breathe."

Lura clings to my neck with the strength of Atlas. Thank the gods. I can bear her tight grip, but I do not know if I have the strength to hold her.

The mare struggles under our weight. I feel her breathing, too, but she will not fail us, this I know. She rides for my mother, fueled by the love she had for her, this beautiful beast, and it is my mother I feel in this moment, guiding her beloved mare to the home of the witch of the woods. I have very little to do.

I see the witch outside her cave, sewing a quilt, of all things, various squares of pelts, coming together to make a blanket. She clocks our approach, casually stands, and waves us over, as if she expected us hours ago and is bothered by our tardiness.

She guides Petros to the ground with the strength of two men.

"Put the child down. She's safe here," she says to me, calmly. I do. "Carry him to the cave as he did you," she continues.

As we enter through the waterfall, I remember Petros hauling me into this cave as I begged to be let go, to die. I put Petros on the bed of straw, already prepared.

My host moves to her cabinets, her clay jars and pots. She extracts the ingredients for her mushroom tea, adding the caps and stems to a steaming broth. I open Petros's mouth so she can pour it in, but she waves me off. "He has a reason to live, Band," she says with a wry smile, and she downs the hot liquid herself in one gulp. She hums softly as she takes rags from a basin, boiling on a separate flame, and washes down Petros's wounds.

He moans, and all at once my body spasms, and I fall to my knees. Where I have not allowed myself to before, I feel now. I feel all at once. My heart bursting, I clutch Lura to me as if she might be able to keep the organ in my chest. I thank the gods for her. I thank them for bringing us here, to this place of healing, when all other places this day have been transformed to places of death by my own hand. I will not cry. I do not deserve tears. I do not deserve this mercy. I bury any pity I feel for myself.

My next thought is of my men, of Thebes. Those spirits, still bound by earthly bodies. They call to me, too, I remember. I have orders.

I look to the witch, and she nods. She knows what it is I am thinking. "Their fates are set, Band. There's only one soul who matters now," she says. She is right. I can not run back to my orders now. Her words and her cave hold me here. Until Petros wakes, I am by his side.

Chapter 52: Alexander

Alexander's captains surround him. Helena listens on. Hephaestion, too. There are multiple chess pieces on the board. Alexander does not know if he see them all, but he's confident he sees more than any other one person. There is the rebellion of Thebes, of course; and which of the other Greecian states might offer the Thebans support. Those are the external threats. Internally, within this very room, there's more at play, Alexander's Captains, some of whom belonged to the king before him, each with an agenda. There are the true military men who are gauging Alexander's ability to lead, looking to see if Alexander's decisions will put their men in harm's way unnecessarily. Alexander likes these men. *Let them judge*, he considers. There are the Captains looking to advance themselves, to move up the ranks either by agreeing with the new King or betraying him when the moment is right. Alexander understands these men. They think like he does. They are predictable. *They may stay*, he decides. Then, there are the Captains of noble birth who listen for hints of empathy towards Thebes based on rumors of Alexander's kinship. Motivated by their own dogmatic belief, that their bloodline is superior to another, they hope Alexander will show mercy towards Thebes, that city for kin, so that they can spread more rumors and turn the plebeians against him. *They may die*, Alexander decides. But he can't kill them without cause, unless he'll turn them into martyrs. Alexander even turns a suspicious eye to Helena. She is still a Greecian Pythia. She could use the network of Temple Priestesses to rally the Greecians to the Theban cause. All these things, ingredients in a curious and deadly soup.

And while Alexander recognizes that there may be more threat that he does not see, he also knows that Hephaestion does not see the most important one. He does not see the threat of their love. It pains him that Hephaestion will not understand why Alexander must do this thing, speak these actions into existence.

“We take the entire army. We destroy her walls. We burn her to the ground. Every man within is to be killed. Every woman, every child to be sold to the Spartans. If they won’t buy, then we give them away.” Alexander says.

“Sir?” A Captain says, as if he misheard.

“We leave at dawn. That was your question, was it not?” The Captain nods his agreement, pretending that it was. Hephaestion winces at Alexander’s tone. *Let him wince.* Alexander thinks. Not out of annoyance, but because Alexander has no other choice. Hephaestion’s face always gives away his heart. Alexander cannot change him.

“You all have work to do.” Alexander returns to his maps, as King Philip would, to signal that the meeting had concluded. Perhaps Alexander was his son after all.

The others stand and leave. Hephaestion and Helena remain. *I wish Hephaestion wouldn’t. At the very least, I wish he would leave with the others and then come back to me later. I wish his decision to be alone with me was not seen at this moment*, Alexander thinks to himself. He considers sending Hephaestion away but that will only draw more attention to them and so Alexander stays silent on the matter.

“We have business to the east.” Hephaestion says, once the three are alone in the room.

"Persia can wait. With Thebes so goes the rest of Greece. We must break her." Alexander offers more than he needs to, his eyes remaining tightly pinned to the maps.

"But the entire army?" Hephaestion pushes.

"The entire army. That includes the cavalry. They need to be alerted. You know what we're up against." Alexander sends his hint. *It's time for you to go.*

"Alex -"

"See to your men, Captain."

With that Alexander steels himself against Hephaestion, against Thebes, against his own heart. He steels himself for his men, his country, his future.

Even so, Alexander's soul moans as Hephaestion walks out the door.

And that leaves only Helena to contend with.

"I'm sorry. I know you're fond of Thebes," Alexander says, softening for her, in the way he feels he is expected to with women.

"The band safe guarded my sorority for two hundred years." She says, anger swelling up inside her.

"You don't think I see? I see you, Alex," she continues. "And I will shave that beard from your face with a flick of my wrist."

“What is this nonsense you speak?” Alexander asks, knowing full well her meaning.

“I asked for three things from you. Delphi was to remain a holy place. My sisters were to remain protected and -”

Alexander interrupts, not wanting to address the third, “I have delivered upon these promises and will continue to do so,” but he has not forgotten the third.

“Monuments for the fallen Greek heros.” She says it anyway.

“This is not a peace making mission,” Alexander says, mustering a tone of finality that she cares not about.

“A monument for the band, give them their lion,” she demands.

“In due time,” Alexander says, trying to maintain himself.

“Now. Or I will snip the beard clean from the face. They will be remembered. By the gods, I will not let the world forget them. You may not care to be, but they will be seen,” she says.

Alexander has no response. He is not unaccustomed to living with determined women. Helena goes back to her quilt, sewing on another patch to join the others.

Chapter 53: Leksi

I watched as his wounds stopped bleeding, perhaps because there was no more blood left in him, but his breath continued in and out, in and out. And so I watched his hallowed breaths for as long as I could will myself to remain awake. But sleep must have overtaken me.

Now, I wake to more blood on the floor, and I panic. I have never before winced at the sight of blood, but now my heart beats at a gallop, and I rear back from it, fearing it is Petros's blood, fearing it is the last of his life now pooling at my feet.

The witch laughs. I turn to her and see the slain goat, already butchered, at her feet. "It's goat blood," she manages to get out through her chuckles. "My knife took its life so that we may continue with ours. It's the way of things. It's a noble dying."

My attention is drawn back to Petros, still breathing, in and out, in and out. I calm.

A few moments later, chunks of the butchered beast, skewered on sticks, roast over the witch's flame. Lura, on my lap, watches with eager anticipation. In the next few moments, I watch Petros breathe, listen to Lura's babble, smell the meat cooking. Or perhaps that all happened inside of the same moment. Time does not exist in this cave. But I know I have somewhere else to be, if only I could remember where.

Petros breathes. Lura eats. I eat, too. Not from hunger, but because I know my body must remain strong. I still live. I still have work.

I try to remember time but cannot. How much of it has passed? A moment or an infinite number of lifetimes spent eating and watching Petros and his shallow breaths, listening to Lura's sounds. Finally, there is something more from Petros: a sharp inhale, a cough. Either death spasms or his awakening.

I look to the witch, but she only takes Lura by the hand, gently pulls the toddler to her, tempting her with goat flesh. She gestures me towards Petros.

I put my hand on his cheek. He opens his eyes. He sees me. He manages to take my hand in his. He looks to Lura, squeezes his eyes shut in relief. He opens them again, and they stay on me. "Aello," he manages to croak out. It is not a question. It is a mourning.

"I know. Don't speak," I say.

"Your father," Petros says. Another burial. He uses his first waking words to honor those fallen in battle, without knowing the custom. His soul tells him to. He's a better soldier than I.

"I know," I say. Then, "Petros, we won, Thebes is ours."

He closes his eyes. I hoped my words would bring him relief, even if they feel hollow as they come out. I know they have not. I do not have to be told. I feel his annoyance. Petros does not care about Thebes.

"Water," he requests.

I give him the cup, tilt it into his parted lips. As the water oozes down his throat the world outside floods into my own mind. His eyes are open now. There are others who need me. There are others who may die without me. A moment ago, I knew I had work but I could not remember exactly what, like the remnants of a dream, but I feel the pull of my duties once again.

"I must return. I will come back with a proper cart. We'll take you and Lura home, okay? To Thebes proper. There are doctors in the city. Alright? I won't be long," I say, desperate for a smile from him, a nod, desperate for his permission.

"Fool." Not the word I was hoping to hear from him, but it is what he gives me. "You won nothing. This war will continue on and on and on until Thebes is a pile of rocks."

"No, quiet now, you must save yourself." I am more concerned with him conserving his energy than I am the harshness of his words, but they do hurt my soul.

"Go, get your cart, Leksi," he says, with spite on his tongue.

"I will and I will return to you," I respond, pretending that I do not hear his tone, telling myself that what he said before was the result of his fragmented mind, weakened by the loss of blood.

"You come back, and you take us to the port, an island," he says, proving that his brain is not fragmented. He is on his mission. I move to leave but Petros's back spasms and he groans and his body contorts. I put my palm on his chest. His body calms with my touch,.

"Thebes can be a place for us now. A place where we can live in the light. We don't need a ferry to take us to an Isalnd," I say, recognizing how rehearsed my words sound, no better than the latest slogan, but I want to give him hope before I go.

"A place where kin can die for them?" Petros says. I stop breathing. "Take us to an island, the three of us. I want to grow old with you," he begs, before his eyes drift closed in sleep, my hand still on his chest. I would not have known how to respond with my words.

I will my fingers away from his heart. I try to remember my orders, my country, my duty. I try to remember that which Petros has destroyed. I repeat the slogans to myself: *For the Band, for Thebes, to the death.* They lack their resonance, but still I move, still I go. I am a soldier. There are battles to be fought.

Chapter 54: Hephaestion

Alexander asked to ride alone, but Alexander is a king so alone is a relative term. There are guards riding in a tight but unseen circle around him. He's never alone, trully. Hephaestion was his guard at night, in the darkness. That's the role he had been reduced to, but now even that has been stripped away. And yet, Hephaestion considers, *I am not a peasant.* And he's not. Hephaestion's been taught to circumvent or destroy all obstacles and take what it is he wants. He is no pawn. He moves freely.

And so he rides towards his king, even though the king has asked to ride alone. The guards see him but they dare not stop him. They know, even if the great Alexander pretends not to, that these powerful men are more than friends, any fool would be able to see it. The fear of their knowing lies solely within Alexander. This fear inside Alexander, and the blindspot to others knowing, are the obstacles to Hephaestion achieving his desire.

Alexander sees Hephaestion coming and his jaw locks. Alexander hates it when Hephaestion defies him.

"Captain," Alexander says.

"Alex," Hephaestion responds, reminding his oldest friend who he is.

"We're in the field, Captain," Alexander says as a reminder of his own.

"Outside of earshot, from anyone," Hephaestion responds, in a tone that is less than submissive.

Alexander says nothing. Hephaestion's innards boil. Should this have been even a year earlier he would have thrown Alexander from his horse.

"It would be nice to hear you call me Hepha again." Hephaestion says, not so softly. Alexander turns away from him in a way Hephaestion has never seen before.

"Alex -" Hephaestion begins to ask but Alexander cuts him off with a turt wave of his hand.

Angry, Hephaestion leans over his stead's mane to try to force Alexander to look him in the eye. Hephaestion calms upon getting this closer look. He cannot be sure, but he believes his friend is crying.

"I'm sorry," Hephaestion says, thrown from his intent. "This mission has got me feeling outside myself," Hephaestion offers as an explanation.

"Perhaps you should not ride so close to me," Alexander manages, his voice tight and wavering. He is crying.

"Why's that? Explain," Hephaestion asks sharply. Hephaestion rarely offers apologies and this one was rejected. And so he dismisses his first instinct to offer mercy.

"For the reason you're outside yourself, Captain," Alexander says, regaining his voice.

"And why do you suspect I'm outside myself, your majesty?" Aries has Hephaestion now.

"This city. What it represents." Alexander spits back.

"And what does it represent?" Hephaestion understands Alexander's code, but it does not satisfy him. He wants him to say it. *Say it aloud, you fool,* Hephaestion thinks.

"Kin. A different way, a very non Macedonian way to be kin," Alexander says it. *The bastard.* Hephaestion thinks, *he said it.*

"And you insist on burning it all to the ground." *If Alexander can speak truth, so can I.*

"I do. And I insist on finding him and killing him. You know who and what he represents, too. And for that reason, Hepha. Do not ride so close to me." His voice waivers again, tears returning. This was not an order. It was a plea. Hephaestion's heart breaks for he knows he can deny his beloved not a single thing, and this was a request from his beloved, not his king. Hephaestion pulls up on his horse's reins. He stops the beast in her tracks.

He watches as the rearguard passes him.

He rides off to the side as the infantry marches by, masking his face, unsure what he'd reveal should he be seen, forgetting that they all already know.

He stays hidden as the massive cart, hitched to an entire team of draft horses, pulls Helena's statue past him. A giant lion, a grave marker for the Sacred Band of Thebes. Alexander may want to burn their memory to the ground, but Helena will not let them be forgotten. In their honor, Hephaestion remembers. *I am Hephaestion. I do not hide.* He lets his face be seen. It is not much, he knows, but it is his own silent salute.

Chapter 55: Leksi

The mare resists the journey back to the City of Thebes with every step, even turning to nip at my heels when kicked.

This is not her way. She is calm and gentle. I tell myself that, in her age, the journeys back and forth, back and forth, were too much on her, but I know this is not true. She is plenty strong, and she has never shown me anything but love and kindness. It is the destination that she does not approve of. And it is my solitude that makes her bite. *Where are Petros and Lura? How could you leave them?* This is her message.

But I demand this journey of her, and I tolerate the nips.

I arrive back at Thebes. My men do not greet me at the gate where I expect to find them. They were supposed to have been positioned there. I ride into the city to find it quiet. There are no celebrations. The markets too are closed. There are no people in the streets, only the occasional ghost.

I lead the mare to the senate, where I tie her to a post.

And so here I am, at this post, wondering where those that call themselves Thebans are. After an extended moment an officious man walks up to the broken down door.

"Are you with the resistance, the Dragon's Teeth?" he asks.

"I am. I am their leader. My name is Leksi. I was of the Band." I suddenly feel very young as this wrinkled man looks down at me from the steps.

"I see," he says, not unkindly.

"I was acting on the orders of my captain. In the event of a Grecian defeat: return to Thebes, lead a resistance, repel the occupiers." I don't know why I feel the need to explain myself, but I do. I want to be congratulated. I want him to run to me and take my hand in his and smile wide. I want him to call me liberator. I want him to tell me, *job well done, son.* I did not know I would want any of these things, to hear those words, but in their absence, I do.

"I understand and thank you for your service," he says. He is not insincere but his tone is cold. Still, I feel my body relax, partially satiated by the gesture. "Would you come with me?" he asks.

I hesitate.

"Your men said that they were told to put a civilian in the speaker's office," he continues.

"That is correct," I say.

"They've accomplished that task. And he would like to speak with you," he says.

The officious man leads me into the building, where several old women wash the statues of the gods, those stained with blood during the battle, but not destroyed. I watch them watch me. Any one of thesecs women could have been my mother, with their soft, brown skin and dark eyes. When these women look at me, it reminds me of the way my mother would look at my father, with this strange mixture of defiance, disappointment, pride, and empathy in equal parts.

I continue to follow the officious man, hoping for a sight of my men, holding each other, talking out the horrors of battle so the wounds will not fester in their souls, like I would with Sigorin. But I do not see them.

The officious man arrives at the Speaker's office, the very one where I slayed the Macedonian captain. He opens the door and motions me to enter. I enter to find another aging man in a fine, white toga at the desk.

"My name is Georgian," he says. "Thanks to you, I am currently the Speaker of the Theban Senate. You were a Bandsman, I understand?"

"Yes, sir. I am still." I mumble.

"You were a shield boy, before Chaeronea? You are too young to have been a swordsman," he says. I do not like his tone.

"That is correct, sir. I am also the highest ranking member of the Theban military," I say, finding my voice again.

"You are," he says "And in Thebes, final command in military matters ends in civilian leadership, so you are under my command then, are you not?"

"I am. That is correct," I respond.

"Very good, then," he says. He pauses for a moment. He is a man who believes direct communication is the kindest form. This pause, however brief, is an apology for what comes next.

"You are to surrender your shield and your men to Alexander."

"What?" I ask. Do my ears fail me?

"You heard me correctly, son." He continues. "Alexander will be here by sundown with his entire army, complete with wall crushers and torches. He'll disassemble our city brick by brick and burn what remains to the ground. This process was detailed in the treaty I signed following Chaeronea. I've written him, asking for mercy, explaining that this was the act of a small group of kin terrorists and did not represent the hopes and feelings of the Theban populace. I hope by turning over you and your men, his appetite will be appeased."

"Coward." My thought escapes my lips against my will, but let it be heard.

"Perhaps, but I am also not a fool," he says.

"Thebes has walls. We close them and we fight. The grain stores are full," I counter.

"He'll tear down our walls," he responds.

"Then we pack up every man, woman, and child, and we leave. We take what we are, what is in our heads, and we take it somewhere else." I don't know how these words find their way to me, but they do, and they move him. I see it

"It's a beautiful notion, but he will hunt us down," the Speaker says, as if he were trying to push down the hope the idea brought to him.

“Then we split up. They won’t catch us all,” I say, continuing the fight. I think for a moment that I have him, that there is a Theban in him yet. He closes his eyes. He considers.

“When you became a member of the Band, you swore to protect all Theban children as if they were your own. That’s how the oath goes, right?” he says.

“Yes,” I respond, bothered that he had to ask the question.

“If that meant dying for them?” he asks.

“Then may the gods strike me down,” I say.

“That’s what they need from you, son. They need you to die for them,” he says it with regret in his voice.

“No,” I say, surprising even myself. “If my men die, if I die as an act of surrender to Macedonia, then Thebes dies too.”

“Convenient way to look at it,” he says, the tone of regret gone.

And I no longer have words. My fist grabs the stray, grey hairs on his head and slams his face into the desk. He laughs as blood trickles down his cheek. He laughs? My blade finds the edge of his throat. My blade will not accept laughter.

“Where are my men?” I ask.

Chapter 56: Petros

I wake in the cave.

Lura sits beside me. For a moment, I'm happy, despite the pain in my body. I'm happy. This little thing is mine. But it's a fleeting moment before I'm run through by a searing guilt, the face of Aello in my mind's eye. Aello was my friend. Now that she's gone, I get to truly call Lura mine. And with any happiness I might temporarily draw from that fact comes an equal serving of responsibility for Lura's care. She will see tomorrow and tomorrow or take me from this earth.

And with that thought, my pain retreats to the back of my mind. Lura is my world now. I must get up. I must attend to her.

I struggle to my feet. The old witch smiles at me as she sews her quilt. I wonder why this creature of the woods helped us, twice now, but I don't bother her with questions. Her quilt is almost done and she sews as if time were about to expire. She makes the final stitch and squeezes the fabric to her, as if it smelled of an old lover, when there's a noise outside, a rustling. The witch narrows her eyes and falls still.

"Ayo, tracks," we hear from a Macedonian tongue beyond the waterfall that masks the entrance to this cave.

The witch puts down her quilt and walks to the falls. I shrink back against the wall, holding Lura close.

"I smell goat," the Macedonian calls out, hungrily.

The witch looks to her cauldron, scents emerging from the pot.

"What, a herd pissed in the water?" another calls out. There's more than one.

"It's here, coming from the falls. I know, trust an old herdsman," the first Macedonian says with a laugh, his voice just outside the cave, feet away from us.

I watch as the witch pulls out an old pair of sandals. I recognize them. They're Leksi's from when we first met. She slips them on her feet. She holds her butchering knife as if it were a sword. Her eyes go wide and she sets her feet to charge.

I want to cry out, *no, don't!* These Greeks are always throwing themselves on swords, stupid donkeys! And this witch is no different. But I don't call out. I need her to do this thing, even if I don't understand why she would. She takes an inhale and lets out a battle cry, she flies through the watery threshold and out of her cave.

"Argh!" I hear one Macedonian scream out in pain, followed by the splashing of a body hitting the water.

"I wear the shoes of the Sacred Band, who fought and loved and showed no shame!" I hear the witch call out.

"Stand down!" another Macedonian commands. It's a familiar voice, but I can't place it, and I don't have another second to, because the witch's scream steals my attention.

She stumbles back through the falls. There's an arrow through her gut.

She turns to me. "Do not forget my quilt. Do not forget us," she says.

She turns back to the falls and charges through them once more. A moment later, the now-familiar sound of a body collapsing into the pool sounds out again.

For what feels like an eternity, all is quiet. But then, Lura lets out a cry. I cover her mouth, but I suspect the worst, and the worst comes.

He walks through the falls. I know who he is immediately because, despite how I fear him, he is objectively the most handsome man on earth. I pray to Athena that Captain Hephaestion doesn't recognize me.

He sees me by the light of the witch's fire. "You," he says.

So much for prayers.

Chapter 57: Leksi

Any question of the mare's strength is forgotten as she carries me with haste back to the cave. She gallops with the pace of the river we follow. She battles against her own desire for home with no intervention from me. She does not want her old barn, nor the old way. Her nose points to Petros and Lura.

I only have to guide her away from the enemy's trail. The speaker spoke truth when he said Alexander was bringing the entire Macedonian army. I can hear their horses and the pounding of their marching drums from here. Petros was right, too. Thebes will be destroyed. What a fool I am, but there's no time for that now.

I did what I could to save my people before I left. It was not much. I found the jail where my men were held. They had surrendered themselves voluntarily and were prepared to hand over their swords to Alexander at the order of the speaker. They are good soldiers. I would have done the same two years ago, two days ago maybe, but not now. I am done following orders.

I advised Deimos on a plan, albeit a simple one. Take as many citizens who would agree to go with him and flee the city. Go to the ports, make a new home elsewhere. I went with him to help load the grain onto the wagons. By the time we completed the task, word had traveled throughout the city. Alexander was coming. The resistance was leading an evacuation. No more than a dozen civilians chose to evacuate with us.

In mass, the people would not follow my boy soldiers. Nor would they follow me. I suppose the speaker was right. Kin die for them; we don't lead them. They would sooner put their fate in the gods. Not that there was room for the masses, but we might be able to escape with these twelve.

I told Deimos to board the first ship out tomorrow morning. That will give me time to get Petros and Lura and join him. That is should Deimos make it at all, should Alexander choose not to hunt down those smart enough to run. But that too is up to the gods now.

All I can do is ride. The mare has figured out that she is to avoid the smell of Macedonian horses, and we do not encounter the scouts I feared would harass us on the way back to the cave. For a moment my heart is light, perhaps the gods are with us. But then I see her.

At the foot of the falls, the witch lies on the rocky shore. The river has stripped her of her clothes, and an arrow has pierced through her stomach. She still has life in her, though. More importantly, her eyes hold a purpose. I run to her, kneel before her.

"Playing your silly games has made you late, Band," she manages to say, a look of chastisement on her brave face.

"I am sorry, my lady," I respond as I prop her up, my eyes scanning the tree line for evidence of Petros.

"They're alive, Band, but they have them," she says. I know who she means. The Macedonians have taken Petros and Lura.

"The Band lived in the light, so let them die in the light, too, yes? You save our little spark…let him light the fire for tomorrow's kin? You can do that, Band?"

She speaks in a death riddle that my mind understands not. But my body does. The mare does too, and she neighs, calling me forth, back into battle.

Before I know what I am doing, I am atop the beast and we ride towards enemy lines. I remember my slogans: *For the Band, to the death*. I remember my purpose.

It will be a good death.

Chapter 58: Alexander

Alexander stands atop this hill. His captains surround him, except the one he wants most to be by his side. He understands why Hephaestion would not want to see him give this order because he himself does not want to give this order, but he feels he must.

An officer hands Alexander a looking glass. From this perch at the foot of the statue of Hercules, Alexander looks down to the walls of Thebes below. He sees his soldiers at the foot of the gate. As promised by Theban leadership, they are not greeted by arrows or threats. The gate lowers down. This once great city knows her time is past. She would rather not live in the world to come. This is her suicide. Alexander is reminded of his tutor's tutor, Socrates. He too chose to drink the hemlock.

An old man exits and offers his sword. He expects mercy. He receives none. Alexander is involuntarily relieved that this man is not the Bandsman. Those around him can't know it, but the Bandsman was a brother, in a sense. Alexander knows that now. He can admit it to himself even if he can't say it aloud. He would not want to kill his brother, at least not in a way as unhonorable as this.

"Kill him." Alexander orders, ending the man below. It's an easy command for him to give.

Flags wave from Alexander's bearer, ordering his commands to the Macedonian soldiers at the wall, and whoever this old man who offered up his sword is, he meets his death.

"Proceed," Alexander says. There's nothing more to say. Everyone knows the plans.

The bearer waves that command and Alexander watches as a stream of soldiers storm into the city's walls with ropes and torches. Thebes will by ash by morning.

The deed is done now. *May Aries forgive me. I don't want to watch. I know what I've destroyed.* Alexander thinks to himself as he walks back to his tent.

He enters, expecting to find the usual stack of messages awaiting his attention, but that's not what today has in store. It's Hephaestion. Alexander's heart swells to see him, but he's not alone. There's a prisoner with him, strange in that all Alexander's men were given orders to not take prisoners on this mission. The man is bound. He's short and he's familiar.

"He's Macedonian, my lord," Hephaestion says.

The prison guard. *This is the man who guarded the Bandsman*, Alexander remembers to himself.

"I found him in the countryside with a little girl." Hephaestion says.

"The girl is mine. She is of Macedonian blood. She's only three." The little man is quick to add.

"You will only speak in response to a question. And kneel in the presence of your king." Hephaestion orders. And the little man kneels.

Alexander considers what he sees before him. Perhaps the man deserves mercy, even kindness, had he been a Theban hostage for the last three years, but he's declaring this child to be his own blood. How would he have had the chance to sire a child as a hostage? What's more, there's something undeniably kin about this man. *I hardly see him siring a child at all,* Alexander thinks to himself.

"You were responsible for a prisoner, a member of the Sacred Band of Thebes. What is the status of your prisoner?" Alexander asks.

"I do not know." He answers quietly.

"I do not believe you." Alexander responds, holding his stare.

"He ran off. I followed him for as long as I could, looked for him, but never found him." He says.

"Seems like you had plenty of time for other activities, if the child is truly of your blood." Alexander says. And to that the little man lowers his head.

"It was made clear to you that should your prisoner escape you would be put to death," Alexander continues, hoping that if he does know the whereabouts of the Bandsman this will pull it out.

"It was made clear and I accept my fate. But the child? Please, my king, spare her," he says without a thought to his own life. "She's Macedonian." He says again, holding back tears.

"Half at most and even that's extremely questionable. She'll go with the Theban women and children," Alexander says. The little man gave Alexander the coin by which to bargain with. Alexander would feel no instinct for compassion here, but the look on Hephaestion's face gives him pause. This man is kin and Hephaestion feels kinship. Alexander understands and feels it, too. *Perhaps that is the danger of kin*, Alexander considers. *Perhaps my people are right to fear us. Our loyalties are divided.* And Alexander reaffirms to himself that he will not let his kinship blind or distract him to his duties as a king.

The little man's face is desperate. He knows not how or will not betray the Bandsman.

"This is all?" Alexander says as the prisoner looks to Hephaestion, sensing that he might have an ally in him. Alexander's not sure what the guard picked up in Hephaestion's gaze, but it emboldens him. Hephaestion senses it too. It freezes him in place.

"Take him away." Alexander says, trying to snap Hephaestion back to his duty, trying to end this affair before it becomes complicated, as he senses it may.

"His name is Leksi." The little man blurts out. "And he wasn't my prisoner. Not for long. Nor I his hostage. That was only how the gods saw fit to bring us together. I was his love. And he was mine. We were partners." The man declares.

"You admit your treason. I'm glad." Alexander says, refusing to be moved, eyeing Hephaestion, who looks upward, his eyes dampening.

“If living in the light, if being in love and not caring who knows is treason, then let the gods know it. I loved. I was loved and that love kept the child alive. I am kin.”

“And you’ll be dead by nightfall. Captain, take him away. Now,” Alexander says as he turns away, further locking down his heart.

“Please, help the child, please,” the little man begs of Hephaestion as Hephaestion takes his arm and leads him off.

Alone now, Alexander wonders what that would feel like, to declare his love. *Is it not enough to love? Must I declare it for it to be real? Must I speak it to the world?* And then, he wonders why his chest is numb to this. *Where has my heart gone*? He asks himself.

Chapter 59: Hephaestion

Hephaestion ponders what inspired the little man to offer up those final words.

It might have been the look on Hephaestion's own face. Helena has called his attention to the way he can look at Alexander at times, when Alexander angers him. *Heart hurt,* is how she describes it. He can't help it. Perhaps this is what clued in the little man, *my heart hurt*, he concludes.

Hephaestion still does not know the little man's motive. It got him nowhere and was never going to. Hephaestion cannot save his life, or spare the baby he cherishes from a life of slavery, if she's lucky enough to survive long enough to be of use as one. These things are set now. His words only served to hurt Hephaestion's heart all the more. *Maybe that was it*, Hephaestion considers. Maybe that was the only weapon he had available to him and so he used it. *But are my feelings for Alex really that transparent?* He asks himself.

As Hephaestion walks back to his camp, having left the prisoner with his men, this is what occupies his thinking, that and the ache in his heart, and the smell of Thebes burning in his nostrils.

He thinks how it might feel, if only once, to share his love of Alexander with the rest of the world. *Is it just my pride? Is it only that I want to show him off?* He wonders. *How would it change anything if others knew?*

He approaches his tent, passing a tree, when something grabs his hair and yanks him to the ground.

His mind races away from its previous bone, *what is this beast that has me? What monster have the gods sent forth to devour me?*

A fist, if it is a fist, feels more like a hoof, lands firmly against his cheek. He weathers the blow and he sees that it's a man, but a man whose strength he has never known. He tries to push him off, but he's too strong. He tries to move out from under him, but he's too fast.

Hephaestion opens his mouth to scream out but no sound comes forth as the other's arms are around his neck, holding the air in. This foe thrashes Hephaestion across his body and thrashes him back the other way. *I've done this to other men,* Hephaestion thinks. *I've dominated them. I've squeezed the consciousness from their persons.* Part of him enjoyed it, too, and he cannot help but wonder if his assailant is enjoying this. *Is this fun for him? It is a game? Or is it a duty?*

Hephaestion breathes only if this other will allow him. And the other does not allow. The blackness comes all at once.

A sliver of light comes back to Hephaestion a moment later as he's pulled to his feet, the foe's arm still around his neck. He's moving Hephaestion into torch light, as if he were but a puppet. *What shame?* Hephaestion thinks, *please... back to the darkness.*

"Captain?" A voice call out. Hephaestion's thoughts are muddled *Captain... not my voice, but that's me. I am Captain. The voice is asking about me.*

"Captain!" Another voice calls out.

"Back." *That is him. That is my better.* "Or I bleed him out." Hephaestion knows this voice. The Bandsman. Then Hephaestion feels the blade against his belly.

"Hold, good sir, hold," another voice pleads. Hephaestion sees it now, through the swelling of his eye; the soldiers gather but do not attack, Hephaestion's life in the balance.

"Bring me your king." The Bandsman says, to Hephaestion's horror.

"No." Hephaestion says aloud. "No, just kill me." Hephaestion says with all the strength he can muster. *Let Alex never see me like this. Never.*

"Bring him." The Bandsman calls out.

"Attack, you fools, my life matters not. Attack!" Hephaestion screams, his wits coming back to him. But they don't. They know he's lying. His life does matter. He's Hephaestion and there's only one Hephaestion.

"Alexander!" The Bandsman screams, deafening Hephaestion's ear.

"Alexander. I have him. I have him!" The Bandman says. And all at once it makes sense to Hephaestion. *The Bandsman knows what it is between Alexander and myself. He's known since the tent in Chaeronea. He's known this whole time.* Hephaestion remembers in the prison tent, the scene playing in his mind's eye, like shadow puppets, before Alexander's and his first kiss. The way the Bandsmen eyed them. He saw all. *He knew what we were, what we would be, before we did.*

"Alexander!" The Bandsmen calls for the third time.

"Please…" Hephaestion begs, but the Bandsman does not hear him. He's fighting for his own love, Hephaestion gathers. The group of soldiers part and Hephaestion sees through to behind their mass. Alexander. *May the gods strike me down. My love, Alex, sees me like this.* Now, Hephaestion knows what it means to be heart hurt.

"Let my captain go." Alexander says, and where his face shows terror his voice stays strong.

"Your captain, no captain. Say what he is!" The Bandsman calls out. "Or he dies here and now."

I can not survive this shame, Hephaestion thinks to himself. He wants to lean into the point of the Bandsman's knife, now pressing into his neck, but some force deep within his own self stops him.

"Say it!" The Bandsman calls out once more as the blade's tip presses deeper into Hephaestion's neck.

"He is my love! My love. I love him. By the gods let him go!" And Alexander means it. *Alex means it.* And he said it before all of his men. And Hephaestion's heart stops hurting. And now he knows what it means to be seen.

Alexander does not take his eyes off Hephaestion to see how his men react to the proclamation but Hephaestion's eyes do see. The men do not react. They stand as they were before, at the foot of their young King, ever loyal.

"I love him." Alexander says it again. And with this repetition Hephaestion forgets his shame and his will to die.

“A love for a love then,” the Bandsman says. “A love for a love.” He repeats.

“Get the prisoner and the child,” Alexander orders a nearby soldier.

“Safe passage for him and the babe,” the Bandsman bargains.

“For the night. I can’t promise more,” Alexander says, stepping closer.

“You will not send trackers,” The Bandsman offers back.

“I will not,” says Alexander.

“Swear it!”

“Before my men, my honor as a king, I will not.”

And behind Alexander, the little guardsman appears.

“Leksi!” He calls out.

Alexander turns to him. “Remove his binds,” Alexander says and the guards obey.

“Petros,” Hephaestion hears the Bandsman say to himself, as if it were a prayer, and Petros runs towards them. The Bandsman lets Hephaestion go and Hephaestion stumbles forward, passing Petros.

Hephaestion falls into Alexander’s arms, his legs failing him. Alexander lifts Hephaestion up tall. “I’m sorry,” comes from

Hephaestion's lips before Alexander silences them with a kiss, plucking the guilt from Hephaestion's soul.

To Hephaestion, the kiss feels as if it lasts hours. He feels the eyes of their men on them but he does not care. And Alexander does not care.

Alexander finally pulls away only to watch Petros walk through their ranks, the little girl in his arms. He stands taller than anyone else.

The Macedonian men swarm in on the Bandsman, their hands grasping at him, holding him in place, waiting.

Alexander turns to Leksi. Alexander draws his sword.

Ash from the burning city falls down upon them.

"Goodnight, my brother." Alexander the Great says, as he thrusts his blade through Leksi's throat.

Chapter 60: Petros

I sit on the docks waiting, hoping, but all I can really do is remember what happened, over and over, as if my whole life from this moment onward will simply be this night repeating itself in my mind's eye.

The guards came in, grabbed me and Lura. I heard screams outside, and I thought I heard Leksi's voice, but I always hear his voice in my head, and I thought it must only be his memory calling to me from within. I had learned to separate his phantom voice from his real one, but these screams confused me.

When the soldiers entered, I felt a wash of fear. After all I'd been through, I had never felt fear like that. They were here to take me to my death, but I wasn't ready to die, not for this, not like this, not without a cause. To save Aello, Lura or Leksi I'd die a thousand times, but to die because I lived?

But the haste they pulled us with made no sense. Why were they rushing me to my death?

They pulled me to a field, where I saw the backs of soldiers all poised to do battle. They turned their heads to see me, and the group split so I could be led through. And I saw what they stood against.

Hephaestion, bruised and beaten, a sword held to his throat. My heart sped at the sight of the sword bearer, Leksi. I knew at once what he had done, what his plan was. He was trading my life for Hephaestion's.

Alexander and Leksi traded a few quick words, and I was released at the same moment as Hephaestion.

I knew the next step of Leksi's plan, what I was meant to do, because it had been my plan all along. I was to run away from here, to take Lura as far from here as possible, to an island somewhere to live a long and glorious life. But my heart and my legs fired me to Leksi. I saw his heart crack, but I ran to him anyway.

We wrapped each other in our arms, and we kissed, Lura squirming between us.

"You must go to the ports, you'll meet the others there, take my shield," he said, as he handed me the weapon.

"You'll come too," I said. It was a stupid thing to say. There was no way Alexander could allow him to live after this. I knew that.

Leksi smiled gently at me. "You live for us both," he said. "You live in the light. I love you. I will find you in the next life."

"I love you," I said back. It sounded so predictable, but no other words would do. He kissed my lips once more.

"Run for me," he said. I turned my body so that my back was to him. But I didn't run.

"Don't look back." He offered. That was his final gift. And I would not deny him that.

Still, I didn't run. I walked through the ranks of Macedonians, but their eyes weren't on me. They were moving towards Leksi now.

Gods forgive me, but I prayed he'd take them all down, one by one, that he would do Aries proud, but I knew he could not. He had given me his shield.

Once I made it to the tree line, I did run.

While the gods felt it necessary to take Leksi, they left me with Lura, and they guided me to the mare, drinking at the river.

As ash fell around us, I mounted the mare and we rode.

We stopped at the cave, guided by an immobile star. Here we picked up the old woman's quilt and the dried food that the Macedonians had missed. She'd left us everything we needed.

We pushed on into the night, towards the northern ports, and arrived before the sun.

These are the memories I will live with for the rest of my days. I will always remember. I will not forget.

The sun rises, though. Lura smiles her greeting. I find other refugees and travelers beginning to gather. I feel alone. But then I see a familiar face in the masses. It's Deimos.

He sees me, too. I see tears form in his eyes. He knows what it means to see me without Leksi. He subtly waves me forth, and all at once I know that we are not Thebans or

Macedonians now. We are a new people, brought together by the gods.

I guide the mare to Deimos and his group. Like me, they are survivors. We will live and make new memories.

We load the boat, thankful for the coins the others had stashed away.

The rowers eye us. They probably know the story: Thebans on the run from Alexander. They're probably not too glad to have us onboard; we risk inciting their new lord's wrath. One, though, handsome and strong, about my age, smiles at me, and offers a shy wave. I know what that smile means now and I'm glad for his kinship.

"Are you warm enough?" I ask Lura, bundled in the witch's quilt.

She smiles up at me.

"Da," she says. "Da."

Chapter 61: Leksi

I did not hear what Alexander said to me before he drove his sword through my neck. I cared not that it was him doing the deed or how the deed was done.

I saw only Petros, the ash from my burning home raining down upon him, holding Lura in his arms, walking, too proud to run, too stubborn to heed my orders, away from this place.

This was worth dying for. This was a good death.

This is the thought, the memory, that swims through me as I come to this new awareness. I am on the boat, alone this time but for the cloaked figure at the helm. He silently steers me to our dark port. My eyes adjust to the darkness. It takes me a long moment to see them.

My brothers, two hundred ninety-nine soldiers of the Sacred Band of Thebes await me in rank and file, fully dressed in shield and armor, battle ready.

I see Sigorin. He tries to remain at attention, but his face beams with pride. I step into the empty space beside him, the space left for me. Sigorin keeps his eyes fixed to the front as a good soldier does. There was a time when I would have turned and done the same, but I am different now. I touch his hand and watch as his eyes fill with tears, though they stay focused straight ahead, awaiting orders, guarding what lies behind him: a sun rising.

This light, this divine embrace, calls to me. I step out of my place. I break from the rank and file, and I turn to face its warmth. Sigorin bangs his sword against his armored chest, once, twice, three times. And all the Sacred Band joins in, drumming to the beating of my heart, urging me forward.

And I alone step forward into the light.

The End.

Printed in Great Britain
by Amazon

47660881R00159